Some Kind of Life

This book is dedicated to the memory of Alan Cole. His life among us brought joy and laughter. He is missed. "Put that in your little black book, Buddy."

Prologue

Life. Death. No matter who we are; no matter where we're from; no matter our ethnicity or backgrounds; we share those two things in common. Despite all our differences, we all have a beginning and an end. That should be just enough common ground to get something started. At least it would be if either one of them mattered.

I'd grown to become rather callus to both of these common denominators. I guess it's sad really. I suppose in some way, I'd allowed myself to see life as somewhat mechanical. We're born; we eat, we live, we spread, and we die. I even found it difficult to feel empathy towards others much more deeply moved by either event.

I'm a geek; a nerd; strictly driven by reality and facts, not nearly as controlled by emotion as my gender is stereotypically considered to be. I look at the numbers, and I see a sum. Evolution explains my path, both past and present. Not only could I accept that, I practically worshiped it. It's not much different you know, being compelled by science as opposed to religion. Either one can consume.

My parents were products of the sixties; free thinkers, carefree and children of mother earth. As far as I could tell, if they had any ounce of religious conviction, it had probably burned away between the teeth of a roach clip somewhere during their youth. They taught me to think for myself or at least that's what I believed. Who knows? Somewhere under all that free thinking, there always seemed to be some alternate agenda, a current dragging me along; influencing my thoughts much as the traditional beliefs against which they had railed.

Anyway, in my few young years on Mother Earth, I'd grown to see life as a function; just like watching bacteria grow in a petri dish. Life ends, and we turn to dust, feeding the planet upon which we had fed. It wasn't much to get worked up about and if we all shared the same fate, what was the point in trying to prolong the experiment.

I saw these people all around me looking for everything from the fountain of youth to a cure for cancer, and I couldn't for the life of me understand what was so darn important about adding another day. It all ends people!

Callus, huh? I didn't see it that way. To me it was merely a matter of facing the facts of reality. Of course, that was before...before I met Cole.

Chapter One

Golden brown stalks of wheat waved in the wind, stretching across the plains. The gaps between fields were decorated with dry, crinkled blades of grass and the pale green tufts of sage. Yucca provided some accent to the scene dotted here and there; long, slender blades pointing off in different directions; shriveled pods sticking up in the centers on spindly stalks. Herds of cattle, some black with white paint spots and some brown-red, moved lazily across the pastures looking for something to eat, while others stood in groups around stock tanks, drooling strings of water and saliva dripping from their mouths as they stared off in their curious ways.

I searched the countryside, taking in the view in total amazement. Watching out the windshield as the gray-black thread of a two lane highway lead me further away from civilization. Ahead of me I could see the bunching of trees upon a hill; the apparent indications life may have popped up out of the barrenness around me. As we grew closer, there were what appeared to be silhouettes of buildings and the pointed top of a water tower jutting up into the sky, held aloft on the stilt-like legs.

It was September of 2010, my sophomore year. I was about to become the new geek-girl on campus in Podunk, USA. How in the heck I'd been tricked into this move was beyond me. I guess I didn't have a lot of choice being a minor and under the influence of my freethinking parents. My dad, Will, had just taken a new job. Of course, being an earth child and all, his job had to focus on preservation of the home planet. So riding the wave of conservation he'd taken a position with the soil conservation office. This new office placed us smack dab in the middle of No-where-ville or if you prefer, the Oklahoma Panhandle.

I'll never forget my first sight of this one horse town. Brown grass and sandburs seemed to be the primary agricultural products. We pulled into town, or at least that's what they called it, and right away I knew there was no clear scientific explanation for the way the gears on the clock of history were moving backwards. I expected the Calvary to ride over the hill at any moment.

Having lived in the city most of my life, saying I was in shock would have been a mild way of expressing what I was experiencing. Gone were the concrete speed ramps, clover leafs, shopping plazas, and malls I'd grown up with, and the tradeoff seemed to be Ma's Diner, Bub's Gas Station, and Jack and Jill's Groceries. Of course, my eco-enlightened parents in the front seats were in heaven, quickly bonding with the sand and sage. I swear, if the modular home hadn't arrived before us, they would have been pitching a Tipi on the Buffalo grass of our lot.

"Sophie, isn't it magnificent?"

I nearly choked on Geneva's words. Geneva is my mom. We have one of those modern families where we call each other by our first names. It's supposed to make me feel more comfortable with them. Sometimes I think it's just to make them feel younger; in my less cooperative moods I revert to euphemisms.

"Mom, you've got to be kidding? Please tell me we're just stopping for gas."

She turned in her seat, the astonishment playing clearly on her face.

"You don't like it?"

"What's to like? There's nothing here. It's Precambrian."

Her eyes were telling me she'd already begun to hear the spirits of the earth speaking to her.

"That's what makes it so incredibly special sweetheart. It is so rustic and rugged."

"Well gee, let me get out and rally the rest of the wagons. We women folk are going to have to get the camp ready. Pa, you want I should fetch your rifle so's you can scrub us up some vittles?"

Geneva scoffed.

"Now Sophie, don't be ridiculous. They have a grocery store."

"I wonder if they got rattlesnake hanging in the window. That sounds tasty."

Will had killed the engine on the Toyota and with the air conditioning gone the Camry suddenly turned into a Japanese oven. I glanced at the temperature gauge on the mirror. It read one hundred and eight. For fear of suffocation, I opened the door and immediately slammed it shut.

"Well, we'll save a lot on utilities, no need for an oven. Hey Pa, run down to that there grocery store and grab a side of beef. We'll just throw it on the hood and flip it over a few times."

Now it was Will's turn to put me in my place, glaring into the mirror at me.

"Sophie, there's no smog in the sky, there's no exhaust fumes hanging in the air, and there's no concrete jungle hiding us in its shadow. Why can't you be more positive?"

"Dad, there's no concrete hiding us in its shadows because it hasn't been discovered here yet. I don't know what they build with since there aren't any trees to cut down, but my guess is they probably still rub sticks together to start the stove."

"You're being a little melodramatic. It isn't that backwards. Per capita, they have one of the finest schools in the state. There is no crime to speak of, no gangs or violence. What more could you ask for?

"How far to the beach?"

He wasn't to be deterred.

"Okay, so it isn't what you're used to. It'll grow on you."

"Look around you dad, nothing grows here."

"That's not true. They raise wheat, milo, some corn, and…cattle."

"Beef? You've stooped to using beef as an argument? Dad, you're a vegetarian."

"That's not true; I eat some meat."

"Where do they raise the fish?"

He stopped arguing with me from the rearview mirror and whipped around in his seat.

"Look, this is a good place, and I have a good job. The least you can do is try to make this work."

I rolled my eyes and opened the car door.

"I'm getting out of this sauna. Do they have the air conditioning hooked up yet?"

He glanced at the house.

"I don't know; let's go find out."

With that, the Earth Family from San Diego took one giant leap backwards for mankind and placed our first footprints into the Oklahoma soil. And no, they didn't have the air conditioning hooked up. In fact, it was nearly a week before they had it hooked up. I filled the tub up with cold water and camped there for the first seven days of my new residency. I have to admit, having grown up in the city, the only time I'd experienced water that cold and clear was on a back-to-nature trip into the Rockies.

It didn't take long before the locals came calling. Word quickly spread that there was a new family in town, and they didn't even have a pickup in the driveway.

I was destined to be an outcast from the beginning. I looked different, acted different, talked different, and I wasn't related to a soul in town; while most of my peers were either closely or distantly related. My plain, geeky style just didn't fit in with the Levi's and Wranglers crowd. The only thing that saved me was the other new girl in town. She was even more different than me. However, as I was a product of my parents' liberated philosophy, Tisha was setting her own course. With short-cropped, jet-black hair dyed red on the ends, a nose stud, ear piercings, and her eighties hair-band clothing style--she was just enough of a distraction to allow me to assimilate into the upper-lower popularity level with relative ease.

I didn't meet Cole right away. He was away at football camp when I arrived in town. In fact, I didn't meet him until the second week of school. Cole wasn't exactly Mr. Popular either, though it wasn't from lack of effort. He was a re-plant as well, second generation. His straight blond hair seemed to wander from unruly to wild. He had one lock of hair that spent most of the time falling down in front of his eyes. Skinny and lanky, he was just above me in the food chain. He had an advantage though; his humor was intoxicating. With comedic timing that would have made Robin Williams jealous, he often diverted disaster with laughter. In fact, if it weren't for his re-plant status and his severe allergies, he would probably have been a potential candidate for popularity promotion, but two things that can't be overcome in a small town are lack of genealogy and nasal congestion.

I'd seen him around and caught snippets of his comical musings. We shared the same biology class, but we'd never sat beside each other. He sat at the table near the front of the class, where he was often the center of attention. Though he was not what I'd call a troublemaker, he did have a tendency to speak when he wasn't supposed to speak. Rather than getting in trouble, he'd end up causing Mr. Johnson to break out in laughter. The trouble came when Mr. Johnson tried to regain control over his composure and the rest of the class. Cole didn't seem to know when to stop and would end up in the crosshairs.

One day after a particularly amusing class I ran into him in the hall.

"Hey, new girl. I'd call you by your name, but I don't know it."

"Sophie."

"Oh, yeah. Sophie. Got a last name?

"Carter."

He stuck out his hand.

"Cole Allen."

I clutched my books to my chest and reached for his hand.

"Nice to meet you, Cole."

"So, Sophie Carter, how'd you do on the test?"

"I got a ninety-six. How 'bout you?"

"Ninety-eight."

"Which one did you miss?"

"Number six."

I was puzzled.

"That was one of the easiest ones."

"Yeah, I had a brain cramp."

"What'd you put?"

"Green suit, red beard, Irish accent."

"The question was: What are the characteristics of a lepton? You gave the characteristics of a Leprechaun."

He smiled.

"I told you, brain cramp."

I gave him a knowing smile in return.

"Right."

"So, how's the assimilation going? Making any new friends?"

I shook my head.

"Not really. They're pretty cliquish."

"They're not cliquish; they're clannish because they're cousins. It's really not so bad after a while."

"No one's been mean or anything, I just get the feeling they don't want me around."

His face crinkled.

"Nah, that's not it at all. It's kind of like walking into a room full of rabbits. They're comfortable with each other, and you're moving into their space. They scamper to the other side of the room. Once you've been there a while they start moving around again like you're not in the room."

"Rabbits, huh?"

"It's the first thing I could come up with."

I rolled my eyes.

"Want to sit together at lunch."

"Sure."

I closed my locker, and we started walking to the lunchroom.

"Hey, have you seen that other new girl? Now that'll scare those rabbits right out of the room."

I smiled.

"She's actually kind of nice. She's just really expressive."

He raised his eyebrows and nodded.

"So you are on the football team?" I prodded.

"I'm not just on the football team. At this phase of the season, I'm one of the most important elements of the team."

As I considered his build, I couldn't hide my skepticism.

"What position do you play?"

"Tackling dummy."

I laughed.

"I can see that would be an important position. Do you get a letter for that?"

"Not unless they put me in to let the other team practice too."

"Why do you go out?"

"Uh, because I like it."

"You like getting pounded by everyone else?"

"No, I like football. I may get pounded this year, but next year I'll be better."

He held the cafeteria door open for me, and we lined up with the other students. When we had our trays, we found a table in the back. A few minutes later the ever outrageous Tisha joined us, and shortly after that Cole's best friend Duane became part of the newly formed group. It happened that quickly. From that day forward, we sat together at lunch each day.

Duane was a rather unlikely best friend for Cole. Whereas Cole had high hopes for being an athlete, Duane *was* an athlete and one of the stars of the basketball team. Upon first appearance, Duane might be mistaken as a tall, carefree farm boy, but once on the court he turned into an aggressive and athletic machine. His aggressiveness stopped at the court, however, because Duane was as socially backwards as they come. Although not exactly popular because of this trait, he was still treated with a healthy amount of respect. Hey, even in a small town the guy who carries the team has his privileges.

We made quite a group. Cole had his smart and zany wit. Duane had his awkward social skills. Tisha had more brass than any guy I ever met. And then there was me, the plain, ordinary, geek girl. We had somehow formed our own social group. It was at least a beginning, and I finally started to feel like I fit somewhere. It didn't change the way I felt about being far from everything familiar. It was still a boring little town, but we could be bored together. And sometimes we even found ways to beat the boredom.

The Earth children (aka: my parents) seemed to be happy enough. They continued to thrive on the back to nature feeling that had brought us here in the beginning. Mom was reveling in staying at home, and she was even showing signs of being normal. I found myself calling her mom more and Geneva less.

I started to notice changes in my dad as well. When we were back in San Diego, he'd come home each day seeming to be stressed to the max. Here it was almost like he was coming home from a day at the golf course. And that's another thing, with the golf course at Spring Creek so nearby, they even took up playing golf together on the weekends.

I guess some people adapt differently. As bored as I was, I couldn't help being happy for them. They seemed to bloom in that dry, dead environment.

Chapter Two

Pom-poms danced in the chill of the fall air as the band played the school fight song. It was one more cheesy feeling to mark on my list of reasons for wanting to escape from this place. I'd never been to a football game, high school or otherwise, and I wouldn't have been at that one if it weren't for Tisha pleading with me to go. She hadn't struck me as the type to be mesmerized by school pride, so I couldn't for the life of me understand her reasons for wanting to attend.

The lights cast their glow on the field, and we watched as the players bounded out through the spirit line. I looked for Cole's number when they lined up along the edge of the field. I was amused by his image when my eyes had finally sifted through the group to locate him. He looked like a piece of spaghetti contrasted with his teammates.

As I glanced over at Tisha, I suddenly understood the real reason she'd wanted to be here. Duane sat between us, his eyes zeroed in on the field, not wanting to miss a second of the opening kickoff. Tisha's gaze was on him; goo-goo eyeing his every move. It was evident if things went the way she was hoping, I'd soon be a third wheel to the little bicycle of love she was riding.

"Great," I mumbled under my breath. "I could have been at home watching an episode of Dr. Who."

As a distraction from my boredom, I asked Tisha if she wanted to go get some popcorn. She hardly broke her gaze on Duane, who, of course, still sat mesmerized by the battle taking place out on the field.

"No, you go ahead."

I rolled my eyes as I slipped off to the concession stand.

By the end of the first half, Tisha had all but abandoned me. Although, she still hadn't gained Duane's attention. Bored beyond belief, I'd counted the number of lights beaming down on the field, the number of fence posts surrounding the field, and the average number of popcorn bags leaving the concession stand per hour. How did people get into this game?

After exhausting all the ways I could find to occupy my time, I resorted to the only thing I could find – trying to understand what was so exciting about a bunch of guys pounding each other. We had the ball, and we were progressing towards the goal line. That would have made us the offensive players. They, on the other hand, were trying to prevent us from scoring; that would make them the defenders. Our players lined up, and their players lined up. The lines seemed to be relatively close to evenly matched, so unless someone made a mistake there was a stalemate there. We had two men in the backfield and one who received the ball from the line. I nudged Duane.

"What do they call the guy who takes the ball?"

"Which one?"

"The one who gets it from the guy on the line?"

I got an annoyed look from Tisha. What the heck? It was her fault I was asking in the first place.

"The center takes the ball and hikes it to the quarterback. The quarterback can run with it, pass it, or hand it off to one of the other backs in the backfield." Duane said as he pointed out each position.

"Oh."

I watched a couple of plays. The quarterback tried to run around the right side, but he was stopped. On the next play, he was hit just as he was handing it off to one of the guys in the back. The ball spun across the grass, and someone jumped on it.

I nudged Duane again. I got another irritated look from Tisha.

"What happened then?"

"He fumbled, but we jumped on it, so it's still our ball."

"What would have happened if we hadn't?"

"They would have taken over the ball."

"Oh."

The next play we moved the ball forward down the field a little. The referee blew his whistle, and the time stopped ticking off the clock.

Another nudge, another look. I stuck my tongue out at her.

"What happened then?"

"We got a first down," Duane replied without taking his eyes off the field.

"What's that mean?"

This time I got an annoyed look from him, but at least he looked at me. That's more than I can say for any attention he was offering Tisha.

He took a deep breath.

"We have four downs to move the ball ten yards. If we make it, we get four more. If we don't they get the ball."

"Oh."

On the next play, the quarterback started back the opposite direction.

"What's he doing?" I asked, my voice elevated. "He's going the wrong way!"

Duane didn't look at me; he just shook his head.

"He's going back for a pass."

"Oh."

The ball went into the air. It floated down the field...ten yards...twenty yards...thirty yards. The hands of both our players and their players stretched up into the air.

I jumped up out of my seat.

"Get it!" I shouted, then stomped my foot on the bleachers as the ball fell to the ground.

"Dang it!"

I looked at Duane, as I sheepishly sat back down.

"Sorry."

He just grinned.

"No problem."

Tisha glared again.

"Sorry." I mouthed the words to her.

On the following play, the quarterback again went back for a pass and that time he connected with his receiver down field. The Bulldogs scored their first touchdown of the night, and I jumped out of my seat along with everyone else in the stands. Okay, so maybe a person could get a little excited when they started to understand what was going on out there.

Our team rallied and came back with two more touchdowns by the end of the second half. We got an extra point with a kick after each one of them. We won the game twenty-one to eight. I figured I had annoyed Tisha enough during the game, so as soon as it was over I slipped off by myself. I decided to head over to the locker room to wait for Cole.

After a little while, he came out of the locker room with a few of the other guys.

"Well, what did you think?"

"It was okay. I was kind of bored at first, but once I started figuring it out, it didn't seem so bad. Sorry, you didn't get to play."

"It's alright. I didn't expect to. I probably won't unless we're way ahead or way behind."

"And you're okay with that? Spending all your time on the sidelines?"

"Sure. I'll be better next year," he said with sincerity.

"I'm sure you will," I encouraged.

"Want to go down to the Dawg? I'm starving."

I rode with Cole down to the Grumpy Dawg. It was a local hangout. Pretty much everyone was there, except Duane and Tisha.

"Where's Duane?" Cole asked.

"I don't know. I left him with Tisha at the game."

"Hm. I wonder where they went."

"So, why doesn't Duane play football? He seems to know quite a bit about the game."

"Oh, he used to play, but since he got so into basketball, he practices all year long. He doesn't want to take a chance on getting hurt during football season and then having to sit out the basketball season. I think his dad had something to do with it. He's been grooming him for basketball for years. His dad was a big basketball star back in high school."

"Oh, well, I guess if he likes it that much maybe he's making the right decision."

"So, are you going to go out?"

"Out where?"

He laughed.

"Are you going out for girls' basketball?"

"Uh, no."

"Why not?"

"I don't do sports. I'm not that athletic."

Cole grabbed my arm and squeezed my bicep.

"Hey, you have a little muscle there. What makes you think you aren't athletic?"

"I'm just not. Besides, when I run too much my asthma flares up."

"Exercise-induced?"

"Huh?"

"Do you have exercise induced asthma?"

"I don't know. I have asthma."

"Does it only flare up when you run?"

"Um, mostly. Sometimes when it's real humid."

"They have medication for that."

"I don't like medication."

"Doesn't fit with your world view, huh?"

"Don't start."

"I'm not starting. I was just making an observation."

"Let's observe something else."

"So you figured out the game?"

"Pretty much. I'll probably have it down by the time you start playing on the first team next year." I winked at him.

"Good. I don't want you to miss anything." He said grabbing for his soda.

We were quiet for a while before he spoke again.

"What are you doing tomorrow?"

"Uh, I don't know. I'll probably sleep in."

"You want to go fishing?"

"Fishing? Like for fish?" I squawked.

He laughed.

"No for alligators. I just call it fishing to keep from scaring the girls off."

"I don't know. I've never been fishing. What do you do with them?" I asked, ignoring his obvious sarcasm.

"Usually just throw them back."

"You touch them? But aren't they all slimy and stuff?"

"That shouldn't be a problem for a girl of science like you. Should it? Haven't you ever dissected a frog?"

"I used gloves."

"Oh, come on. It's no big deal. You can wash your hands off in the lake."

I scrunched my nose.

"I didn't think you were a girly girl."

"I'm not, but I'm not a squirrelly girl either."

"That was a good one. Sophie made a joke…Sophie made a joke." He sang out.

I punched him in the shoulder.

"Fine. I'll go. What time?"

"How about seven?"

"Seven in the morning? On a Saturday? What? Do the fish take a nap in the afternoon or something?"

"No, it's just better if you get there early. Besides, it won't be as hot."

"It's fall; it won't be hot anyway."

"It'll be hot-ter later in the day."

I rolled my eyes.

"Fine. Seven."

"I better get you home then. You won't be able to roll out of bed in time."

"I have an alarm clock and I get up at six-thirty every morning for school."

"Six-thirty? I get up at fifteen till eight."

"I'm a girl."

"But you're not a girly girl."

"No, I'm not." I smiled as we stood up to leave.

"Well, wear an old pair of jeans, Girly Girl. I wouldn't want you to get all that slimy stuff on something nice."

Cole was there bright and early the next morning, and I was ready. I wasn't about to give him the satisfaction of making fun of me for being late.

"Wow, I'm impressed. I didn't even get to wake up your parents by honking the horn."

"You wouldn't have anyway."

"Why's that?"

"Well, first, you're not that rude and second, they've been up since six. They're teeing off at eight."

He smiled.

"Okay, then. I guess we're off."

The drive out to the lake was a long one. I'd never been out that far into the countryside. The lake was fed by a stream that wandered down through a pasture and into a valley between hills. Lined along one side by sandstone cliffs, the other side was largely grass with sandy beach in spots. Tall grass grew along the edge of the water with small scrub trees dotted here and there. With the exception of a grove on a small finger of land which jutted out towards the middle of the lake, there were few trees. On that point, there stood a group of cottonwoods, tall and thin. The dam stretched across the north end of the lake.

We pulled up along a sandy beach, and Cole began to unload the truck.

"Have you ever been fishing?" he asked as he opened his tackle box.

"No, never," I answered. Looking at the tackle box and fishing poles, I got a sudden sense of queasiness.

"You're not going to make me stick my own worms on the hook are you?"

"What's wrong, Girly-Girl, you a little squeamish of worm guts?"

"Okay, so maybe there is a little girly-girl inside of me."

"Relax; I don't usually use live bait."

"What are we going to catch them on?"

"We'll use lures."

"Don't they know the difference? I mean, don't they smell them or something?"

"Catfish smell, bass use their sight and touch."

"So we're fishing for bass?"

"Generally. Maybe some crappie if it looks like they're hitting today."

"Will we use one of those floatie things you watch?"

He chuckled.

"A bobber? No, not with lures."

"I get bored just sitting around, you know."

"You won't get bored using lures. You'll be busy the whole time. You have to work the lure to catch the fish."

I nodded.

Cole rigged up the fishing poles, and we made our way down to the edge of the lake.

"Now watch what I do."

I watched as he cast the lure out into the lake near a bunch of cattails. As he reeled the lure in, he worked the fishing rod in an up and down motion. He cast it out again, and the surface of the water exploded with a splash.

"There he is," he said as the fish fought back against him.

It was amazing to watch as it danced up out of the water and along the surface. The end of the rod bowed and straightened, then bowed some more. When he finally lifted it out of the water, the colors of the fish were amazing -- varying shades of gray, white, black, and green – a touch of yellow.

"What is it?"

"A largemouth bass. Want to hold him?" he asked as he removed the lure.

My eyes widened as he held it up with his thumb in its mouth.

"I don't think so."

"Aw, come on. Give it a try," he encouraged.

I cautiously raised my hand toward the fish. It flipped its tail, and I jerked my hand back.

"It won't hurt you."

"Will it bite?" I asked timidly.

"It might, but it won't hurt."

I raised my hand up.

"Stick your thumb in his mouth." He directed.

With Cole's help, the fish transferred from his hand to mine. It was heavier than I thought it would be.

"How much do you think it weighs?"

"Oh, probably about two pounds." He pointed toward the lake. "Okay, you can put it back in."

"What do I do? Just toss it?"

"No, just bend down and put it back in the water."

I followed his direction and as soon as the fish touched the water it tossed its tail around splashing water up into my face. I dropped it, and it took off.

His laugh gave him away.

"You knew it was going to do that, didn't you?" I asked, looking at him while the water dripped down my face. "You butt."

He stopped laughing long enough to wipe the water away from my face with the tail of his shirt.

"I guess that wasn't very nice of me."

"I'll remember that," I cautioned.

"I guess you won't trust me very much next time, will you?"

"I shouldn't have trusted you before. I know you better than that."

"No blood, no foul," he said, shrugging his shoulders.

"What's that supposed to mean?"

"It means you didn't get hurt, other than your pride, so you're okay."

He picked the rod up off the bank.

"Okay, now you try."

"I don't know what to do."

"Didn't you watch me?"

"Yes, but I don't know how you did it."

He stepped behind me. I could feel his body against me as he placed the rod in my hand.

"Okay, see this button...hold your finger on it...don't let go yet...Okay, now pull it back over your shoulder like this..."

He stepped away from me.

"Now, when you fling it forward, let go of the button."

I lunged forward letting go of the button and the lure splash into the water about three feet in front of me. He took the rod from my hand and reeled the lure in again.

"You let go too late. You have to let go as you cast forward. Kind of like throwing a ball."

"I don't throw balls. I told you; I'm not athletic."

"You don't have to be athletic."

He stepped up behind me once again. I could feel his warmth against me. His cheek brushed against my ear.

"Let's try again. Now, push the button...pull it back..."

This time he kept his hand on mine. It was innocent and meaningless in the scheme of things, but the simple touch of his fingers against mine was electric.

"Now, nice and easy...cast forward and let go of the button." I felt his breath against my ear as he spoke softly.

Our arms moved forward together. I watched as the lure sailed out into the lake.

I jumped up and down in one spot.

"I did it! I did it!"

He smiled.

"Now don't let your emotions get the best of you, Girly Girl."

I smirked at him.

"Now what?"

"Just reel it in...slowly... Lower the rod tip. Raise it back up."

I felt a tug.

"I felt something."

He smiled.

"Next time you feel a tug, pull back on the rod to set the hook."

I continued to move the rod as he'd directed, but when the lure came back up to the bank, there was nothing on it.

"I didn't catch anything."

"Well, you just have to keep trying."

He bent down and started rigging up another rod.

"Now try casting it out by yourself."

I pushed down on the button and raised the rod over my shoulder as he had shown me. Then I cast forward. It wasn't as pretty, but it landed near the edge of the cattails. I suppressed my excitement.

"Okay, now work the lure."

There was the tug. I pulled back on the rod. The water broke as the large bass leapt from beneath the surface.

"Oh my gosh! I got one!"

"That's great. Now just kind of play it a little. Don't pull it in too quick. You don't want him to let go. Pull back and then drop the tip and reel. There you go. Just like that. Keep going."

As I worked the reel, I felt the fish swim off in zigzagging directions. Closer. Closer. It worked toward the bank.

"When you get it close, lift the rod and pull it out of the water."

Moments later I stood proudly holding my first fish while Cole took a picture with his phone. When it came time to place the fish back in the lake, I was prepared for the splash.

We fished throughout the morning. About nine o'clock Cole placed his rod down on the bank.

"Want something to eat? I brought some snacks."

"I really need to pee."

He pointed toward the grove of trees.

"There's the bathroom."

My eyes widened.

"I have to go in the trees?"

"It's either that or hold it."

"You've got to be kidding."

"Sorry, no bathrooms out here."

"Why would you bring me out here where there aren't any bathrooms?"

"You said you wanted to fish."

"You could have warned me."

"Well, I guess I could have, but I didn't think about it. It's pretty simple to me."

"It's pretty simple *for* you."

"Yeah, that too."

I glanced at the trees and then around the lake.

"What if someone sees?"

"We're the only ones here and I promise not to peek."

"I can wait," I said, stubbornly.

"Suit yourself."

He reached into the cooler.

"Want a bottle of water?" he asked with a smile.

"No, I think I'll pass."

Thirty minutes later, I was about to explode. I'd spent the last half hour trying to convince myself that I didn't really need to go, but all I'd done was make it worse. I finally reached a point where I simply couldn't wait any longer without a disaster.

"You promise not to peek?"

"I'll just be concentrating on the fish."

"I've never had to go outside before."

"It's no big deal. Just go into the trees and do your thing."

"It's a little bit easier for you."

"Yeah, I guess it is, but even if we left now, it would be another thirty minutes before we got back to town."

"I can't wait that long."

"Go ahead. I won't watch."

As I made my way toward the trees to do my duty to my bladder, he called over his shoulder.

"Just watch for snakes."

As if I didn't have enough on my mind. If he called me a girly girl again after this, I'd throttle him.

"See any snakes?" He asked as I stepped up to the edge of the lake, a snicker in his voice.

"You just had to say that when I headed out into the weeds."

"Would you rather I hadn't warned you?"

I thought about it for a second.

"No. And thanks for not peeking."

"No problem. You hungry?"

"No, not really. Thanks anyway."

I caught a total of six fish. Cole caught four, but his were all bigger than mine. We got back to town around two in the afternoon. He dropped me off.

"Guess I'll see you later," I said as I turned to head into the house.

"You want to come over later and watch a movie?" he asked. I walked back to the driver's side of the truck.

"I'll have to see. I don't know what my mom and dad have planned."

"Okay, just call me later."

I stood at the door and leaned in to kiss him on the cheek.

"Thanks. I had fun."

"I'm glad," he said with a grin. "Are you up for another trip out to the lake tomorrow morning?"

"At seven?"

He nodded.

I rolled my eyes.

"I guess, but you're cutting into my beauty sleep."

"Don't worry. You don't need any beauty sleep," he commented, his face beginning to blush as he realized what he'd said. I felt the blood moving to my face as well.

"Thanks."

There was an awkward pause.

"Hey, you did pretty good for a girly girl."

I punched him in the arm.

"I caught more fish than you; I peed in the trees; I got fish slime on my hands…You can't call me that anymore."

He shrugged.

"I guess not. I'll have to think of a new nickname."

"How about just calling me Sophie?"

"That'll work for now," he said as he put the truck into gear.

I watched as he drove off.

"Yep, that'll do for now," I thought as he disappeared down the road.

Chapter Three

"I can't!" I whined.

"Sure you can. I thought you'd lost the whole girly girl thing," Cole encouraged.

"I can't! It's too gross."

"We've already covered this. You've dissected frogs for the pure enjoyment of it."

"I explained that; it was for biology, and I was using gloves and a scalpel."

"I saw you; you were practically sticking your nose in its innards."

"I was not," I said defensively. "Besides, this is different."

"It's just a little worm."

"But black stuff gushes out of it when you do it."

He laughed.

"Black stuff? Now there's a scientific term for you."

"Okay, the black gooey mix of castings, intestines, and partially digested food."

"That's better," he said contentedly.

"I still can't."

"Yes, you can. You just slide the hook up inside...like this..."

He demonstrated, and I turned away.

"I can't. I thought you used artificial bait, anyway. That's what you said yesterday."

"Well, sometimes I use the real stuff. It depends on what we're trying to catch. Today, we're fishing for catfish."

"I can't."

"Then you're gonna starve today because the only way we'll be eating anything is if we catch something."

"We're going to eat the fish?"

"It's catfish. Of course, we're going to eat them?"

"Can't we just throw them back like we did before?"

"These are different fish."

"What's so different about them? Huh? Why do the other fish get to live, and these have to die?"

"These are great to eat. The others are more for the sport. They're just fun to catch."

He paused.

"Besides, what do you care which ones live or die? That's what they're here for, right?"

There he went again; taking a stab at my world view.

"I'm not going to bite on that one," I said smiling at him.

"Oh, Sophie made another joke. Too bad no one was here to hear it but me." He said it with a little grit in his voice. Apparently I was starting to irritate him.

"I'm not hungry and maybe I don't like fish."

"That won't work. You've told me all about the seafood on the coast and how much you enjoyed eating it."

"Well, I was talking about seafood from a restaurant. It wasn't a fish with which I'd developed an acquaintance."

"Now you're developing an acquaintance with a fish? We'll let me introduce you to them all."

He turned and made a bow toward the lake, stretching out his arm like some kind of butler.

"Fish, this is Sophie."

Then he turned to me.

"Sophie, these are the fish. Now, you have an acquaintance with them all." He smirked.

"Look, I'm not trying to make you mad, but can't we just throw them back like we did before. I don't care if we don't have anything for lunch."

"Well, we could, but we have to catch them first," he said as he cast out his line into the pond.

"Now, your turn. Just bait your hook."

"I can't."

He grabbed for my hand and thrust a squiggling worm into it. I picked it up and watched as it curled and twisted as it dangled from my fingers.

"I'm not afraid of worms. See?" I said holding it in front of his face.

"Just the black gunk inside of it," he said with a smile.

"Yep."

"Okay, okay. I'll bait the first one, but after you lose it don't get mad at me when you don't have any bait on your hook, and I'm catching all the fish." He grumbled as he took the worm from my fingers and started sliding the hook into it, causing me to look away once again.

"I can't believe, being the mad scientist you are, you can't handle seeing some worm guts."

"I can handle seeing worm guts...in a lab...with a pair of gloves."

He rolled his eyes, then flipped the fishing rod. I watched as the fishing line snaked out into the air, and the sinker pulled the mistreated worm down into the water with a plop. The surface of the water broke into circular waves which danced out wider and wider until they finally disappeared. He handed me the rod and I watched as the little red and white plastic ball floated around on the reflection of the morning sun as it began to rise.

"So now what?"

"We wait."

"Wait for what?"

He pointed out toward the water at my bobber.

"For that."

I glanced in the direction he was pointing just in time to see my bobber dart below the surface.

"Oh my gosh! Do I have a fish?"

The bobber popped back to the surface.

"Probably not anymore."

"What am I supposed to do?"

"You have to watch for it to go under. When it goes under water, you have to start reeling it in."

"Do I reel it in now?"

"Not unless you just want to check it to see if you still have any bait."

"You mean they already took my bait away?"

"Probably."

"That's not right. They took my bait, and I didn't even get to catch a fish?"

His mouth screwed up into a smirk.

"I told you; you have to be ready. You weren't ready."

I looked back out on the water to contemplate my next move and watched as the bobber sunk below the surface once again.

"It went under again."

"Then reel it in."

"Now?"

He dropped his head back in exasperation.

"Well, do I?"

He gathered his patience.

"Listen carefully. I can't believe I have to draw a picture for a genius. You reel it in when it goes down, not after they let go of it."

"So do you need to reel yours in now?" I asked pointing out at the pond. "Or now?" I quizzed again as his bobber popped back up to the surface.

He grabbed for his pole and started to reel.

"I missed it." He mumbled.

"You have to reel when it goes down, not after they let go of it," I offered mockingly.

For a time, we sat in silence. I watched as the round red and white ball floated lonely on the still surface. I fidgeted with the zipper on my jacket while I stared out at the water, trying to lose my impatience in the beauty of the morning. The blending of the orange sun lifting into the blue sky began to morph into a crimson color casting a reddish glow on the water and the world around me. As the sun moved higher, the crimson gave way to burnt orange, to orange, to yellow, and finally a bright white center surrounded by a yellow starburst. It was almost as if someone had slid a filter between it and the earth, sucking away the color and washing out the sky.

"Should I reel it in now?"

He smiled.

"You're not good at this waiting stuff, are you?"

"Well, you said they probably got my bait."

"Yeah, probably. Go ahead."

I picked up the fishing rod and tried to reel it in, but the handle didn't move. He reached over and turned the rod in my hand, so the reel was hanging down below the handle.

"You need to hold it that way. Now try."

I turned the handle once again, and the center of the reel started to spin collecting the fishing line.

"Well, I didn't have to put it down and wait, last time. I just got mixed up," I explained as I watched the line gathered on the spool. Looking out over the pond, I could see the bobber move across the surface creating a wake as it darted toward the water's edge. When it neared the edge, the tip of the rod started to bow.

"I got one! I got one!" I exclaimed, my excitement getting the best of me.

"You're hung up on the reeds."

"Oh."

He stood up and took the rod from my hands. I watched as he worked the fishing rod back and forth trying to free the hook from the reeds; his image silhouetted against the morning sky. I couldn't help but smile. He looked so natural and at ease. Though I knew I had been trying his patience, he was maintaining it well.

Cole got the line loose and reeled it in.

"Looks like you've lost your bait. You know the rules. You have to bait this one," he chided.

I squinted at him, the morning sun in my eyes.

"You're going to stick with that aren't you?"

"Yeah, I am. If you need some sunglasses, there's another pair in the top of the tackle box."

I stood and put my hands on my hips, trying desperately to give him my best pleading look.

"Nope. It's not gonna work. This one is yours."

I moved over to the tackle box and found the sunglasses in the top tray. An idea came to mind, and I began to rummage through the box. There were all kinds of little fish lures with hooks, rubber lizards and worms, and these yellow fringy ones with shiny dangly things kind of like earrings with hooks. I picked one up and held it behind my back.

"I'll bait my own hook, but you have to show me how to put it on again."

He shrugged.

"Sure, no problem."

"Okay, I choose this bait," I said holding it out in the palm of my hand.

He smiled.

"I gotcha, didn't I."

"Yeah, that was pretty tricky."

"Can I use it?"

"Yeah, but you're not going to catch catfish with it."

"I don't care which kind of fish I catch. I just want to catch a fish."

He set his rod down on the bank.

"Here, let me show you how to put it on."

He took the lure from me and sat down in the grass.

"Okay, now watch."

He took the end of the fishing line and looped it through the lure, then twisted it a few times and ran the end back through the loop. When he pulled the line tight, the knot shrank, and when he held it up in front of me, it dangled from the end of the line, the little metal blades catching the light.

"What kind of lure is this?"

"It's a spinner bait; as it moves through the water, these little blades spin catching the light and the attention of the fish."

"What is this fringy stuff?"

"It's called a skirt. It serves a couple of purposes. The color and the movement of the fringe help to catch the attention of the fish, and it also helps keep the hook from hanging up in the weeds."

"Okay, so what do I do with it?"

"You cast it out and then you reel it back in just like we did last time. If you can get your cast to land where you want it, you would do better getting closer to the reeds. Fish like to hide over along the edge, but you probably want to stay away from there until you get used to casting it."

I took the rod from him and brought it back over my shoulder, trying to do it like I did before. This reel was different though and it didn't have the little button to push.

"You have to cast this one a little different."

He stepped around behind me and helped me line the rod up over my shoulder. Just as the day before, I could feel his body at my back, the warmth seeming to envelope me. As he reached forward, his chest touched against my back. His hands slid over mine as he positioned my fingers on the reel.

"Okay, see this silver thing?"

I felt his breath against my ear, causing me to lose my concentration. When I'd collected myself, I nodded.

"Flip it back like this and hold the line with your finger."

As he instructed me, I turned my head to watch and my face met his, our noses touching and our lips just inches apart.

I felt a tingle begin inside of me, and my heart skipped a beat. Just the movement of a few inches and I could taste his lips for the first time. It would have been an easy move, but it would also have been a big move. It would have changed everything between us, and I so loved what we had. I was comfortable with Cole and as strong as the pull was to take a chance; I was desperate not to lose something I treasured more than nearly anything else I could imagine.

I know he felt it, too. It was there, the hesitation in the air, a moment of decision and I'm not sure if I was disappointed or pleased when he took charge and pulled back.

"Sorry," he said clearing his throat. "Anyway, I'll just kind of show you where to release the line. See, as you move forward let the line go about here."

Amazingly, there was no awkwardness hanging over either of us. Life went on just as it had. My first cast with the new reel didn't go all that far, but with a little practice I got better. I was able to direct the lure to the general area in which I wanted it to land with a plop. As I watched it move closer to me, it looked like a colorful butterfly floating through the water, the spinning leaves of metal sending out reflections of light as it moved. It took a number of casts before I felt the first tug on the lure. At first I thought it had gotten stuck on something, but when the fish broke the surface of the water, I felt my stomach lurch.

"I've got one!" I screamed with greater confidence than I did the time I got it caught in the weeds.

Cole moved over beside me.

"It's a bass. Okay, start reeling it in, but remember how they fought yesterday, so be ready."

The fish pulled against the rod causing it to bow. As it moved closer, I could feel it trying to change directions and do the zigzagging thing like the day before. Just as it got near the bank, the fish started to thrash around. My adrenaline was flowing, and I could feel the excitement coursing through me.

"It's a big one. Keep working it until you get it close. I'll help you get it in." Cole instructed.

The rod bowed when I lifted the bass from the water. Then with one final wiggle, it dropped from the lure and splashed back down into the water, leaving me empty handed and disappointed.

"Get it!" I screamed at Cole, the disbelief causing me to lose control.

"It got away."

"Don't you have a net or something?" My voice was shrill.

"Sophie, it got away. A net won't do us any good now."

My mouth hung open. My face was blank of expression.

"What happened?" I asked still trying to absorb the loss.

"You didn't get the hook set good?"

"I didn't what?" I heard my voice squeak.

"You didn't set the hook good."

"What is that? You didn't tell me about setting something." I said suddenly finding a way to place the blame for my lost fish.

"Yes, I did. Remember yesterday when we were using the other lures. I told you; you have to get the hook set."

"You should have reminded me."

He laughed.

"I'm sorry. Maybe I should have."

"Sorry?" I looked at him incredulously. "Obviously that was an important point or I wouldn't have lost the fish!"

He started laughing at me.

"What?"

"An hour ago you wouldn't touch a worm. Now you're ticked off because you think I made you lose your fish."

"Well, if you're going to teach someone how to do something, don't you think you should include all the important stuff?"

He was still amused.

"I did."

"But I just learned yesterday. You should have had a recap or something."

"Oh, like a pre-test in biology."

"Yeah, something like that."

"Hey, some things just have to be experienced. You'll get another one."

"I don't care. You said it was a big one."

"You were just going to throw it back anyway."

"But not before I could say I caught it."

"Well, it's too late now."

I crossed my arms in disappointment.

I glanced around. Across the pond, a turtle climbed up on the bank to lie in the sun. The head of another popped up through the water. At the edge of the water schools of minnows darted back and forth while a couple of dragonflies appeared to be chasing each other swooping and diving like combat aircraft, their wings fluttering as they zipped by me. A bullfrog took the opportunity to spring from the reeds breaking the water's surface, leaving behind a series of swelling ripples and the sound of its splash.

"If I help you catch another one, will you forgive me?" Cole asked, his eyes teasing me.

I could feel my face breaking into a smile.

"I'd forgive you anyway. After all, you have given me a beautiful morning."

He shook his head.

"No, God gave you the beautiful morning. I'm just spending it with you."

"Either way, I'm having a great time."

"That's all I could hope for." He said with satisfaction. "Now, let's try again."

Chapter Four

Chatty sounds surrounded us. The bustle of orders being taken and served mingled with conversations. The big screen on the wall displayed a major league baseball game. The walls were decorated with high school, college, and professional sports memorabilia. We were at the Grumpy Dawg.

Cole took a big bite of his burger. He could eat more than a guy twice his size. I was always amazed at how he could consume so much and stay so thin. I picked at a plate of French fries. After he had swallowed he continued to critique my world view.

"So it's all just a chemical reaction," he responded with cynicism.

I nodded.

"Yeah, basically. Electrical responses as well, but those have a chemical basis too."

He looked at me with his head tilted.

"Mind, spirit, soul? They don't mean anything?"

"I see no scientific basis to believe we have souls," I replied indifferently.

"So what makes you who you are?"

"My experiences make me who I am."

"Your experiences shape who you are and who you become, but what makes you – the conscious you – who you are? Suppose your slate was blank, with no experiences, you would still be different from me or Tisha. What makes you the conscious person you are?" he quizzed.

"Consciousness is simply the firing of neurons in the brain exchanging information. It is a physical, material act. This exchange of information, influenced by experience makes us conscious."

"But before the experience, you were you. Even if nothing happened, if there were no experience, you are you."

"Well, consciousness has been debated for years and will be debated far into the future. It doesn't get around the fact that the brain and the body are simply a physical reaction."

He took another bite while he turned it around in his head. We'd been at this for months. It didn't take him long to realize my way of thinking was rather different than most of the students at Smalltown High.

"So with this purely physical view of human consciousness in mind, what's the purpose of life?" He questioned, taking up his argument again.

"We're animals, living creatures. Our instincts tell us to continue life."

"So, we're just seed machines."

"Well, not exactly. We do have the advantage of intelligence. We can learn more about our world and our universe."

"Why?" he asked.

My face scrunched.

"Why what?" I asked missing his meaning.

"Why would it matter if we learn more?"

"So we can gain more knowledge. We can discover more about how the universe formed. We can improve our way of living. We can extend the life of our planet."

He was unmoved.

"Why?"

"To advance society and humankind," I said, stating the obvious.

"But why?"

He was starting to sound like a parrot repeating the same phrase over and over, and it was beginning to annoy me.

"Why do you keep asking why?"

He leaned his elbow on the table and scratched his head.

"Because I just don't see the purpose if we only exist on this planet. If we are simply a chemical reaction; if life ends when the neurons quit firing; if the light goes out when the switch goes off; then why seek knowledge? Why improve our way of living? Why extend the life of the planet? What's the point?"

"The point is to perpetuate the species."

"For what? If it all ends in a box, what's it matter? I just don't get it."

"Because that's what we do. We grow, experience, and evolve to become better."

"Better for what?"

"We're here aren't we? We live here; we all depend upon each other; our societies are interconnected. Why wouldn't we want to improve our situations?"

"Why don't we just throw the main breaker and turn all the lights out?"

"That's a stupid question."

"What's stupid about it? Why go on?"

"Cole, were not going to agree on this."

He took a different stab.

"Okay, so when we die, that's it?"

I swirled my straw in my strawberry shake. The Dawg had the greatest shakes, thick and rich, lots of strawberry chunks.

"Yeah, basically. We're born; we live, we populate, we learn, and we die."

"That's kind of a depressing way of seeing things. So again, what's the point?"

I sat up.

"Cole, why do we have these conversations? We never agree."

"I'm just trying to understand your point of view. That's all."

He paused.

"So how do you reconcile yourself with that?"

"I have no problem reconciling myself with my world view. We are the product of evolution and our purpose is to continue life."

"But if you think there isn't anything more to it then why do you keep it going? I mean, if there is nothing more, I just don't get how you find the reason to go on. It all seems so absolutely useless to me with that kind of philosophy. How can any sensible person find a reason to go on if it is all for nothing?"

I dabbed a French fry in some ketchup.

"So what are you saying Cole? I'm not sensible, or I should cut my wrist?"

"I'm not saying either. I just don't understand how a person can wake up each morning knowing their only purpose in life is to produce more seeds. It makes me feel like a weed or something."

I shook my head in defense.

"I never said that was our only purpose. I feel part of my purpose is to add to humanity, more knowledge, more understanding, more experience."

He was silent, staring off at nothing in particular. We'd been friends for a while now; I knew Cole well enough to know he was thinking of a different line of attack.

"So, you're okay with death?"

"Yeah. We're all going to die. It's something we all face. Life ends."

"You seem so casual about it. You don't get worked up over it at all?"

"No, not really."

"What about your parents? Are you concerned about them dying?" he questioned.

"I'm sure I'll miss them if that's what you mean. But it doesn't do any good to get hung up over it. It's inevitable. I don't know why people get so worked up over trying to live as long as they can."

"So if you got a disease or something you wouldn't do anything about it?"

"You mean like treatment?"

"Yeah." He shrugged.

"I guess no one knows until they're there, but I don't think so. It might depend on how extreme

the treatment or how high the odds of survival. I don't know for sure."

"What if you had kids? Wouldn't you want to do something to be there for them?"

"I don't know Cole. I don't have kids. I mean, what if I died in a car wreck? I wouldn't have a choice then, would I?"

He smiled. I knew the ordeal was coming to an end for now.

"I don't know Sophie. I think down deep inside you want to believe all that, but sooner or later you are going to have a change of heart."

I grinned back at him.

"I'll let you know when I do."

"I'm sure you will," he said as he got up to get a refill on his pop.

About that time, Tisha bounced up to our table. I immediately slid over in my seat to make room for her. Her face was aglow.

"Well, someone seems to be having a great day," I commented.

She just smiled and reached over to steal a fry. I paused watching her nibble away at it with an "I've got a secret" look on her face. The silence continued while my curiosity grew. Finally, I'd waited long enough.

"Oh, will you just spill it already?"

Her grin widened.

"I'm going on a date."

"Who's the lucky guy?" I quizzed.

"Guess."

I ran through a quick mental list. She wasn't popular enough for the jocks. I thought a second and then the clear choice came to me.

"Duane?"

"Uh huh," she replied nodding.

"Did you ask him?"

The sudden change in her face as she gave me a scowl was almost comical.

"No!"

"Well, I didn't mean that you needed to, it's just Duane is so awkward around girls," I defended.

"It surprised me, too," she responded. "I mean, we have a lot of fun together and all, but I wasn't expecting it."

"Aren't you afraid it will ruin your friendship if it doesn't work out?" I cautioned.

"Not really. We were friends first. Besides, it's just a date. I'm trying to see it as an extension of our friendship."

"Hm. Seems kind of awkward to me."

She tilted her head and glared at me.

"Don't go being little miss negative reality on me."

I changed my tone.

"I'm not. I'm happy for you. I hope you guys have a great time. I guess I just don't know how I would handle that."

"You know Sophie; I would think you of all people would be willing to take a chance. I mean, after all you're the one who thinks life just happens."

"That doesn't mean I don't feel awkward about things from time to time. Besides, I'm not really concerned with that stuff right now. I'm in the educational phase of life."

"So when do you start the living phase?"

"I am living," I defended.

"No, you're existing. There's a difference. That's the part that doesn't fit with that world view of yours. You spend all your time trying to sterilize life. You can't live life in a test tube. You may find life in a test tube, but if you watch it for a while, you'll see it keeps moving and growing."

"That's rather philosophical for you isn't it?" I assessed.

She lifted her nose in the air.

"You're not the only one who can have a world view."

"So what exactly is yours?" Cole asked as he sat down.

"Mine is 'life is short and we need to make the most of it.'"

He nodded.

"Not bad, Wild Thing."

She smiled with satisfaction, before standing up.

"I've gotta go. See you later."

"Have fun."

Cole looked at me with a puzzled look as she walked away.

"She's got a hot date," I whispered across the table.

He nodded and then added, "I've gotta go, too."

"You have a hot date?"

He smirked.

"No, I have to get back to work. My boss will come looking for me if I don't."

"Can you drop me off?"

"Sure, I think I can squeeze it in."

We cleared the table. When we reached the door, he held it open for me, and I felt him briefly place his hand on the middle of my back as I walked through. It was just a gentle act of chivalry, I know, but it sent a shock of electricity through me.

The short drive to my house was quiet. When we pulled up, he parked for a moment out front.

"So you gonna tell me who Wild Thing has a hot date with?"

I pursed my lips.

"Um. No, I think I'll let you figure that one out on your own."

He smiled.

"Okay. See you later?"

"If you want you can come by after work. My mom's making her veggie pizza."

His brows raised.

"Veggie?"

I laughed.

"It's actually pretty good."

"Alright. I'll give it a try. It's a date."

"See ya."

I got out and waved as I walked toward the house.

"It's a date," I whispered as I opened the door.

Chapter Five

It'd been a lazy Saturday, which had turned into a lazy Saturday evening. Cole was in the floor of my room on the bean bag, while I was stretched out on the bed. We'd just finished watching a movie on the TV.

"How have you handled living here as long as you have? I've only been here six months, and I'm bored out of my skull."

"It's not that bad. Want to go down to the Dawg?"

I sat up on the bed crossing my legs.

"That's the point. Going down to the Dawg is the only thing we have to do in this town. There's no theater, no mall, and no beach."

"Sorry, I can't help there." He paused. "We could go down to the river."

My brows furrowed.

"There's a river?"

He rolled his eyes.

"You cross the bridge over it every time you go to Spring Creek."

"That's a river? I thought it was like a natural drainage ditch. I wondered why there was water trickling even in the summer."

"Funny."

"No, really. I never realized it was a river."

"Ever read the signs?"

I laughed.

"Okay, so I guess I knew it was supposed to be a river. It looks a little more like a wide expanse of sand with a dribble of water down the middle of it, if you ask me."

"Okay, so it's not the Mississippi. It just goes down to a trickle near Spring Creek because of the drop in the water table. There's more water if you go further west."

He seemed to be lost in thought for a few seconds.

"Want to go see it?"

"It's dark out there."

He stood up.

"It's no big deal. Come on."

"You're kidding right?"

"No, I go out there at night sometimes. It's really cool."

He grabbed my hand and started leading me through the house and out to his F150. I climbed into the truck just as he was starting the engine. We headed west out of town, and I fiddled with the stations on the radio. I looked across at Cole's face lit up from the green glow of the instrument panel.

"So how far is it?"

"Oh, just a few miles."

Moments later, he turned off the highway, and we headed down a dirt road. The headlights danced along the tall grass lining the sides of the road. As the truck bounced and swayed I glanced in the side mirror. I could clearly see the cloud of dust lifting in the air behind us in the red glow of the taillights. In the headlights, I saw an image dart across the road in front of us. Then another.

"What's that?" I asked anxiously.

"Just a jackrabbit."

"It looks like a little kangaroo."

As we continued down the road, there were more along the sides of the road and in the ditch. There appeared to be dozens.

"Why are there so many?"

"No natural predators. They aren't native to the country, so there aren't enough predators to keep the population down. In fact, years ago, I think it was in the thirties, there were so many they had roundups and hunted them down."

"Do people eat them?"

"No, not normally. They eat cottontail rabbits."

We continued on down the road, the moonlight bright enough to light the surrounding countryside. I was tossed to the left, my seatbelt stretching tight, as the truck followed a sudden turn in the road.

"What's over there?" I asked pointing to my right.

"A canyon."

"Wow. Have you ever hiked it?"

"No, we've ridden four-wheelers down there a couple of times."

"Sounds like fun."

"Maybe we can do it some weekend."

The truck rumbled as we went through a spot in the fence line.

"What was that?" I gasped.

He chuckled.

"What's so funny?"

"It's just things I take for granted, are so new to you. I never thought about how many questions a city girl could come up with?"

"Am I bothering you?"

I could see the sincerity in his face when he answered.

"No, not at all. It's kind of fun to hear the awe in your voice."

We drove on in silence for a few seconds before he spoke again.

"A cattle guard."

"Huh?"

He pointed behind the truck with his thumb.

"That noise back there. We were going across a cattle guard. It's kind of like a gate without the gate. It's made of pipe with spaces between them. The cattle avoid them because of the spaces between the pipes."

"Oh, I get it. I wonder who thought of that."

He chuckled again.

"I don't know."

The truck rose over a slight rise in the road. On the other side of the hill, Cole slowed. The road split and he turned toward the west.

"So this goes down to the river?"

"Yeah. Well, both roads lead to the river, but this one will get us a little closer so we won't have to walk as far. The other one goes down to the ranch headquarters."

"Who owns this land?"

"It used to be a ranch, but now it is a wildlife refuge. The state owns it."

"Cool. So anyone can come down here?"

"Yep, anyone."

The road we traveled had thinned to where it wasn't much more than a trail. Grass grew high along the road, and I could hear it swishing against the sides of the truck. The trail led up another hill, much steeper than the last, and it seemed the headlights were pointing straight into the air. As we came down the other side, the headlights floated back down to the earth.

"It gets a little sandy here. We'll have to use the four-wheel drive," he said as he reached down to pull on a stick in the middle of the truck.

The truck swerved slightly as it made its way through the sand. Coming out of the draw on the other side, Cole reached down and shifted the stick once again.

As we moved forward, I could hear brush and grass crunching beneath the tires and scraping the sides of the truck. Cole finally eased the truck to a stop and turned off the engine. When the lights went out, the earth was bathed in the white haze of the full moon.

"Come on."

Hesitantly I reached for the door handle. I opened the door and immediately pulled it back into place.

"What's that noise?"

Cole was standing outside the truck with his door open. He paused for a moment, listening to the sound.

"Coyotes."

"What?"

"It's just some coyotes off in the distance."

My eyes grew wider.

"How far in the distance?"

He laughed.

"Far enough."

He reached for my hand.

"Come on scaredy-cat."

I slid cautiously across the seat towards him.

"Are you sure it's safe?"

"Relax; they aren't nearby at all; probably at least a mile away. Besides, they're more scared of you than you are of them."

"I don't know how that's possible."

He laughed again.

"Really, it's okay."

I listened cautiously before stepping out of the truck. Cole continued to hold my hand. Once he had closed the door behind us, I felt his hand against the middle of my back urging me along. He pointed and then took the lead.

"This way."

I followed closely behind him. It was amazing how much we could see without a light. As we moved closer to the river, I could see the light of the moon dancing off the water like little sparkles of silver. The closer we got to the river, the more clearly I could hear the gentle flow of the water.

Cole led the way to a fallen tree along the side of the river. We sat on the tree, and I could feel the rough bark beneath my fingertips when I placed my hands at my sides. The river was about twenty feet wide at the point in front of the tree. As I looked across to the other side, I could see little pools along the bank where the water was as still and flat as glass. In the surface of those pools, I could see the full reflection of the moon looking back at me.

"The moon's so bright," I whispered.

"Yes, it is," he whispered back. "But you don't have to whisper."

"It's so quiet, except for the river."

He nodded in agreement.

"That's because we're here. Or rather, because we just got here. Give it a few minutes, and the night will come alive again."

"What do you mean?"

He motioned around us.

"Well, we frightened everyone in the room. It'll take a few minutes for them to settle down and get back to talking."

"Like the rabbits."

He laughed at my reference to his first conversation with me.

"Yeah, like the rabbits."

We sat quietly taking in the night around us. Gradually, sounds started to pierce the silence. I recognized the crickets. Then a deep echoing noise came from the other side of the river.

"What's that?" I whispered once again.

"That's a bullfrog. He's calling out to his friends."

"What else is out there?"

"Oh, it's hard to tell who will start speaking."

As different sounds made their way to our ears, Cole named them off.

"That's an owl."

"Probably an otter or a beaver splashing in the water."

"A bat out looking for mosquitoes."

The thought startled me.

"Will it come close?"

"No, I don't think so. We don't have the right kind of sound signature."

"Oh, yeah. They use echolocation."

"Ooo. Echolocation. Sophie used a big word," he teased

The coyotes began to howl in earnest, startling me.

He placed his hand on my shoulder.

"You're shivering. Are you scared?"

"No, just a chill," I lied.

He put his arm around my back, placing his hand on my hip and pulling me closer. I could feel his warmth against me and a tingling, feeling zipped through me at his touch. I glanced above at the stars in the sky, mentally trying to change the subject.

"Wow. I've never seen so many stars."

"You could see more if the moon wasn't full. It'd be better if we'd had a crescent, but then we probably would have needed a flashlight to find this log."

"How many times have you been out here at night?"

He thought for a moment.

"Oh, I don't know, maybe ten. I'm not sure."

His closeness was comforting, not just because he made me feel safe, but also because it was just us. I'd never been with a boy like this, away from home at night, alone. We were just friends; I knew that and although we'd had a few of those hanging moments, our relationship had not really bordered on romantic. I certainly had no claim on him or reason to feel jealous. It just never felt like that, but I guess I just had to ask anyway.

"Ever been here with a girl before?"

I just caught a glimpse of his smile from the corner of my eye.

"Well, yes, but not alone. A group of us came out here one night. There were a couple of girls, but we were just getting away from town. It wasn't like a date or anything. Just friends."

"Same as us?"

He smiled and nodded.

"Yeah, same as us."

We were quiet for a few minutes, both of us finding the fit of the situation. It seems we both came upon the same conclusion because we slowly moved back into conversation.

"So, how far are those coyotes really?"

"Oh, by the sound of them, the group is at least a mile away. There could be one or two closer, but they wouldn't harm us. They have plenty to eat right now, and they wouldn't have any reason to get too close."

He paused.

"But what are you worried about? Doesn't being eaten by a coyote fit into your world view?"

I poked him in the stomach.

"Okay, I guess you got me on that one, but I never said I would like to die while being shredded by a wild member of the canine species."

"Yeah, but it doesn't really matter since we're all gonna die."

"How about we don't ruin the moment with a debate?"

He slowly nodded his head in agreement.

"The moon is so big and beautiful," I whispered into the air as I gazed up.

"Yeah, it is. Sometimes when I'm out like this and I see a full moon like that... looking almost so close, I could touch it... I can't help just staring at it. You know it's crazy, we've seen the pictures of its surface, all pimply and pockmarked with hills and craters, but yet from here it almost looks perfectly round. It reflects light down on our night like a galactic nightlight. It controls our tides keeping our oceans moving. It seems to have so much purpose, such perfect design; I wonder how someone can look up there and consider it an accident."

I smiled at him.

"I thought we were going to steer away from the debate."

"Oh, sorry. I'm not trying to bait you into the debate. I just get so amazed when I look up there. I just can't help but wonder. I've thought about this stuff long before we met. It's not a Sophie thing: it's more of a general thing. There seems to be so much timing to the universe, to nature; almost like the gears of a finely tuned watch. Nothing about it seems random to me."

I let him speak. I could hear the wonder in his voice, and I knew he wasn't trying to disturb or taunt me. He was sharing with me; offering me a moment inside his thoughts and feelings. It wasn't just a matter of belief or a statement of his world view; it was pure wonderment at the world around him.

He turned his eyes away from the moon and back to me.

"I'm sorry. I just kind of get caught up on things."

"It's okay. I understand."

His eyebrows raised.

"You do?"

"Yeah, I get it," I said patting his hand.

He paused a moment looking at me. Then he gave me a soft smile.

"Thanks."

We sat talking, not keeping any track of time. The night continued to cool and before long I was squeezing closer to him to stay warm. I felt his hand lift from my hip to my shoulder as he pulled me closer. I leaned my head into his shoulder. I could feel his breath against my hair.

Eventually, it grew cool enough we were both feeling the chill into our centers; we decided to head back home. Cole stood and reached down to help me up. As we walked back to the truck, our fingers lingered loosely together. He opened the door, and I slid over to the other side of the truck, missing the warmth of his body against me.

The drive back was quiet. I know I was certainly lost in my pondering. I found myself sorting through thoughts and emotions. I was desperate not to feel anything that would jeopardize our friendship. Yet, there might have been something.

When Cole dropped me off at home, I expected to face the Spanish Inquisition. However, Geneva was so excited I had left the house for the evening she didn't find it necessary to pepper me with questions. After grabbing a snack, I headed off to my room.

I took a while going to sleep. So many thoughts were flowing through my brain. I wasn't a girlie girl. I hadn't given a lot of thoughts to boys. With the way I looked at things, it seemed an eventuality, but nothing to consider before its time. Suddenly, it was upon me, and I struggled to find a way to explain the feelings inside me.

"Just a chemical reaction, Sophie," I said quietly to myself.

So easily explained in a clinical way; science simplified. Would that really satisfy me? For once I wasn't sure.

Chapter Six

"What have you done to your hair?"

The shrill in Geneva's voice startled me. I stared at the images in the bathroom mirror, suddenly uneasy with the new me. She stood directly behind me, with her hands over her face, and my eyes grew large as I studied my mother's reaction in the mirror. My apprehension grew with each passing second.

"I love it."

I exhaled.

"Are you sure?" I quizzed.

She moved behind me and placed her hands on my shoulders.

"Yes, it's gorgeous."

"Tisha did it."

I watched in the mirror as she turned and looked at Tisha, who was sitting on my bed. Tisha raised her hand and bent her fingers down in a small wave.

"Tisha, this is beautiful," Geneva oozed.

I glanced back at my reflection. Tisha had highlighted and straightened my normally kinky hair, but before that she had cut nearly two inches from its length, bringing it just above my shoulders. With my glasses off, I was staring at a stranger.

"Why don't you try a little makeup?" It was Geneva's idea.

"Mom!"

"Just a touch. Maybe some eye shadow and some lip gloss."

"Mom."

"Okay, okay," she said putting up her hand as she left the room.

I saw Tisha move up behind me.

"She's right you know. You have beautiful skin. You wouldn't need much."

"Tisha."

She took my hand and spun me around to face her.

"Come on. Let me try it. If you don't like it, you can wash it off."

I let her drag me back to the bed where I sat down while she worked.

"I can't believe I'm letting you do this."

"Why? It's just a little makeup," she said with a smirk.

"Next thing you know you'll be trying to get me to paint my toenails."

"You're on your own there, sister. I don't do feet," she was defiant.

She lifted the swab.

"Close your eyes."

I complied.

"I said close them. I didn't say squeeze them shut."

I relaxed.

"That's better. Now sit still."

As Tisha worked her magic with the makeup, I wondered what had led me to this point in time. I'd never been all that obsessed with my looks. To me it's all so superficial; there are much more important things in life with which to be concerned.

"Cole's gonna love this," she whispered as she worked.

I opened my eyes with a start.

"What's that supposed to mean?"

"Keep your eyes closed unless you want this stuff plastered to your eyeball."

I complied.

"I just mean he's going to like your new look."

"Why do I care if Cole likes it?"

She stopped.

"Open your eyes, girl."

I opened my eyes.

"No, silly. I didn't mean literally. I meant figuratively. As in: Can't you see what is staring you right in the face? Now close your eyes."

I complied.

"What do you mean?"

"I mean, he likes you," she teased.

"Of course, he does. We're friends."

She stopped.

"Open your eyes."

She waited.

"I mean, open your eyes and look at me."

This conversation was getting confusing, but I complied.

"Have you had your head so stuck in a science book you can't even tell when a guy is crushing on you?"

"We're just friends, Tisha. What makes you think he's crushing on me?"

"Girl, he lights up like a disco ball when you show up."

I tilted my head and stared at her.

"Cole is just very upbeat. It's just his personality," I offered.

I could see the disbelief on her face.

"Really, we're just friends," I pleaded.

"Just friends? Do friends lose their concentration during conversations just because another friend walks into the room? Do guys tell their best friend what an awesome night they had down at the river with a certain other friend if they were just feeling like friends?"

I shrugged.

"Yeah, they might."

Tisha laughed.

"Okay, Cinderella, think what you want. But I thought you were the one who dealt with reality." She paused. "Now close your eyes."

I complied.

"But you really should open them," she mumbled.

My mom's reaction sent mixed feelings through me.

"Oh, my gosh. You look like a model." Geneva swooned when I walked out of my room.

"Take the glasses off," she commanded.

I slid the glasses from my face, and her face became a blur.

"We've got to get you contacts."

My shoulders slumped.

"Mom."

"That would be awesome," Tisha exclaimed from behind me.

"We have to, Sophie. You are so beautiful; it isn't right to hide that behind those glasses," Mom continued.

"Mom, I don't care about the glasses."

She was confirming my fears. I'd taken a step toward the superficial, and now I was being urged onward by my mother. One step just leads to another.

She was undeterred.

"Well, I do. Sophie, if a pair of contacts can keep you from hiding your beauty, then we're going to get contacts."

"So, you only think I'm beautiful without my glasses or with makeup?"

"No, dear. I think you're beautiful no matter what, but it doesn't make any sense to hide it behind a pair of frames."

"I like my glasses. I don't want to have to mess with contacts every morning when I'm getting ready for school."

"Okay, we'll compromise. We'll get you contacts, and you can wear them when you feel like it."

I rolled my eyes and slipped on my glasses.

By the time I had returned to my room, she had already grabbed the phone book to look for an optometrist.

Tisha was gathering her stuff when I walked back into the room.

"Hey, Duane is coming by to pick us up and take us to the Dawg."

I shook my head.

"Oh, no. I'm not going out like this."

"You have to. I already told him, and he told Cole."

I felt the lip gloss ooze between my lips as I pressed them together.

"What did you go and do that for?"

"I wanted them to see how hot you look. Now change clothes so we can go. I picked something out for you."

"Why do I need to change?"

"So you can complete the transformation."

I shook my head.

"This is getting out of hand. I should never have agreed to let you put makeup on me. I was okay with the hair, but this is going too far."

She picked up the outfit she had laid out on the bed, handed it to me, and pushed me towards the bathroom.

"Just change. He'll be here any minute," she said as she closed the bathroom door behind me.

I just stood there looking at the skirt and top in my hands. It was something Geneva had picked up. I'd never worn the skirt and had only worn the top one time with a pair of jeans. I grudgingly started removing my clothes. Moments later I uncomfortably emerged from the bathroom.

"Oh, man. You are one hot piece of girlfriend. This'll get Cole's attention."

I put my hands on my hips.

"I'm not trying to get Cole's attention."

Just then I heard a honk as Duane pulled up outside, then the sound of his motor revving. Tisha grabbed my hand.

"Come on."

As she pulled me to the front door, she called out to my mother.

"Geneva, we're going down to the Grumpy Dawg."

Just before the door slammed shut, I heard Geneva's reply.

"Have fun girls."

Duane stopped revving the engine on his Dodge pickup the moment he saw us exit the house. His eyes were still hanging out of his eye sockets when we got to the car.

"Dang," was all he said.

Tisha slid in next to him, and I was next to the door.

"We're in now. You can stop staring any time," she said as she urged him to put the truck into gear.

When we got to the Dawg, they both made me wait outside so they could go inside ahead of me to catch Cole's reaction. I fidgeted nervously for a few seconds before I got the courage to go inside.

Tisha was right. I got Cole's attention and just about every other male in the building. With the skirt that only went down to mid-thigh and everyone staring, I felt like I had just walked into the restaurant naked. My uncertainty grew with each passing second. I felt as if all eyes were upon me and I didn't know if it was because I looked good, or if it was just because I looked different. So, I simply tried to act as casual as my nerves would allow, when I walked up to Cole.

Tisha spoke up first.

"What do you think?"

"Man," was all that came out of his mouth.

I couldn't help but notice the look of amazement on his face. It certainly didn't help my comfort level any. Tisha grabbed Duane's hand,

and they walked up to the counter to place their orders, leaving me alone with Cole.

"Is it too much?"

"Uh, no," he stammered. "You look incredible."

His compliment helped to build my courage a little.

"So a little bit of makeup was enough to get your tongue tied."

He smiled.

"It's not just the makeup. Your hair...the outfit...nice package. Was this your idea?"

Since he seemed to be recovering, I relaxed a little.

"No, it was Tisha's. I feel so silly like this."

He put his hands on my shoulders and looked me straight in the face.

"You shouldn't feel silly. You are absolutely the hottest girl in here right now."

I looked around the room. It was a pretty big compliment, since almost every popular girl in town seemed to be present at the time.

He motioned toward the counter.

"Ready to order?"

"Yeah. I'll have the usual."

As we walked up to the counter, he couldn't resist teasing me.

"So, how's this fitting in with your world view?"

I looked up into his eyes.

"At the moment? It feels like it is crumbling beneath my feet."

Chapter Seven

Life in a small town isn't without its difficulties. In a large school, there are more kids, and it's easier to find a group in which to fit. Although, I'd found my group, it sometimes paired me against the other groups in the hierarchy. Of course, the Popular Girls were at the top of the food chain and though they could be rather exclusive, they weren't out to be hateful. Hateful doesn't always blend well with popularity, and they were more about being liked by all.

Under the Popular Girls, there were the Wicked Girls. They were exclusive. You had to be both pretty and evil to fit into this group. They derived pleasure in demeaning anyone who might get more attention than them. Although, almost everyone would try to find a way to either get along with them or avoid them, there was no one who couldn't be a target for them. From time to time, usually when they felt their approval ratings were slipping, or they felt they had attracted too much attention; they would call a ceasefire to allow the stage to reset.

The popularity groups fragmented below these two levels as each student struggled to find their niche. The majority of students fell into the splinter groups and got along quite well. They have the same problem in the big schools, but there the groups are bigger; it's easier to find a place in which to slink away. In a small school, the groups are smaller and more exclusive. If you can't find someone you fit with, you're on your own.

It started simply enough. I was in American History. The Wicked Group had taken over the back corner of the room, and they were whispering among themselves as they did so often. You always know you're a target when they all laugh their fake laughs and stare in your direction. Apparently, my new look was disruptive to the stability of the populace, and it was time to take the new girl down before she had a chance to move up a level.

The hour went by slowly, their whispers going largely unnoticed or unchallenged by Mrs. Whann, who most often had trouble maintaining control of the class anyway. Mrs. Whann was technologically stuck in the past. While other teachers use whiteboards, computers, and dvd movies to complement their curriculum, Mrs. Whann was strictly old school. While she spent the main part of the hour flicking slides of the Civil War on the screen at the front of the class, the Wickeds continued to interrupt her with their hushed laughter.

As we were exiting class, I was met at the door by the top two officers of the Wicked Club. Jaima Sanchez stepped through the doorway at the same time and "accidently" knocked my books out of my hands. As I stooped to pick them up, Leza Wilson "accidently" bumped into me from behind, sending me spilling forward onto the gym floor.

"Oh, careful Leza. We don't want to mess up Sophie's new look."

They giggled.

"I heard she went to O' de Tisha for her doo," Leza added.

Again, the group-giggle.

I glared up at them from the floor, before starting to pick myself up.

"Ooo. Someone seems to get worked up easily over a little accident. Careful Sophie, they may send you to anger management," Jaima prodded.

Of course, Mrs. Whann was nowhere in sight, although it wouldn't have mattered if she'd seen the whole thing. She wouldn't know what discipline was if she'd been strapped to a chair.

Tisha pushed through the doorway and reached down to help me up, glaring at them.

"Oh, her boyfriend is there to help her. How chivalrous," Leza teased.

Tisha turned on her.

"Keep it up and I'll snatch your pretty black locks off your head."

At that, they took their exit, smiling as they walked away.

Darlene, one of the girls from a splinter group, picked up my books and handed them to me.

"They are so hateful," she commented.

"It's okay. Someday life will pay them back." I stated.

"Whoa, someone almost made a reference to Karma," Tisha scoffed.

She was right. I'd just made a statement to indicate life had an order. Maybe it wasn't always as random as I wanted to believe or maybe at the moment I just wished it wasn't.

It wasn't the end of my encounters with the Wicked Group. They continued to take swipes when they thought they could get away with it. They were generally strategic in their efforts and didn't waste a strike unless it was going to help achieve their goals. The next major encounter was at the Dawg. I was there with Cole, Duane, and Tisha.

I'd just picked up one of my favorite strawberry shakes. As I turned, Leza was there to lend me a hand and toss the shake on to a brand new, peach top.

"Oh, my bad," she offered. "Can I get you another shake Sophie?"

"Uh. No, I don't think so," I replied, looking down at the strawberry goo sliding down my chest.

"Yeah, on second thought, you better get your top into the washer, before it stains."

Cole was at my side right away.

"Come on, Sophie. I'll take you home."

With a flair for drama, Leza patted me on the back.

"It's such a good thing Cole is here to take care of you. Be careful though, if he sneezes you'll have to wipe off the slime before you wash it."

Cole turned on her.

"You know, it must be pitiful to have such a disaster of a life you have to find entertainment by bothering others. You try to distract from your own insecurities by running down other people because you know down deep inside, there isn't a person in here who doesn't loath who and what you are; other than maybe your twin over there," he said tossing a finger in Jaima's direction.

She was momentarily stunned. She wasn't often challenged.

"Uh. Cole, you're so disgusting."

"That was an incredibly intelligent comeback, Leza. You must have burned off the majority of your brain cells thinking that one up."

"Like I care what you think, sneeze boy."

"Obviously, you do. You look like someone just slapped the snot out of you. Pardon the pun." He laughed at his remark.

"Ouch, that hurt. Go on and take little miss new dweeb home, before she stains."

We turned to go; then I pulled on his arm.

"Wait."

I walked up behind Leza.

"Hey, Leza. This shake was so good, I just thought I'd share it with you," I said as I dumped the remainder of my cup over her head.

The entire restaurant erupted in laughter as she screamed and ran out the door dripping strawberry ooze with each step.

I turned to look at Cole, who was struggling with holding back his laughter.

"I shouldn't have done that," I confessed.

"Probably not," he said. "It's just playing into her game."

He paused.

"But it felt good, didn't it?"

"It sure did," I said with a smile.

Chapter Eight

One-quarter of the way through the school year, Charlie Waters became the new target of the popularity machine. Charlie was unique in that he didn't fit a social class at all. He was sharp as a tack, as the saying goes, but he didn't give a flying flip about his grades. Charlie would have been pinging at the maximum on the Nerd-O-Meter if he had any care at all for structured education, but Charlie rarely turned in his assignments on time, if at all.

Judging by appearance, one would have figured him for a Beatles follower since he looked a little like a young John Lennon, complete with the thick dark frames Lennon wore in his younger years. Charlie's straight bangs fell just above them. His wardrobe didn't contain a single "designer" anything. Flannel shirts, colored t-shirts, and store brand jeans seemed to top his choice of dress.

Although far from repulsive, he did suffer from acne, which didn't help him among the higher-ups in the popularity food chain. His music choices didn't pull in a big group of followers either. While most of the school could be split between rock, pop, rap, and country or a blend of them all, Charlie was strictly a classical music guru.

Charlie's most redeeming quality was that he was the nicest, sweetest person you'd probably ever meet. Upon first contact, he seemed shy, but such an assumption was simply a misinterpretation of what could only be described as genuine humility. He didn't try to impress anyone. He believed in individuality to the extent he accepted everyone equally. He treated those most annoying individuals the same as those who welcomed him. He was a true pacifist and didn't take sides on anything or with anyone.

Some of us found Charlie a refreshing change from those who were constantly in the midst of or creating the issues surrounding us. Others saw it as a weakness. He was immediately the target for the most severe attacks.

Our little group tried to pull Charlie in; we sought him out to be one of us, but true to his nature, he remained neutral and independent.

"Hey, Charlie, want to come over and hang out tonight?" Cole asked him one day at lunch.

"Nah. Thanks, but I don't really hang out."

"So what do you do in your spare time?" I asked.

"Um, listen to music, surf the net," he said with a shrug.

"Do you ever watch movies?"

"I watch documentaries from time to time."

"No movies? None at all?"

He seemed lost in thought for a few minutes.

"I think I watched some Disney videos when I was around four or five."

Cole's eyebrows lifted.

"You haven't watched a movie since you were four or five?"

"Not that I can recall, and I can, usually, recall about anything I try to remember."

"Isn't that almost impossible? Does anyone in your family watch movies?"

He perked up.

"Oh, sure, my little sister watches them all the time."

"You don't ever watch TV together?"

"Uh, no. I spend most of my time in my room."

Duane shook his head.

"If I spent that much time in my room, my mom would freak out and think I was on drugs or something."

We all laughed, but he was right. Our folks would think we were up to something if we spent that much time hiding in our rooms. I could hear Geneva now.

"Sophie, come out here and let's spend some time as a family."

Of course, I would have rolled my eyes at the comment and reluctantly conceded.

Although I'd never spent any time in his world, I could imagine Charlie's room as a collection of books, artifacts, papers with scribbled thoughts, and classical music albums. It wouldn't have surprised me at all to find him to be one of those individuals who was solely dedicated to vinyl albums, but he wasn't as his near constant companion was his iPod.

Usually arriving at school in his faded red VW Beetle just in time to meet the bell, he was still pulling the earbuds attached to his iPod from his ears as the teacher started to speak.

"Mr. Waters, in our current studies of the novel Anna Karenina, which character most mirrors Tolstoy's personal characteristics?"

"Levin is generally considered to be an autobiographical character. His beliefs, characteristics, and life experiences appear to parallel Tolstoy's. Additional support for this understanding is found in the fact that Tolstoy's first name was Lev, and in Russian the surname "Levin" means "of Lev," Charlie responded without missing a beat.

Mr. Scott nodded his approval.

"Ms. Sanchez, what form of POV does the novel make use of?"

Jaima looked like she'd been smacked in the side of the head with a brick. Clearly clueless, she made a weak attempt at being cute.

"Um. I think Charlie wanted that question. Didn't you Charlie?"

"Ms. Sanchez the question was directed at you. Which point of view is used in the novel?"

"I don't know."

"Thank you. Mr. Waters, would you mind helping Ms. Sanchez out with this answer?"

"Tolstoy utilizes a third-person-omniscient perspective; switching attention to several major characters throughout the eight parts."

Jaima leaned toward Charlie when Mr. Scott turned his back.

"You're such a geek," she whispered.

Charlie smiled.

"Thank you," he whispered back.

Showing up Jaima was one sure way to become the next target of the Wicked Girls, and it didn't take long for them to attack their target. At lunch, Charlie felt the sting of the first strike. As he was leaving the lunch line and about to head for his table, he suddenly found his tray of food "bumped" by Stacy, one of Jaima's underlings. In a matter of seconds, Charlie Waters found himself staring down at a bowl of chili as it slid down the front of his t-shirt and onto the floor.

Strike two came when gym class ended and the locker room door was conveniently left open while he was in the shower. Exiting the shower to find Jaima's little crowd standing in the doorway, Charlie was facing total humiliation. When he couldn't find his clothes, he went over the top. Poor, pacifist Charlie started screaming at the top of his lungs.

"Get the heck out of here! Leave me alone! All I did was answer a question you were too dumb to answer!"

Of course, Jaima and her friends were long gone before Coach Winston showed up and found a hysterical Charlie ranting in the nude in the locker room. His clothes were lying outside the locker room in the hallway, and Charlie was treated to a trip to Principle Myers' office.

Strike three came the next morning when Charlie found his faded red VW decorated with Tampons and toilet paper as he was preparing to leave for school.

When Charlie showed up at school the next day dressed like a Ninja out for blood, he sent the school into lockdown. After the police were summoned and it was determined he had no weapons, he was promptly suspended and escorted from the premises.

It was a sad situation, and my heart cried out for him as I watched them lead him out to a police car, his head hanging in despair. Although most of us didn't see Charlie as a threat, in the world we live in, the school wasn't about to take any chances. I understood the school's dilemma. Still, it was a miserable day in America when someone like Jaima – who threatened, bullied, and humiliated others on an almost regular basis – was free to walk the halls. While someone like Charlie – who wouldn't normally bother a fly – was marched away in handcuffs.

Of course, once the school came off lockdown, and we were moving around as normal, Charlie was the topic of conversation. Most of us knew why he did what he did, and few of us had any fear he would do anything dangerous. It was widely acknowledged he had dressed that way to send a message to Jaima and her crew that he was prepared to fight back and wasn't going to live in fear of her or her taunts.

As I walked through the hall, I saw Jaima with a few of her little minions gathered around. She was speaking in her loud, boisterous, irritating tone.

"Did you see the geek? Dressed like some Ninja warrior? What's wrong with Charlie?" Jaima quipped.

I lost my cool. Yep, I snapped and it was a good thing there wasn't any faculty to view it or they might have carted me off with Charlie.

"What's wrong with him? I'll tell you what's wrong with him! The same thing that's wrong with everyone around here who doesn't fit into your little box. If he was the best looking guy in school and the girls were all crazy about him, he might stand a chance. If he was the best athlete and everyone worshiped him, he might stand a chance. If he had the right last name or his family was made of money, he might stand a chance, but he doesn't and therefore he doesn't matter. We don't matter. Our feelings and our self-esteem are disposable as far as you're concerned. We are insignificant scraps of flesh you think you can walk all over like the rug in front of your door. That's what's wrong with Charlie!"

I could tell it was too much information for her small brain to process. If it didn't start with "as if," 'like," "ewww," or similar single syllable thoughts neither she nor her minions could process it. Her response seemed to underscore my thoughts.

"Tool," she said as she rolled her eyes and walked away, Leza and Stacy slinking along behind.

Chapter Nine

His jet black hair hung nearly to his shoulders, and his strut echoed with over confidence. Tate Jordan was the quintessential egotistical jock. The captain of both the football and basketball teams, he was the kind of guy all the sports fans admired. I can't say as I blamed them. He was extraordinarily athletic, and they only saw him operate on the field or the basketball court. They had no idea what he was like when they weren't around. He could be engaging and likable, combine that with his ability to rule whatever sport he happened to be playing, it made him seem like the all-around great guy they thought they knew.

Walking the halls of the school, he seemed to bounce from personality to personality, depending upon who happened to be around. His groupies were almost as brain dead as Jaima's, and when they were his only audience, he could be a real jerk. He harassed the underclassmen, made fun of the weaker players, and made life miserable for those who didn't happen to make his circle.

The jocks operated under a separate code of conduct, namely if Tate Jordan did it; it was okay.

He was the star of the show and as such, he could operate in his own theater. Oh, he wasn't bad looking, but he had obviously transferred some of his brain cells to his muscles. He had the coaches fooled as well. They had no idea the kind of torture he put on weaker players when they weren't around. And since he was the captain of the team, they naturally consider him as a leader, which allowed him to pretty much run the team any way he wanted. Thus Mr. Jordan got to dole out the discipline as he saw fit. Stay on his good side, work in his circle, and you were okay; cross him up, and you were doing laps or running bleachers, or worse, dealing with his locker room wrath.

"Hey Allen, you need to clean up the locker room," Tate commanded.

"Why me?" Cole responded.

"Because I said so," came the reply.

Cole finally showed up at the Grumpy Dawg an hour later.

"What took you so long?" I quizzed.

"I was sentenced to locker room cleanup." He sulked.

"So what? You guys take turns or something?"

"No, it usually falls on the guy Tate wants to pick on that day."

"Tate Jordan?"

"Yeah, they pretty much let him decide who he wants to clean the locker room."

"I thought the janitors took care of it."

"No it's supposed to be a team building thing."

"A team building thing? How's that?"

"You tell me. The only ones who get stuck with it are the ones Jordan has a problem with. That's the way it goes with everything."

"Why do you guys listen to him?"

"Because if we don't he'll take it out on us during practice."

"Sounds like a real team leader."

"Yeah, he is. None of them are really team leaders. They argue all the time and blame each other for their mistakes. It gets annoying."

"Then why do you play?"

"Well, I like the game and I keep hoping that when I'm a senior, I'll be a better leader."

While we were talking, the man of the hour walked in. He moved through the restaurant like he owned the place. As soon as he showed up the groupies gathered.

"Why do they fawn over him like that?" I quizzed, scrunching my nose up and feeling nauseated at the thought.

"I donno," Cole replied absentmindedly, while he picked at his fries.

"I can't stand that little shake he does with his hair. It's like he thinks he's Fabio or something."

Cole giggled like a girl at that one.

"Well, it's ridiculous. And about that hair, doesn't everyone else have to follow some kind of dress code? You said last week the coach said you had to get a haircut."

Cole rolled his eyes and nodded.

"So, what's the deal? How come he gets away with it?"

Cole just stared at me.

"Because he's Tate Jordan," I said, answering my question.

Cole just dug back into his burger.

"Doesn't that stuff bother you?"

He nodded again.

"You don't act like it bothers you."

He looked at me while he finished chewing. Then he took a swig of soda to rinse his mouth.

"What am I going to do about it? He's fifty pounds heavier than me, has muscles like a Duane Johnson double, and has the temperament of a hungry lion."

"Well, you could tell him what you think. That doesn't mean you have to fight him."

"I just told you he has anger management issues. While I'm sharing my feelings and offering my Dr. Phil insights on his aggravating projections, he'd be separating my teeth from my gums. My folks didn't spend twenty-four hundred dollars on braces two years ago so that I could let a jock with a steroid problem jack my smile back up."

I gave him a harrumph and crossed my arms in front of me.

"So you're just going to let him get away with demeaning you."

"Hey, my self-esteem is just fine as long as I don't allow my jaw to get out of alignment with my brain."

"But what about personal dignity?"

"Look, I keep my mouth shut, he graduates and moves on to some college campus with other members of his species, and I'll make the most of my junior and senior year. I open my mouth; I might not make it to my senior year."

I decided to let it go for then, but the gears kept turning. It was people like Tate Jordan and Jaima who made life hard for the rest of us. We couldn't just let them always get away with it. If evolution was right and it was survival of the fittest, then sooner or later the smarter among us had to put those mindless imbeciles in their place. Besides, our school wasn't a bad school. With a few exceptions, most of us got along, and most of the teachers were people you could trust and respect. Surely they would want to know what was going on.

I got an opportunity to take a swipe at the gorilla with the dangling bangs a few weeks later. Never let it be said that Sophie Carter knows when to keep her mouth shut. I guess foot in mouth disease has gotten me and those around me in trouble more times than I care to mention. Maybe it has something to do with the way I was raised. My folks had always been rather liberal with their thoughts and conversations; I suppose some of it rubbed off on me.

We were standing in the hall when Mr. Opportunity came knocking. The school stud was prancing down the hall, kind of doing his own version of the Travolta strut. As he walked by, he tossed his mane, and it nearly made me want to toss my cookies.

"You ever throw your neck out when you do that? I'm surprised it doesn't give you brain damage, not that anyone would notice."

My eyes grew wide. Had I just said that out loud? His reaction was a certain answer to my question.

As one might expect when dealing with a person of Tate's intelligence, it took a moment to register. He walked on past me a few steps, and I swear I could almost hear the Bee Gees singing

"Stayin' Alive" in the background. Then when he'd had a few seconds to process the thought, it was like the needle of the phonograph scratched across the record. He stopped so quickly; I could almost hear his Nikes squealing like a set of Goodyears under locked brakes.

That's when I knew I'd gotten his attention and when Cole started wishing he was a shape-shifter so he could turn into a glob of the slime they used to dump on people on the Nickelodeon channel. Looking back, I'm surprised either of us survived the encounter, and it took a month before I could get Cole to forgive me.

"What'd you say?" he thundered from above me.

You know, he was a lot bigger close-up. I held my composure though.

"I just asked if you ever threw your neck out when you do that little hair-flippy thing you do."

"I heard that part. I'm talking about the other part."

"Oh, the part about the brain damage?"

"Yeah, Geek Girl. That part."

"Well, you know with all the talk about incidental head injuries these days, it's bound to be a potential for disaster."

"You run your mouth a lot. Maybe I should take it out on your boyfriend at practice today."

"Oh, he's not my boyfriend. We're just friends. It wouldn't really be fair of you to take it out on a non-participant anyway."

"A what?"

I knew it! Throw a few big words at him and he'd get so confused he'd forget what he was mad about.

"A non-participant. You know, one who doesn't participate in vocal elaborations or dubious discussions of a subject or in this case one's obvious cerebral inadequacies."

"Oh." He said, his brain stumbling over everything I'd said that involved more than one syllable.

"So, have you?" I asked sweetly, giving him the cutest smile in my arsenal.

"Have I what?"

"Have you ever thrown your neck out?" I offered, tilting my head like an expectant cocker spaniel.

"Nah. I just gotta get it out of my eyes sometimes."

"Oh. Okay, I just wondered," I said turning back toward Cole.

There was no doubt the dumb jock was lost in the conversation because he stood there with a blank look on his face for a moment before he tossed his hair to the side and continued on down the hallway. He was at least fifty feet away from us before Cole remembered how to breathe. When his lungs finally started to work again, I saw the blood rush into his face.

"If you ever do something like that again, you won't have a chance to baffle the baboon with brilliance; I'll kill you myself," he said allowing the words to squeeze out through his clenched teeth.

However, I didn't let him bother me. I was on an intellectual high. I'd just insulted the biggest guy in school several times, and he walked off thinking nothing of it; that is if he was capable of thinking anything at all. I was now as certain as ever Tate Jordan had less capacity for comprehension than a pet rock.

"That was awesome!" I squealed with delight.

"I mean it Sophie. You were just playing with fire."

"Seemed more like playing with Play-Doh."

"You almost got me killed and I'm still not sure you haven't. He'll probably figure it out about the time we start practice. Then he'll make mincemeat out of me."

"Oh, you're being a little dramatic. By the time practice comes around, he'll be lucky if he can find enough brain mass to remember his football plays. He won't even be thinking about it."

"You better hope so."

The first bell rang for our next class, and we wondered toward Mr. Scott's room. While I was still reveling in my intellectual victory, Cole was checking the front of his pants to make sure he hadn't had an involuntary bladder response.

Cole didn't stop by my house that night after practice. I figured he was still sore over my nearly getting him killed before lunchtime. I decided to give him the space to sulk, so I didn't bother to call him. I figured he'd get over it in due time.

The next day at school Cole looked like he'd been run over by a truck. His gait was slow and stiff. I reached for his arm, and he pulled out of my grasp.

"Ouch."

"What's wrong?"

He lifted up the sleeve of his t-shirt to reveal a dark bruise.

"What happened?"

"Tate Jordan."

"He did that?"

"Under the auspices of a lead block."

My hand went to my mouth.

"He did that in practice? Was it because of what I said?"

"Couldn't say for sure, but he slammed me. Stuck his facemask into my arm."

"Let me see it again."

He lifted his sleeve again. The distinct outline of the facemask grid had left its mark as a dark purple splotch.

"I'm sorry Cole."

"Oh, he would have hit me either way. He may have had a little more motivation than usual."

"Did you say anything to him about it?"

He looked at me and rolled his eyes.

"Sophie, there are some things better left alone. I don't need a bigger target painted on my back."

"But people like Tate shouldn't get away with being bullies. It doesn't stop if no one does anything about it."

"Tate is more of an egomaniac than a bully. Whereas some guys just pick on people for the brutality of it, Tate just likes to display his physical prowess."

"I don't care what you call it; it's still bullying. It's just like what Jaima and her friends did to Charlie. They found a way to humiliate him. They didn't leave bruises on his body, but they left bruises on his self-esteem."

"High school is tough that way."

"But should it be?" I asked.

"Hey, you're the one who believes in the survival of the fittest. In your world, they are just eliminating the weaker among the species."

He'd slipped in a punch on that one.

"Survival of the fittest isn't necessarily displayed through brute strength. We are smarter. Besides, just because we got here through survival of the fittest, doesn't mean we need to act like animals to each other," I offered.

"So evolution should stop once we become human?"

"No, it should cause us to evolve into something better, something higher than a human."

"We do after we leave these vessels behind." He said placing his hand on his chest.

"How'd we move from a conversation about bullies to a conversation about religion?"

He smiled.

"It's not so much a conversation about religion as it is a conversation about the evolution of our spirituality."

"That's a big deal to you isn't it?"

"It's the only one that matters."

"Well, I still don't think people like Tate and Jaima should get away with treating other people as lesser beings."

"No, they shouldn't," he admitted. "But they do."

The bell rang, and he closed his locker. As he turned to head to class, Tate Jordan bumped into him spilling his books from his arms. Jordan stopped just long enough to point and laugh; then he flipped his hair and moved on with his little group.

Cole gave him an annoyed stare before bending to pick up his books. To his astonishment, Kevin Nelson the quarterback had already gathered his stuff from the floor.

"Sorry about that, Allen. He can be a real jerk sometimes," he said as he handed Cole the books.

"Thanks," Cole replied.

"Hey, no problem," Kevin said as he waved him off and continued down the hall.

"Well, I guess there's still some hope in the world." I marveled out loud.

"Yep, I guess so." Cole agreed.

Chapter Ten

As the credits rolled, I wiped at my eyes with a tissue, trying to avoid Cole's amused look. Though the room was dark, except for the glow of the television screen, I could see his mischievous smile from the chair across the room. I knew he was just dying to tease me.

"What?" I asked through my sniffles.

"Oh, nothing," he replied holding back a chuckle.

He continued to watch me.

"What?" There was a degree of aggravation.

He just shrugged.

"Just go ahead and say it."

"Say what?" He tried to sound innocent.

"You know you want to give me a hard time about this."

He shook his head, but he was not at all convincing. Besides, I knew him too well.

"Cole, don't play dumb with the geek." I stopped to wipe my eyes again. "You know you want to harass me for getting so worked up over a movie."

"Well, it was a Nicholas Sparks story. I guess you couldn't help it."

"Look, it was sad. I have emotions too, you know."

"What made it so sad?" He was in his debate mode, and I was going to fall right into it.

"I just didn't think it should end like that."

"He just died; no big deal. Right? It doesn't matter that they had just discovered they were in love."

There was an argument brewing, and he was orchestrating it.

"Look, I didn't say there was no emotion involved in death. I said I was alright with it."

He rose from the chair and moved over in front of me sitting down in the floor crossing his legs and staring up at me.

"I'm not trying to make fun of you. I just want to understand how you feel about things."

"What kind of things? We've talked about this stuff so many times it's ridiculous." I complained.

"Okay, so I know what you think about life and death, what about love?"

"Love?"

"Yeah, how do you explain love? Is it just an emotion? What about people like the ones in the movie who seem to be soul mates? It seemed like they were connected by something bigger than either one of them."

I shifted in the chair. How was I supposed to explain this to him when I didn't understand it myself?

"Alright, to be honest, I don't know. I mean I can explain the actual coupling by instinct and attraction, pheromones, scent glans, and of course chemical reactions. Beyond that, I don't know."

He was quiet for a few moments.

"Have you ever felt anything that made you feel like you were in love?"

I hesitated. I wasn't sure just how much I should say.

"I've felt some feelings I questioned, but I'm not sure. What about you?"

"Kind of the same. I mean, it felt good and comfortable, but I wasn't sure."

"When was it?"

"Not long ago," he answered with his head down.

"Is it someone in school?" I asked, not sure if I wanted to know. His answer might disappoint me.

"Yeah."

He didn't offer anymore.

In a moment of boldness, I reached out and touched his shoulder. He looked up, meeting my eyes.

"Can you tell me who?"

He looked away.

"I'm not sure if it's such a good idea. It might make you feel different about me," he said

"No, Cole. We're friends. I'd understand. I doubt there is anything you could say that would make me feel different about you." Even as I said it my stomach was churning.

His eyes met mine once again.

"It's Leza."

I'm sure my eyes looked like they were about to pop out of their sockets. I couldn't have been more surprised if he'd swung his fist at me. My chest felt like it was about to explode. My stomach was doing flip-flops.

And then... he started rolling on the floor laughing.

"You butt!" I shouted.

He was laughing too hard to respond.

"Cole Allen, you are a freaking jerk. I was serious."

He sat up and in between his amusement he pointed at me and sputtered.

"You should have seen your face."

"That was mean. I don't know if I like you anymore."

He wiped at his eyes as he finally started to settle down.

"I thought you said nothing I could say would make you feel different."

"That was before you turned into a butthead," I said as I punched him in the shoulder.

He suddenly looked at me seriously.

"It's you, Sophie."

"Don't mess with me anymore, Cole."

"No, I mean it. It's you, and I just don't want to ruin our friendship by making it into something more."

I smiled awkwardly.

"Same here."

"So, what do we do now?"

"I don't know. I guess we just do what we've always done. We'll be honest with each other. What's different about it? We spend most of our time together. We tell each other our secrets. What are we afraid of?" I asked.

He shrugged.

"I don't know. That it might turn into something more and we might find out that it shouldn't have."

"Okay, so we just go on like normal and we see where it goes. I think people who love each other are just on the high side of friendship. You know?"

He smirked.

"Like a friendship on steroids?"

"Yeah, sort of," I said with a smile.

"How do we handle the other stuff?"

"What other stuff?"

"Stuff like holding hands, kissing, hugging?"

"We do what feels comfortable."

"How do I know what you're comfortable with?"

I stared at him blankly.

"Uh, duh. You ask me."

"Oh, so I say, 'Sophie, are you comfortable with a kiss?'"

I rolled my eyes.

"Okay, I guess that's a little corny. But we can talk about how we are feeling; just like we're doing now," I suggested.

"I don't know; it seems pretty mechanical."

"Okay, then we just ignore it?"

Neither of us knew what to say. He fiddled, rubbing his hand over the surface of the carpet. Finally, he spoke.

"Maybe we already screwed it up."

"I don't think so. I don't have any desire to bolt for the door."

"That's good."

"Why's that?"

He smiled.

"We're at your house."

"Goober."

"Want to go down to the Dawg?"

"No, let's just watch the other movie," I suggested.

"Okay."

I got up and put the DVD into the player. He slid back resting against my bed. After I had pushed play, I sat down next to him. As the movie started, he placed his arm around me, and I leaned my head against his shoulder. I thought about our conversation while feeling the warmth of him next to me. I didn't want us to change. He was the most comfortable place in my world.

How could I describe what I felt for him in any way without using the word love? I loved the time we spent together. I loved how he made me laugh. I loved his touch and his smile. Whether we were to be just friends or something more, he would always be someone I loved. And yet I wondered, what did that mean? Was it just an emotion, or was it something deeper as he suggested? If it was an emotion, it was the deepest of all emotions.

It was something I would eventually come to terms with, but there were so many experiences that would influence my understanding. I was just beginning to know what love was or just how much it would cost to really find out.

Chapter Eleven

We sat on the tailgate of Cole's truck. It started out pretty tame, just some casual conversation under the warm rays of the sun. That lock of hair fell down into his eyes, and I reached up to wisp it back. His hair had warmed under the sun's reflection, and I felt it against my fingertips.

He smiled casually; his eyes squinting against the glare of the sun.

"The sun's bright today, isn't it?"

I closed my eyes as I looked up into the sky.

"Yeah, it feels good. I'm tired of the cold weather."

"Guess you weren't used to this out in Cali?"

"No, not at all. Sixty degrees was a cold day out there."

"Do you miss it?"

I nodded.

"Sometimes. I mean, I've grown to like it here for the most part, but there are things I miss. Mostly the beach. I mean, it was so close. We spent almost the entire summer taking in the sun, sand, and saltwater."

"Did you have a lot of friends?"

"Yeah, I guess. Probably just a few I was really close to, but there were a lot of people who gathered for parties on the beach."

He raised one brow in question.

"A party girl? Doesn't really seem to fit you. You're too much of a geek."

I slugged him on the shoulder.

"Thanks. Even geeks like to take in the sun sometimes."

"Hmm. A geek in a bikini. Sounds good."

"I rocked it."

"I bet you did."

This time he raised both brows like he was doing an imitation of Groucho Marx.

I gave him my best 'wouldn't you like to know' look.

"I did."

He continued, despite my attempt at a flirt.

"No, really. Being out in the sun, taking chances on skin cancer; it just doesn't suit you."

"I'm sorry. I'm not all geek. Sometimes I'm girl."

"Oh, I know that," he assured me.

"That's good to know," I said, feeling the blush move over my skin despite the warmth of the sun.

He glanced up into the sky.

"Isn't it incredible how much that big ball of fire affects us?"

"Yep. We wouldn't be here without it."

"So, I guess you figure it's up there by accident?"

I rolled my eyes.

"Are we going there again?"

He put up his hands.

"Hey, just wondering."

"I don't like to use the term 'accident.' I prefer to think of it as how the universe developed."

"You know, Stephen Hawking says he knows how it all happened. I guess he was there or something."

"Don't be so obtuse. He's a smart man."

"I'm sure he is, but he seems so intent on proving God doesn't exist that he isn't willing to recognize his work proves the opposite."

"How's that?"

"Order. There's too much order."

"Order? How's that? Give me an example?"

"Okay. He expects me to believe the laws that govern the universe have always existed. In fact, all of science is more than willing to realize, discover, and promote certain laws which govern the actions of the world, but for some reason neither he nor they seem to recognize that laws don't just happen. Laws and rules are established."

"Mmmkay."

"Why can't they acknowledge the possibility that they were placed there by the Creator of the universe? Einstein acknowledged that science requires faith in the absolutes of the laws which regulate the universe. Why is it okay to have faith in science, but not okay to have faith in God?"

"No one said it wasn't 'okay' to have faith in God. They just don't share it."

"Okay, hear me out on this," he said, like I had a choice.

"Those big thinkers, like Hawking and Einstein insist there are undeniable laws which govern the universe. Laws that I acknowledge and believe exist. They fit my world view. They see these laws as unalterable. In other words, they believe those laws are just and affect everything equally."

"Okay," I said cautiously, wondering exactly where he was going.

"Well, I accept these rules dictate the order of the universe, but I can't acknowledge they exist on their own. How is it that these scientists can so easily place their faith in the eternal presence of laws, but cannot find a reason to believe in the eternal presence of a law writer?"

"Uh, I'm not sure what you're getting at."

"As humans, we understand laws as something put in place to dictate how something should function or to maintain order. Without laws, society would eventually decay into chaos. Without laws our roads would be hazardous to travel, personal belongings would be plundered by others, life would be reduced to something without meaning as one man takes the life of another for his benefit. Life, and even the universe, has to have boundaries, and laws establish those. Laws are designed for a purpose. Laws are put in place for a reason. Laws do not create themselves. If laws had the ability to create themselves, society would not need them to be written or expressed. They would be inherent to each of us."

"But you are speaking of laws of justice and society. They are talking about laws of nature. Things that just are."

"Oh, so I'm supposed to believe these laws of nature "just are," but you can't believe that God "just is?"

"I didn't say God didn't exist. I said I don't know. I don't see it."

"And, by the way, according to Hawking and Einstein, the laws of nature are laws of justice as well. They are undeniable. They affect everything equally. They serve as the laws of justice for the universe. The universe can't act out of order because it is bound by those laws."

"Okay, I guess."

"And yet, even though they believe in the laws of justice for the universe, Einstein said, 'I cannot conceive of a God who rewards and punishes his creatures."

"Yeah. So?"

"So, if he can believe the laws of the universe are just and unalterable, how can he not understand that the Creator of those laws would be bound by the same rules of justice? God has rules as well. He set forth the rules that affect the universe and all His creation, so He is bound by the laws He has instilled within His creation. Of course, due to our freewill we choose to follow those rules or not. There are consequences, or outcomes, for each of those choices."

"Einstein believed in the orderly nature of the universe and likened this to God. He just didn't believe in a personal God who concerned Himself within the lives of His creation," I retorted trying to be part of the conversation.

He switched gears on me as if I hadn't said a thing.

"Let me ask you this. If you happened upon a watch lying in the sand and opened the back to see how it worked, would you consider the watch to have spontaneously created itself?"

"No, of course not."

"Why not?"

"Because I could tell it was made by somebody. Watches don't exist in nature or come into being on their own."

"Then why would you believe in a universe which spontaneously created itself?"

"Because that's what the scientific evidence suggests."

"How? You see order in the design. Certainly you can acknowledge that. If you can't imagine a watch was created spontaneously, how can you not equate that with the universe?"

"The watch carries the mark of its creator. Besides, it's mechanical, not organic."

"Suppose it didn't have any marks. Suppose there were no markings on the watch to indicate who made it. Even if you don't know the creator, you can see the craftsmanship and the intelligence in the design, so you know it was created."

"A watch is a known man-made item. It isn't evidence for the creation of the universe."

"No it isn't, but it is an example of design."

He paused in his thoughts and I was sure he was about to take a stab in another direction.

"You know, one thing I don't understand is Einstein's belief as it relates to morality. He said that he didn't believe in immorality of individuals, and he considered ethics as exclusively human concerns with no greater authority as the basis behind them."

"Yeah, so?"

"Well, how can one believe humans are capable of the concept of morality without any greater authority? Without God, concepts like ethics and morality have no meaning."

"Maybe he felt man imposes his own authority."

"If we, as a society, had no higher legal authority to enforce our laws, would anyone follow them?"

"I don't know. Maybe?"

"Seriously? You think people would just naturally create boundaries on their behavior if there were no laws or at least a community expectation of acceptable behavior?"

"Maybe."

"What would be the point? If there were no higher authority, no one to enforce consequences, and no external force, why bother? And why are we to be burdened with things like morality or ethics? Life is a party. Live and let die, right?"

"Of course not. We still have commitments to society and to each other as humans."

"What commitments? Life has no purpose and therefore has no value. In the light of that kind of thinking, there would have been no issue with Hitler's goal of making a superior race and his genocide against another race. If you think no one is holding us to a higher standard and we are animals meant to multiply and evolve, then he should have been praised for what he was doing. Those who are too weak to carry their weight should be extinguished, right?"

"I think that's a little extreme, don't you?"

"Yes, I do, but that's based on my world view. If I shared either Hawking's or Einstein's worldview, I wouldn't feel that way at all."

"Well, I think it's extreme and I don't share your worldview. How can you believe that just because someone doesn't believe in God they have no humanity?"

"Because there is no basis for humanity without God. From where do you begin to have morality?"

"From the simple fact that we are here to help improve our world; to share with each other and to make a better place for all humans."

"Again, for what reason? It doesn't matter."

"It does matter. We're here. We should care for our species and our planet."

"But why, Sophie? Why do we care if it is all temporary? If our moment here is just that, a moment, and there is nothing more, where do we find a place for compassion, for love, for helping our brothers and sisters?"

"It comes from inside of us. It is just what it means to be human."

He smiled.

"Inside of us? You mean like part of our souls? Part of the human spirit? Who put it there?"

He had me frustrated.

"I don't know. Maybe it's just part of our DNA."

"Sophie, it's there because we were designed and yes, we are all connected to the collective by the Spirit of the God who made us. Morality isn't a physical trait."

He wasn't done.

"Of course, Einstein had his own opinion on the concept of souls which live on after we die. He said, "Since our inner experiences consist of reproductions, and combinations of sensory impressions, the concept of a soul without a body seem to me to be empty and devoid of meaning." He believed morality was an exclusively human concern, but morality isn't just a conscious thought. Morality is part of our inner being, and though some, like Hitler, can ignore or pervert morality, it is part of the human spirit which makes you -- you. I suggest that the concept of morality without a soul is empty and devoid of meaning."

As I took in his words, I sat amazed at this guy in front of me. He came off acting so simple and casual. He used humor to defuse the seriousness of situations. These conversations, debates, we had from time to time were the most serious he ever allowed himself to become. He was kind and honest. He was cute and fun. But inside, he was a thinker.

"You've obviously studied this a lot."

"I poke my nose in a book from time to time," he said with a grin.

"It means a lot to you, doesn't it?"

"What's that?"

"Presenting your world view in a way that it can be taken serious."

He shook his head.

"Not so much. I believe what I believe. The next guy can take it or leave it."

"Then why do you work so hard at it?"

He smiled.

"It keeps me on my toes. You never know when a pretty little geek girl might come along and challenge me."

"Challenge?"

"Yeah, you know, make me think; try to put the pieces of the puzzle together."

"I never realized I was challenging to you."

"In more ways than you know," he offered with a slight flush of his cheeks.

I took his hand and pulled him close to me, my head leaning on his shoulder. It was my favorite place. Sometimes he could be perplexing. Sometimes he knew just how to push my buttons. Always he was the right guy at the right time.

Chapter Twelve

My eyes had been glued to the television. It wasn't the latest top rated drama that had captured my attention. It wasn't a television comedy or a natural disaster being reported on the news which kept me from flipping onward through the channels. It was the commercials. One after another they appealed to the hearts of the viewers. The cancer commercial where the older guy talks about being given more time with his family, the public service announcements talking about how smoking kills and destroys the body, and the guilt ridden commercials showing starving children in Somalia; they all stressed the importance of living longer or helping others to live longer.

They were moving, but they avoided the truth. We can't escape death. The end of life is inevitable. It's going to happen. No matter how much people fight against it; no matter how much money they donate for research against disease or to feed the bloated bellies of children, they are going to lose the battle. Develop a new drug and

that cancer patient will just die a little later. Feed
those children and they will die of dysentery rather
than starvation. What was so amazing about living
longer when the results are going to be the same?

If we're going to die anyway, why prolong the
agony? It wasn't that I wasn't touched by the
emotion of the stories; it's just that it didn't matter.
Was prolonging the struggle against death really
worth it? Why?

I was still letting the thoughts float through my
head when Geneva entered the room. I guess I
must have had a funny look on my face or
something. Maybe I just looked more stupid than
normal.

"You okay?" she quizzed.

Her voice startled me.

"Yeah, I guess."

"You looked like you were a thousand miles
away."

"I was just thinking."

"Must have been pretty important to take you
so far away."

"No, not really. I mean, I don't guess it
matters."

"You don't guess what matters?"

"I'm just curious. Why do people talk about
living longer? I mean, why do they want to go
through the pain and agony of radiation and chemo,
if they are just going to die later? Even if they get
well, they'll still die sometime."

Geneva saw a chance for a conversation, so
she sat down on the other end of the couch.

"I guess because they want to spend more time
with the people who matter to them."

"But they're just putting off what happens naturally."

"Yes, but they may have another day to make a memory or to do a good deed. It might give them time to tell someone how they feel about them or to spend some time showing their family how much they mean to them."

"But all that goes away when you die. It disappears once you're dead. There aren't any more memories after your brain dies."

She smiled.

"Well, I guess that all depends on what you believe."

"What do you believe?"

"I'd like to think that our memories go with us. Maybe the love we shared stays with our spirit."

"Spirit? You mean like a soul. You sound like one of those people who believe in an afterlife."

Geneva gave a slight toss to her head while shrugging her shoulders.

"Yeah, sort of."

"Doesn't that seem kind of childish to you to believe that there is some afterlife? I mean there just isn't any evidence to support it."

"Sophie, I'm glad you're a thinker. I am impressed with the fact that you reason things out and try to take a sensible approach to things. That kind of maturity will keep you out of a lot of trouble as you get older and face some of life's challenges. But you can't go through life thinking the only things which matter are the things you can see and touch."

"I'm not limited by what I can see and touch. I can't see the air, unless I go back to L.A.; I know it's there though. There is scientific evidence to prove it. I can't see the see a virus unless it is magnified by a microscope, but I know it's there."

"I'm talking about the things science can't show you, like the love you feel for someone or the life force that inhabits your body."

"They're all the result of chemical reactions."

"Really? Love doesn't feel real to you?"

"I don't know. I guess, but emotions are just a reaction of the body."

"Sophie, if you're intent on explaining life strictly through the eyes of science, then I guess I have to admit, I can't provide any evidence to dispute your arguments. But I have a strange feeling there's going to come a point in life when you just know there has to be more than science can tell you."

"That's what Cole says."

"Well, maybe Cole is right."

"I don't know. It just all seems kind of futile to me."

"Keep your heart and your mind open. It'll all make sense one day."

"You're really confusing me, you know. I thought you and Dad were such freethinkers. You are starting to sound like a normal parent."

"People change as their thoughts change. Life tosses things at you; things you can't explain. You begin to come up with other ways of understanding them."

We didn't press each other over the issue. I still didn't understand what drove people to seek miracle cures or the fountain of youth. I was sure it was something that would come up again sometime especially with Cole looking for any opportunity he could find to challenge my thoughts.

The sounds of a dreary song floated out from the speakers of the television, pictures of cats and dogs with sad faces and injuries rolled and slid across the screen.

"Save the animals. Now that's another subject altogether." I mumbled, flipping the channel to the Cartoon Network

Chapter Thirteen

Spring in the Panhandle is a beautiful thing. I never thought I'd say that, but the truth is the truth whether we want to believe it or not. Watching the green grass emerge from the dry, browns of winter; the contrast of the dark soil against the young, green wheat; looking out upon the rolling hills or the wide, flat countryside; are all experiences you have to see to understand. A baby blue sky with those light, whispers of clouds moving across it is so unbelievably inviting, and it was a complete contrast to the mornings I'd seen back in San Diego.

The explosion of the morning sun as it lifts over the edge of the earth, its orange, yellow glow illuminating the clouds or the gentle way it slips into the prairie sea in the evening can't be experienced from the city like it can on the great wide open. California has its wonders, the rolling of the Pacific onto the warm sands being just one of them, but the magnificence of staring out for miles on an Oklahoma morning can't be discounted. There is freshness in the air, when the dew is heavy upon the grass.

But out in the Panhandle, the Oklahoma spring gives way to an Oklahoma summer, and that very often ends with dry, hot afternoons which lead to a search for shade and comfort. Heat waves lift from the highway as rattlesnakes and tarantulas -- turtles and skunks make their way from one side to the other seeking their forms of relief. The grasses and wildflowers which had grown tall along the highways begin to shrivel into browns and grays as the sun sucks the moisture from within them and beneath them.

While I spent my free time over at the pool in Spring Creek, working on my cool more than my tan, Cole spent the majority of his days out in the heat on a local farm. I didn't get to see him much except for in the evenings. He even worked most of the Saturdays, since farming doesn't take a rest. He did have Sundays off, but I, usually, didn't see him until after church was over.

Between the farm work and spending about an hour a day in the weight room at the football field, he was growing into a rather magnificent young man. His shoulders and his chest had filled out and when we went to the pool one Sunday afternoon I was chilled to discover his chiseled abs. He was dark from his work in the sun, and his normally dark blonde hair was bleached around the edges from beneath the cap he wore when he worked. I couldn't deny the physical attraction I was feeling for him.

I watched as he showed off on the diving board. I wasn't the only one paying attention. I could tell he'd caught the eye of a number of other girls. Thankfully for me, he hadn't seemed to notice, or if he had, he didn't allow it to take his attention off me.

He waved at me just before getting air and curling his knees into a cannonball. The splash sent water spraying across the pool and up onto the concrete where I was laying out. My eyes stayed on him taking in his image as he climbed the ladder along the side of the pool, water streaming off his sculpted body. His incredible smile made me giggle when he started walking toward me, but that quickly changed into aggravation when he stood over me and allowed his hair to drip onto me.

I guess you could say, I'd filled out as well, I had curves where once the terrain had shown more resemblance to the Great Plains. The tan I'd picked up over the summer had given my skin a golden look. I had greater confidence in my appearance than I'd had in the past. And when he sat down beside me to dry off, I knew it was me he was most concerned with impressing that day.

"Man, it's a hot one today. I'm glad I'm here instead of out building fence," he said as he stared off into the sky.

"Me, too. Will you rub some lotion on my back?"

"Sure. Turn over."

The coolness of the lotion as his hands spread it over my surface was a sharp contrast from the heat radiating off my skin. The strength in his hands formed another contrast as he moved them gently over my back, my shoulders, and my legs buttering me with the sunscreen. When he began to massage it into my skin, I found myself moving past the arousing feelings of his sensual movements into a state of total relaxation. I felt like putty beneath his touch and every muscle in my body was at his disposal. He never took advantage of what he most assuredly knew to be a state of vulnerability.

When he finished, he leaned over and kissed my neck, then sat back on his towel, his hands behind his head. As I looked over at him through slivered eyes, he looked so calm and confident lying back with the shades over his eyes, the muscles and tendons of his arms stretched and bulging. Drops of water still lingered upon his rock hard chest. I smiled contentedly at simply having him near me.

Ours was a strange relationship as far as high school romances were concerned. Not quite crossing the line into a serious couple, but certainly more than friends, deeper than friendship. He'd been right about that, when he spoke of relationships that seem to have some deeper bond than mere emotion. We'd connected on a different level, so clearly attached that one knew what the other was thinking, feeling, and experiencing.

"I like that smile," he said, interrupting my thoughts. "It looks so contented."

"Umm. It is," I replied lazily.

"What'd you want to do tonight?"

I rose up on my elbow, by head resting in my palm.

"I don't know. What'd you want to do?" I countered.

"I thought we could go to Liberal to a movie. Maybe get some Chinese food first."

"I don't know. I'd just like to lie around the house and enjoy the air conditioning."

"Mind if I tag along?" He teased.

I threw the tube of lotion at him.

"I meant with you, Bozo."

"What do you want to do for supper?"

"Tell you what, if you stop by the grocery store, I'll get Geneva to help me fix you some Chinese food. She's great at it."

"Sounds like a deal I can't refuse. Want to go to church with me afterward?"

"Cole, I don't know how comfortable I'd be there."

"Just give it a try. I won't bug you about it again."

"I'll think about it."

"Fair enough."

We stayed at the pool for another hour or so and then stopped at the grocery store on the way home. Geneva was so excited to fix supper for us; she rushed us both out of the kitchen.

"But mom, I wanted to help."

"Go spend time with Cole. I'll let you help when it's just us."

I showered while Cole dropped down in front of the television. When I walked back into the living room, Will was there with him, and they were watching a baseball game.

"You want to watch the game or a movie."

"Do you mind if we watch the game for a while?"

"No, not at all. It will give me an excuse to help mom in the kitchen."

Once she knew Cole was being entertained, Geneva was more than happy to accept my help.

"So, how's it going?" She probed.

"How's what going?" I asked as I tasted the sweet and sour sauce.

"With Cole?"

I gave her a puzzled glance.

"Fine, why?"

"Oh, I was just wondering. You two spend a lot of time together. Are you a couple?"

"Were a couple of friends."

She stopped chopping the cabbage.

"Come on now, Sophie. You two have to be past just friends. You're together almost every hour you can be."

"We're just really, really, really good friends. We've talked about more, but we both want to take it slow. You know? We don't want to mess up the friendship."

She caught me reaching for a water chestnut and slapped at my hand.

"Stay out of that. So, if some other guy came along, Cole would be just fine if you started dating him?"

I tossed it in my mouth anyway.

"Umm. I don't know. I don't think he'd have to worry about that."

She smiled knowingly.

"Okay. So, what if he decided he wanted to date another girl? Are you okay with that?"

"I don't think I have to worry about that either."

"Sounds like you're a couple to me."

"Okay, so maybe we're sort of a couple. Look, if I was out to find a boyfriend, it would be Cole, but as long as he is happy with what we have and I am happy with what we have, then we're not going to rush it."

"You know, that's a very mature and sensible way of looking at it. I'm proud of both of you.

Just make sure you are communicating with each other if you feel something changing in your relationship," she said as she opened the cabinet and reached for the electric wok.

"That's what's so great about Cole. We talk about that kind of stuff all the time. I feel completely comfortable telling him about my feelings. And even though we disagree on a lot of things, they don't get in the way."

"Sounds like a pretty incredible relationship. I'm happy for you."

"Yeah, it is."

I paused.

"Can I ask you a question?"

She stopped what she was doing to give me her full attention.

"Of course, sweetheart."

"We've never gone to church right?"

"Well, your father and I went a few times before you were born."

"But Grandma and Grandpa go to church."

"Yes, they do and they always took me when I was little."

"So, why'd you stop?"

She wiped her hands on the hand towel and moved closer to me.

"Well, when I went to college and met your father, some of my views changed. I didn't see things the same way as I did when I was younger."

"So, you and dad don't believe in God, right?"

"I can't really answer that, Sophie. You know there are lots of different religions. Some of them believe in one God and others believe there is some kind of spiritual force that connects us. I would say that I grew questionable of organized religion.

The older I get, the more I feel there must be something beyond what we see here on earth. Our world works in a way that I can't explain. Why the quiz?"

"Cole wants me to go to church with him tonight."

"Oh. Well, is it important to him?"

"Yeah, he's pretty involved in his church."

"Then what's it going to hurt?"

"But I don't know if I'll feel comfortable there. It goes against all I've ever believed."

"True science isn't afraid of being challenged. And if you want to share in what is important to Cole, then maybe you should give it a try. No one is going to force you to change your mind."

"I guess."

"I don't want you to be afraid of religion. I want you to make up your mind about religion."

I mulled it over through dinner and finally agreed to go with Cole. I can't say that I wasn't a little uncomfortable. After all, most of the people I knew from school knew of my philosophy. So it seemed rather hypocritical of me to be there, but the people were friendly enough and the pastor had an interesting message. It at least gave me some things to think about.

Cole was on cloud nine and after the service he introduced me to the pastor and the youth minister. True to his word, he didn't press me to go again, but he had planted a seed that seemed to grow as I became a little more curious. It seemed that my world view was changing on a regular basis

Chapter Fourteen

The deep rich blackness of the night sky was punctuated by the brilliance of a billion twinkling lights. The Milky Way stood out like a swish of pale whitewash against the dark background. I'd never seen a sky so clear, and I stared up into it while my heart raced with excitement. My breath shuddered with anticipation. The warmth of the hood underneath my back was an incredible contrast to the growing chill of the night air against my skin.

The evening was so quiet I could hear the slight breeze stirring the stalks of wheat causing their heads and whiskers to rub together in an echoing chant. Somewhere in the distance a group of coyotes whined and grumbled amongst themselves. Beyond that, the only sound I heard was the thumping in my chest.

I felt the heat of Cole's body pressing up against me. His nearness sent chills of a different kind coursing through my body, creating a kind of euphoric queasiness. His movements were slow, patient, and considerate. The sound of his voice was soft and soothing as he tried to help me focus my attention. I felt the wisp of his breath moving over the surface of my cheek as he whispered.

"Close, just a little further," he encouraged.

My eyes traced the curves and twists of his muscles and tendons as they stretched and extended. The little hairs of his arm tickled against my face. He continued trying to point me in the right direction, but I was having trouble converging with him, the thoughts and feelings swirling within me were creating a distraction. He didn't seem bothered by my lack of focus.

"Right there?" I asked.

"No, over a little."

I squirmed, realigning my body against his.

"There?"

"No." He chuckled. "That's not it."

"Oh! Oh!" I exclaimed excitedly. "There! That's it!"

"Now, you've got it. Can you stick with it?"

"Mmm. Yeah, I think so," I said my silly grin hidden in the dark.

"Good."

"It's such a small spot. How'd you find it?"

"You just have to search. Once you get it the first time, it's easier."

"Uh. That's so incredible."

"Yeah, it is." He whispered.

The day had started simply enough. Cole was working with the Watson's. He'd helped them with the harvest the previous year as well. It was hot, sweaty work; sitting in trucks all day, with no air conditioning, waiting for the combines to fill the grain beds. After the trucks had been filled with the red-gold grains, the beds were covered with tarps to keep the grain from blowing during the slow, dusty trip to the grain elevators.

The dust and chaff coated our sweat dampened skin. I'd come along to keep him company. It didn't take long for me to wonder if that'd been such a good idea. The temperature hovered just over one hundred degrees most of the day. Still, beyond the heat, the itching, and the dust, there was something exciting about watching the combines cutting swaths through the fields and spitting the golden shafts of straw out behind them. Though they moved along in a cloud of dust, it was still majestic to watch them operate.

As we waited for the trucks to be filled, we listened to the radio and chatted. I laughed at his stories. I sang along with our favorite songs. I felt sweat beading over the skin of my arms. I felt it trickling down my chest and my lower back. I pulled my hair up and allowed the warm wind to blow against my damp neck depositing more dust on my skin. And through it all, I had a great time.

Harvest only stops with the closing of the elevators. Even then, the combines creep along, their lights aglow, cutting into the night to fill the trucks one last time before shutting down for the day. It was there, at the end of the day, when we found ourselves lying upon the hood of a grain truck and staring up into the sky.

"It's amazing to experience something so spectacular and to know it's happening somewhere every day."

"Not everyone experiences it."

"Not everyone has someone like you to help them," I said catching the light in his eyes as I pushed back a lock of his hair.

"It's no big deal."

"I'd have never known anything about it if you hadn't been patient enough to show me."

"Come on. You've never done this before?"

"No. I didn't even know you could."

He glanced up into the sky. Cole had taught me the art of identifying satellites as they crossed the night sky. At first I didn't believe him when he told me we could see them, but after he had shown me the difference between the satellite movements and aircraft passing overhead, I was mesmerized.

"Look. There's another one."

"Where?"

He pointed up into the darkness once again.

"Over there."

I followed the length of his extended arm once again all the way up to where his finger pointed into the dark sky, the hairs on his arm tickling against my cheek once again sent chills through me. There at the end of his index finger a tiny flickering light moved across my line of sight.

"I see it! I see it!" I said excitedly. "Two satellites in one night!"

"See, I told you. Once you've found one the first time, it's easier the next time."

"Now I'm going to be looking up there every night."

He laughed.

"Oh, it'll be cool for a while, but you'll get over it. Besides, you need to be out away from town to see them clearly."

I suppose it seems silly to get excited about something so mundane. There were hundreds of satellites circling the earth both day and night, but I was with Cole, and I was comfortable. It felt so relaxing to lay there lazily next to him and pass the time. It was crazy; something as simple as staring up into the night sky could be so fun and exciting, but that's the way things were when I was with Cole. It seemed like everything became more interesting, less ordinary. He always found these little ways to entertain me and to surprise me.

I couldn't imagine life without him. If Will and Geneva were to suddenly decide to move, I don't think I could have handled it. I'd never had a person like Cole in my life. He was as much a part of me as my own limbs. I rolled over on my side to look at him.

"But it's fun now." I paused. "I can't believe how much I've enjoyed myself today. I've sweat in places I didn't know I could sweat. I'm dirtier than I've ever been in my life. It was hotter than an oven it that truck all day, but I had a blast. How's that possible?"

"I don't know. I've done this for two years, and it's the same every year. I work from sunup until past sundown; I'm worn beyond exhausted and yet I have the time of my life. I don't know what it is."

"Would they mind if I come out again sometime?"

"Nah, they don't mind at all. They'd probably put you to work if you said you wanted to drive."

I scrunched my face.

"I'm not sure I'm ready for that. Watching you pull those knobs and raise the bed of the truck kind of scares me a little."

"It's not hard. You just have to learn what to do."

"I'd rather watch right now."

He brushed my hair back off my forehead.

"You are so dirty. Your mom is going to wonder what you've been doing all day."

"I'll blame you. It is your fault you know."

"Yeah, I took you down and rolled you in the dirt."

"Hmm. Sounds like fun."

"You're messed up."

"I was almost this dirty once before. I think I was about three years old."

"Mud pies?"

"No. Compost."

"Compost?"

"Yeah, my dad was checking out this place where they compost organic waste. I fell and rolled down the compost pile."

He laughed.

"That's nasty." He said with the laughter still in his voice.

"It wasn't trash anymore. It was dirt."

"Dirt that used to be trash."

"All dirt used to be trash." I defended.

"Ancient trash."

"What's the difference?"

"I don't know. There's just something creepy about modern trash."

"Oh, and they had cleaner trash when they didn't have indoor plumbing?" I countered.

He rolled his eyes, but he gave in on the argument.

"Okay, my opinion doesn't make sense. So, was your little roll in the dirt traumatizing?"

"Nothing more than a memory."

"Well, you look cute in dirt."

"Thanks, I use it as a foundation all the time."

"Interesting."

"What time do you have to be back out here in the morning?"

He looked at his watch.

"In about five and a half hours."

"Don't you think you should go home and get some sleep?"

"Nah, I'm enjoying myself. Are your folks going to be mad about you getting home so late?"

"No. We're talking about Will and Geneva here, the liberated couple. Besides, they know I'm with you."

"Why's that matter?"

"They love you."

"Well, that's good to know."

"I think we should go, though. The heat makes you sleepy. If you don't get enough rest, you'll be too sleepy to drive."

"I'll be fine."

I poked him in the chest.

"I said."

"Okay, but I could just sleep here."

"I think you'd feel more comfortable in your bed than on the hood of a truck."

"I'd feel more comfortable with you."

"That's sweet, but I'd feel more comfortable if you got a good night's rest."

"Either way, five hours isn't a good night's rest."

"Then we better get you home before you're stuck with four hours."

I rose from my spot beside him and slid down off the hood. The trip to town was quiet. I suspect fatigue was starting to take its toll on both of us. He dropped me off in front of the house.

"You want me to pick you up at six?"

"Uh, sorry Bud; I need a little more rest than that. Maybe on Wednesday. Besides, I think Geneva wants me to go shopping with her tomorrow."

"Alright. Want me to call you tomorrow night?"

"Sure, but better make it before ten if you want me to get up in time on Wednesday."

"Okay. Goodnight."

"Goodnight Cole. I had a good time."

He waited until I'd gone in the house before pulling off. Will and Geneva were both sound asleep when I went inside. I took a shower and washed all of the grime off of my body. By the time I made it to my bed, I was almost walking in my sleep. My head barely hit the pillow before I crashed.

When I woke up, it was past noon. I couldn't believe I'd slept so late. I never sleep so late, but then I never spend half the night staring up at the stars. In the lazy haze which hung over my awakening, I could still feel him next to me; the tickle of his arms against mine; the warmth of his essence radiating into me.

As my thoughts went back to the evening, we shared looking up into the wonder of the heavens; I felt my lips turn into a contented smile. It was just another example of Cole's ability to turn simplicity into exquisiteness; to transform a simple act into one of marvel. Just a moment with him held as much depth as a lifetime with someone more ordinary.

Chapter Fifteen

It's strange how easily time has a way of changing us. I'd seen the transformation begin, but I had no idea just how much life was impacting me. I'd gone from a girl who never cared about anything but my school work to one who started to find herself daydreaming and fantasizing. I thought I had it all figured out. Because I am a product of my parents, I knew eventually I might find someone I would want to spend the rest of my life with, but I'd always had this rather sterile vision. I had no idea how to explain love and so I dismissed it. The closest explanation I had was some form of instinct that urged us to be fruitful and multiply.

Cole and I had grown closer and closer. Though we tried to sell it as merely a strong friendship, there was something deeper brewing underneath. It was hard to explain. There was this warm, comforting feeling when I was with him. I never worried about how he saw me or about hiding who I was and of course, there as an intense physical attraction.

My outlook was changing as well. I know I've painted a rather drab picture of life in Small-town, USA, but it wasn't nearly as bad as I had first envisioned. My friendships were just as strong as they would have been back in my old school, probably stronger. Except for the Wicked Girls, the kids in my school were kind and understanding. After all, most of us were going through the same things.

With the exception of one or two other teachers like Mrs. Whann, most of them were as dedicated as any I'd had in the city schools. Of course, we didn't have a lot of activities, so sports played a big role in school pride. However, I didn't feel any pressure to participate.

Cole had been right about his role on the football team. Though he might have been a tackling dummy in previous seasons, when his junior year started he was ready. He'd spent a lot of time in the weight room since the previous year, and it had paid off. He had put on about twenty pounds, and he was ripped like an actor in an exercise commercial.

When football tryouts were finished, he came by my house.

"I made it!"

"Made what?" I asked.

"I'm starting at halfback."

"What's that?" I asked. I didn't have a clue. I'd learned a lot about how the game worked the previous year, but I had no idea what the positions were.

"I'll be carrying the ball."

"Oh, so you're like the guy who scores the... uh... the uh... What do they call them?"

"Touchdowns?"

"Yeah, that's it. I knew it; I just couldn't think of it."

He shook his head.

"You know, Sophie, for being the smartest person I know, you're pretty clueless."

"Okay, so I still don't know the game that well."

"Well, you better learn. If you're going to be there to cheer me on, you need to know when to cheer."

Based on the little I'd picked up the previous year, and the explanations Cole offered, I had a better understanding of football by the time the first game came around. After that game, he was so excited.

"Did you see that thirty yard carry I had?"

"Uh, huh," I answered, confident that I had watched the whole game, but not quite sure I knew which particular play he was talking about.

"I took the ball and just looked for the hole. It broke open, and I was gone."

I tried to mirror his excitement.

"That's great, Cole. I'm glad you had fun."

"Fun? It was freaking awesome."

I learn quickly, especially when I apply myself, and this was important to him, so I paid attention as he explained. As time went by, I grew to understand more of the game. Cole was suddenly a rising star at our school. Even the Wicked Girls seemed to distance themselves from any criticism towards him. His confidence grew. Fortunately, it didn't change him that much. He might have carried his head a little higher, but his personality remained intact.

The Bulldogs put up a good fight that season, but the playoffs eluded them. It might have been a disappointment, but Cole didn't show it. He immediately started planning for the next season.

"We'll get it next year." He said with confidence.

"I'm sure you will." I agreed.

"We'll have most of the team back. We'll be more experienced. I think we'll have a good shot."

He was back into regular workouts in the weight room as soon as the season ended. Although, I couldn't see any way he could improve on his body, he continued to work at it.

That year seemed to flash by us, and I found myself fearful at how quickly our senior year would skate by when we finally got there. I often found myself contemplating on it when at my most alone moments. When the melancholy got to me, I satisfied it with music. I loved to let the words and music take me away.

Geneva was sitting in the living room when Cole came in, so I know she put him up to it by pointing him down the hall. I don't know how long he stood at the door watching before the creaking sound of the doorframe gave him away. My back had been turned to him. Though I got that warm, lazy feeling that should have told me I was being watched, I didn't realize he was there until there was a pause in the music. The sound caused me to turn with a start.

I could feel the blush in my cheeks as I looked up into his face. There he was smiling like the proverbial Cheshire cat.

"Not fair. I didn't hear you come in."

"How could you? You were swooning away with the music."

He glanced over at the IPod dock.

"Taylor Swift?" he quizzed raising his eyebrows. "Doesn't seem to be your style."

"I like her," I said defensively. "She sings a lot of ballads and I can relate to the words of her songs."

He nodded in amusement.

"Tear Drops on My Guitar? Who's the lucky guy?"

I blushed again.

"You should know me better than anyone."

"Nope. I don't know. I also didn't know you could play that thing like a pro," he said motioning to the guitar in my lap. "Or that you could sing like an angel. Maybe you're hiding some other secrets from me."

"No, I'm pretty much an open book. Well, except for this." I said pointing to the guitar.

"Well, don't stop on my account," he insisted.

I smiled awkwardly.

"I can't sing if I know you're there."

"Why? You have a beautiful voice."

I looked away, averting my eyes.

"Thanks, but I'm kind of a closet singer."

"Sophie, that was an incredible sound," he said as he entered the room.

"I don't know; I just don't feel comfortable singing in front of people. I just do it to make me happy."

He sat down on the bed beside me.

"I can tell you I was feeling pretty good listening to you. You have one of those voices that just seem to melt my heart."

"My voice melts you? Like a laser melts a piece of metal?"

"No, like a pad of butter that slowly turns from solid to liquid as it warms; or like sugar dissolves into a cup of warm water. It just kind of warms up my insides."

"Boiled from inside; that sounds like a really bad way to go."

He put his hands in the air.

"I give up. You just can't accept a compliment; can you?"

I felt my lips tightened as I considered his words.

"Umm. Well, thanks I guess. I just do it for me."

He looked over at the guitar.

"I had no idea you knew how to play that. It doesn't seem to fit with your world view."

"Are you kidding? I was raised by a couple of California hippie-wannabes. How could I not know how to play a guitar? They had one in my hand when I was six."

"You should join the choir," Cole piped out enthusiastically.

"At school?" I heard my voice crack in astonishment.

"No, the Mormon Tabernacle Choir in Utah," he said with clear sarcasm. "Of course, at school."

I shook my head.

"I couldn't do that."

"Why not?"

"I'd be scared of looking stupid. Besides, I told you; I just do this for me."

"With a voice like that, you wouldn't look stupid."

"Well, either way, I think I'd rather keep this to myself."

"You shouldn't hide that kind of talent."

"Okay, we'll go with your first response. It doesn't go along with my world view."

"I don't get you. You are an amazing person. You have a beautiful voice and incredible talent. Why don't you let more people get to know the real you?"

"Just because I don't share something I do in my alone time, doesn't mean I hide the real me. I've shared myself enough be considered a dweeb among my peers. What good does that do?"

"You don't let people see what a great person you are. You hide behind a world view designed to shock and alienate others and keep them at a distance. Why? Why don't you want them to get close to you?"

"Look, I didn't ask you over here to give me a lecture on social adjustment," I responded with frustration. "In fact, I didn't ask you over here at all. Why are you here?"

He put his hands up in defense.

"Hey, I just thought maybe you wanted to hangout or something. Don't let me come between you and your alone time."

He turned to leave.

"Wait," I spoke up.

He turned to look at me; his eyebrows rose in curiosity.

"What'd you want to do?"

"Oh, I don't know," he offered with a mischievous grin. "Maybe sit around singing Kumbaya or some Taylor Swift song."

I threw my pillow across the room at him.

"We're not singing."

"Okay. Want to go for a drive?"

"Where to?"

He shrugged.

"I don't know. Just down the road."

I tilted my head inquisitively.

"You have no destination; no plan?"

"Is that a deal breaker?"

"A deal breaker? No. I trust you'll find a way to entertain me."

"Oh, yeah, I'm talking to the girl who doesn't believe in plans."

I rolled my eyes.

"You're not going to start again. Are you?"

"I was just referring to your idea that life just happens."

"I know what you were referring to. Why can't you just accept my point of view? I accept yours."

"No, you humor mine. You don't accept it."

"I tolerate it, even though it is in conflict with what I believe."

"Believe? Now you espouse beliefs? I thought you had a scientific explanation for your world view."

"I do."

"But you consider beliefs as questionable."

"Not questionable, unfounded. So, I used the wrong term. Sue me."

He smirked.

"So, you still want to go?"

"Go where?"

"For a drive."

"Yeah, sure," I said rising to my feet.

It was a beautiful early fall day. Still warm enough for the shorts and spaghetti top I was wearing, but definitely telling of the changes to come. I felt the sun's radiance as it filtered through the pickup window and fell in a warm caress upon the bare skin of my legs and along my right arm. The heat upon my shoulder was relaxing, and though I remained alert enough to carry on a conversation, I felt myself slipping into a state of sleepy contentment.

Thoughts seemed to meander through my mind, and I went back to those moments when we were together; at the lake and in my room. I could once again feel the warmth of his body near me, his breath on my cheek, the touch of his hand against mine, and the emotions those moments stirred within me. He warmed me from the inside out and seemed to soften the seriousness which had tended to dominate my personality for the largest portion of my life.

I leaned my head against the window and closed my eyes. As I replayed the time that had passed since I'd stepped into this world, I realized they were easily the happiest moments I'd ever experienced. Even in our arguments there was a lightness, a playfulness, which kept either of us from feeling angry or hurt. Despite our differences, we had a connection. The thoughts made me smile.

"Hey, you awake over there?"

I opened my eyes at the sound of his voice. The contented smile which had turned up the corners of my mouth grew.

"Yeah, I was just lost in thought," I explained.

"What were you thinking about?" he quizzed.

"Us."

He didn't bother to ask me to expound. I think he understood. He just nodded and continued to stare down the road.

Our first stop was a place called St. Jacob's Well. It was nestled within the Big Basin Prairie Preserve. It was a lush area hidden beyond the basin walls at the end of a rocky trail. Little more than a deep pond fed by a spring and surrounded by large cottonwoods, the place seemed like an oasis nestled among the rugged landscape of the Big Basin. The water of the well stood still as dark glass, hidden beneath the canopy of the cottonwood trees. The banks around the rim of the pond were steep, giving it the look of a crater filled with water.

We sat on a large piece of granite which rose above and stretched out over the edge of the pond. The heart shaped leaves of the cottonwoods had turned to a yellow-gold giving the impression they were little dangling mirrors reflecting the yellow sunlight. While the light autumn breeze blew, they fell down from above like golden pieces of confetti. Those which held a grip to the tree branches clattered together applauding us as we took in their beauty.

Cole stretched back on the stone surface; his fingers laced under his head, his elbows pointing out from either side. I leaned forward, laying my head upon his stomach. I could feel the rippled texture of his muscles beneath his shirt. His time in the weight room was evident in the hard, chiseled texture of his abdomen. The warmth of his body heat radiated through the knitted material of his red polo. My fingers absentmindedly traced the shape of the muscles below the surface.

I sensed his movements and a moment later; I felt his fingers roaming through the strands of my hair, pulling them back and hooking the errant wisps behind my ear. Then I felt the tender touch of his fingers as they drifted lovingly over the surface of my cheek. The scene and the gentle caress of his movements were almost hypnotic, and I could have easily allowed myself to drift off into a peaceful slumber.

"You know, there's no way either of us could convince anyone watching us right now that we aren't a couple?" My thought slipped out casually.

"Okay, so we're a couple, but we're a couple who doesn't get hung up on being a couple. We're comfortable with what we have, at least I am," he offered.

"Me, too. I like that you give me those little kisses of affection, and you don't push me for more."

"I like that you don't expect me to push you for more because I want us to be happy with all the decisions we make."

I looked up into his eyes.

"So, you don't want more?"

"I don't want it to be about more. I'm wildly attracted to you. You're cute and sexy and fun, but I like the easy playfulness of our relationship."

I nodded. I couldn't imagine there was anyone in the universe with whom I could have been more compatible than Cole. I laid there with my head against him, allowing the relaxing moments to pass by.

"Can we stay here?" I asked as the little rays of sunshine filtered down between the golden leaves and gray bark of the branches, dancing through the unevenly shaded canopy landing like raindrops of light upon my closed eyelids.

"We don't have to go anywhere else if you don't want to."

"No, I meant forever."

"Uh, that's a lovely idea, but it won't be like this forever. Next week there's a cold front moving in, and we'd probably get a little wet out here."

"Oh, okay." I paused. "It's just so beautiful and relaxing here."

"Did you see the bison?"

"Bison?" I asked popping up.

"Yeah, bison. You know, buffalo. Kind of like cows with furry heads and weird horns."

"There are bison? Here? With us?"

He pointed without rising.

"Yeah, right over there."

"Can they come over here?"

"Uh, well they're not like bolted to the ground or anything, so I guess so."

"What if they come over here?"

"Relax; they're more scared of you than you are of them. Haven't you learned anything?"

"You're not going to try to use the rabbit story again, are you?"

He laughed.

"I guess you catch on quicker than I thought."

My hands went to my hips as I stared at him trying to give him my most sincere look of aggravation.

He just laughed harder.

"Is that supposed to intimidate me?"

"I'm hoping it works better on the bison."

"Don't worry. They won't bother you if you don't bother them."

"Why are they here?"

"They live here. It's a prairie reserve."

"Maybe we should get back in the pickup."

"I thought you wanted to stay here forever."

"No. I'm good."

"Sophie, they're a quarter of a mile away. Even if they broke into a run we'd be in the pickup before they could cause us any harm."

"But I'm not going to enjoy myself because I'll be watching them the whole time."

"You might find it interesting to watch them. It isn't every day you get to see a herd of bison. They were almost extinct at one time you know."

Rationally, it was silly to be concerned by the creatures. They were a long way off.

He reached over and took my hand.

"Seriously, you aren't bothered by them?"

"Well, maybe a little, but I'll get over it," I said, my eyes still trained on the large massive brown spots moving around in the distance.

They were incredibly majestic animals. The large wooly heads and shoulders seemed to be draped over their sculptured bodies like a carpet. The embodiment of the American West on four muscular legs; they were somehow elegant as they grazed -- munching down at the sparse grass with black, stubby snouts -- lifting their heads to scan the countryside with those dark inset eyes.

Any quasi fear I might have had dissolved into respect. I watched them standing, strolling, being part of the world in which they existed; an extension of the past sharing a place in the present.

"It would have been a shame." My voice came out as a whisper, breaking the silence that had fallen over us.

"What's that?"

"If they'd gone extinct."

"Having trouble with your world view again?"

"No, I'm just saying they are such incredible creatures. They somehow look like they belong here, but at the same time they don't seem to fit in today's world."

He let me off the hook as he gazed out on them.

"Yeah, I think I know what you mean."

We sat on the stone watching them; our fingers intertwined for the next half hour. Little was said between us.

"You ready?"

"For what?"

"To move on."

I looked over at him. Somehow I had come to the conclusion this was our destination. With Cole in control of the agenda, I should have known better.

"So where are we going now?"

"You'll see." He said with a suspicious grin.

I watched out the window as the terrain rolled past. Grasslands which appeared as dry gray, brown, and gold vegetation blended with dormant farmland or hints of green where the winter wheat was just peaking up through the dirt. The clusters of cottonwoods which clumped together here and there in the shallow valleys between the rolling hills were bright gold against the fall landscape.

The wood fence posts zipped by strung with what seemed an almost endless string of barbed wire.

"This is a pretty desolate area of the country," I said breaking through the sound of the pickup as we rumbled down the road. "I mean, the ruggedness has an essence of its own, but except for the little groups of towns, there isn't much out here."

"Yeah. You know it had to have been hard back when the only way to get around was a horse and wagon. That's why the railroads played such a big role in populating the area."

"You'd think they'd still be around."

"Society changed. They fell into disuse, couldn't make it. Of course, now they are making a bit of a comeback. Nothing like the rising cost of fuel to recreate the industry."

"Think they'll ever be back here?"

He shook his head.

"No, like you said, there isn't anything here. Oh, there might someday be a rail that splits through here headed out west, but I doubt it. Too much to invest for such little benefit."

I thought about the small towns dotting the countryside. They were spread out like the little black spots on a connect-the-dot drawing. Essentially, they were just the train stops on the destination to other places. The people had followed the flow of progress and settled alongside. Those rails had served as a connection, the ligaments of society. And now we followed the roads. As a highway is re-routed, the landscape changes a little more. Towns dry up, and cities grow. It's a process that continues to develop and morph with a changing society.

I stared down the black ribbon we were following. It wound, climbed, and fell as the landscape changed. We had adapted. No matter what the world threw at us, we adapted.

"Don't you think the changing of society; the adaptations of mankind indicate this is what we've always done?" I suddenly quizzed.

"Are you trying to use the changes in society to make a case for evolution?" he asked with a grin.

"Essentially," I admitted.

"I'll concede that society adapts and changes to its environment."

"You will?"

"Sure. That isn't a matter for debate. Look at the changes in traditional families. Economic impacts have created duel income families. Changes in the acceptance of actions and behaviors have created more single parent families. No one can deny facts like that."

"Okay, so why can you not see that this presents a case for the evolution of mankind?"

"Changes in society and behavior don't necessarily translate into the physical changes that your theories of evolution require. I readily admit that society changes. Some of those changes, in my opinion, are not necessarily for the betterment of our futures."

He paused.

"Besides, you miss the point of my world view. I don't claim to know exactly how we came into being in relation to the process. I just claim that we aren't accidents. I see the world as a design. The Mona Lisa wasn't painted with an accidental spill of the paint bucket and yet it also wasn't painted with a single stroke of the brush. The Golden Gate Bridge wasn't built by tossing steel girders into the air and seeing how they landed, but rather a detailed plan and a large amount of labor. This road wasn't just asphalt poured out with no regard to destination or engineering requirements. How can you believe that the world just happened?"

I listened while taking in his thoughts and preparing for my next stage of the argument.

"You can name nothing else which exists merely by accident. Everything you see had a beginning and yet, you want to believe the greatest, grandest existence of all, the universe, just fell into place? And if one concedes that it did, which seems to require a greater amount of faith than anything I offer, where did the materials come from? They just always existed? Hmm. That sounds like something you'd scoff at me for believing."

"I don't scoff. You scoff. You preach at me and pick at me over my world view. I don't ever start these conversations."

"You started this one."

"Only because I had a thought, an angle of argument, which came to mind, and I always have to react to your constant prodding."

"I don't mean to pick or preach. I just try to understand why you believe the way you do."

"Why can't you just accept me for what I believe? I accept you."

"Do you? Do you really? Or do you believe I am naive to place my faith in my religion?"

I looked him in the eyes.

"I have never belittled you for your faith. I admire your faith and your confidence," I said earnestly. "I almost envy it."

"Envy?"

"You don't question. You just move through life with this confidence that everything will be okay. It's like you don't have a worry in your world."

"Excuse me? Sure I worry. I just don't let it eat at me. I look at it. If I can fix it, I fix it. If I can't, I accept it and deal with it."

"What if it's something you can't fix and you can't accept?"

"If I can't fix it, I have to live with it. What's the other choice?"

I fell silent.

"I believe life has a plan and sometimes those things we see as an inconvenience are just re-direction, a correction of our course."

"So we don't have a choice?"

"No, we do have a choice, but our choices may impact our plan. We can accept our path, or we can constantly try to reroute. Take a GPS for example. You put in a destination. You head out on your trip, but somewhere along the way you take a wrong turn or change your mind. What happens? It recalculates and redirects your path. Did you have a choice? Sure, maybe you wanted to take a more scenic route or maybe you just wanted to take a road you had never experienced. Maybe you were truly lost, but to reach your destination, you have to reroute."

"So, we have choices along the route, but no choice in the destination?"

"No, we have complete choice in both the route and the destination, but we may not like either one of them. If we want life to go the way that will lead to the most wonderful destination, then we follow the route set out for us. If we get lost along the way we can reroute and still hit that destination, or we can choose to aim for a different destination, but it may be one we won't like when we arrive."

"How do you know all this?"

"Search your heart. It is inherent in all of us. Some of us put up a wall around it, trying to push it away because we feel it is taking our freedom away. Some of us don't initially notice it and have to discover it. Some of us seek it, but either way it is there."

This was heavy. And the truth was if he was right, I was one of those people walling it off. I didn't like the idea that I had a path. I wanted to blaze my own path. I wanted to decide my own destiny. The question was whether Cole knew what he was talking about or whether he was just operating on his programming, what he had been taught.

We pulled into Meade, Kansas in silence. It was a quaint little town; clean and reminiscent of the bygone era of Main Street USA. The brick building on the corner by the stoplight gave every indication it had once been a Rexall Drug Store. I could see the large windows and imagine the soda fountain along the wall just behind them. In my imagination, I heard the bell on the door as its patrons entered. A picture was painted upon the canvas of my mind; images of the soda jerks curving above the counter and canisters of flavored syrups waiting to be pumped into a glass.

Little shops and buildings from the past lined the highway which stretched through the middle of town. The museum was housed in what must have been a former business building.

"They have a museum?"

He smiled.

"Yeah."

"Have you been in it?"

"Yeah, a couple of times. It isn't real big, but there's some neat stuff in there."

I saw a sign pointing down a road off Main Street.

"The Dalton Gang Hideout?"

"Yeah, cool huh?"

"Are we going there?"

"We can see if it's open before we leave. If you want to that is."

"Is it hokey?"

"No, it's neat."

I rolled my eyes.

"Really," he insisted.

"Okay."

We continued on out toward the edge of town.

"So, if we aren't here to see the hideout, what are we here to see?"

"You'll see," he said raising his eyebrows.

"Can't you give me a hint?"

"Be patient. We're almost there."

The truck slowed, and I heard the familiar tick of the turn signal.

"The cemetery?"

"Yeah."

"Kind of a morbid destination isn't it?"

"There's a story behind it," he said pointing. "See the sign?"

Above a rock wall, there were black wrought iron letters spelling out the word 'Graceland.'

"Don't tell me. This is where Elvis is really buried."

He laughed.

"No, Elvis is not in the building or the cemetery."

"So, what's the story?"

"Just a minute."

We rolled slowly through the cemetery following along the trails between the headstones. Like many small town cemeteries, there were stones of various sizes and apparent ages. I noticed markers with Mason symbols and military ranks, tombstones with 'Beloved Mother' and 'Sweet Angel.' It reminded me of the uncertainty of life and our conversation earlier.

When the pickup pulled to a stop, there was a large rock monument in front of us. On one side there was a star, its points made from different colors of stone.

"What's this?"

"Come on," he said opening the driver side door.

I released my seatbelt and followed him. We walked around to the other side of the monument. There was a large brass plaque. The plaque explained the purpose of the marker. A young girl, the daughter of a local pioneer, her brother, and her aunt had died of scarlet fever. Grace Brown was buried on the family homestead, and the property on which she was buried had been offered by the family to serve as a cemetery for the territory. The cemetery was named in honor of Grace.

"She was so young," I whispered.

"Yes, she was."

"It's sad."

"Yes, I guess it is, but then we all have the same fate. Right?"

"Using my world view against me again?"

"Sorry, I guess that was kind of a dig."

"But that's why you brought me here. Right?"

"I brought you here because it is a story which rooted itself in my mind. And I find it interesting that this little girl who died in the midst of the struggle between man and nature -- at a time when so many people died trying to carve out a life in a difficult land -- was honored this way."

"Is this your 'Life Matters' tour we are on?"

He chuckled.

"Uh, I guess you could put it that way."

"So, was this Grace's purpose in life? To give a cemetery a name?"

"No, I'm sure her purpose was greater than that. I would imagine her short life offered great memories to her family. She probably produced thoughts which allowed them the strength to endure the hardships they would face."

"Don't you think her death was one of the greatest hardships they would have faced?"

"Probably."

"Then how did her death help them?"

"Who knows? Maybe her death saved others. Maybe her memories gave them courage. I'm not sure."

"If we aren't sure what her purpose was, how do we know she had one?"

"Is it really for us to understand? Maybe the only ones who know are those she impacted. I'm not trying to debate you on the subject. I'm only offering this monument as evidence that her life mattered for someone."

"I'm sure we all matter to someone."

"Well, I guess that's something we can build on, isn't it?"

"Is it really that important to you that we are on the same page on this?" I said locking on to his eyes.

"Yes."

"Why?"

"Because I want you to know you are special."

"You make me feel that way."

"You are. I don't want you to feel like you are just a step in the process. You aren't just a stage in the evolution of mankind."

"Would it be so bad if I were?"

"Yes, it would. You aren't an experiment. You are a planned, well-designed individual."

"Your worldview doesn't make me feel individual at all. It makes me feel like a robot. Am I just some toy to be played with? I was designed for what? Entertainment?"

"No, you were designed for a purpose."

"For the purpose of entertainment?"

"No, for the purpose of greater good."

I shook my head.

"I just don't know, Cole."

"You will."

I smiled at him. There it was; that calm confidence which accepts things as they are.

"When?"

"When the time is right, you'll know. It will come to you. It may strike you like a bolt of lightning, or it may come to you as a whispered breath, but you will know that you have a purpose. You will see that we all have a purpose, and you will understand."

I reached up and ruffled my hands through his hair.

"How do you do that?"

"What?"

"Get me beyond frustrated and then just make me smile despite it."

He winked.

"I guess that's just what I'm here for."

"Can we see the hideout?"

"Sure."

So, okay. It wasn't hokey. It was kind of neat. It was this tunnel that ran from the little house along the road to a barn down by the creek. It didn't take long to look at it, but it was interesting, and I had no idea that piece of history was just a few miles down the road from home. We wandered down through the dark tunnel, our path lit by lights along the walls. When the tunnel turned and went up inside the house, Cole turned ahead of me. I was lost in thought, and when he jumped back out at me, I screamed. My voice echoed down the rock lined path.

"You butt!"

He was laughing so hard, he leaned against the wall for support.

"You should have seen your face."

"I can't believe you just did that. They'll probably come down here and run us off."

"Relax. I'm sure it isn't the first time they've heard a girly scream down here."

"Girly? I thought we had established that I am not a girly girl."

"Me too, but that scream just cast doubts on the whole subject."

I punched him in the arm as hard as I could.

"Ouch," he said rubbing his shoulder.

"Did that feel like the punch of a girly girl?"

"Oh, that's just like you. Revert to violence to make your point. You can't make an intelligent argument; you have to punch someone."

"Whine on."

We finished the tour and then went down to Sonic before heading back home. After leaving town, we stopped by the lake where we finished our meal while sitting on a picnic table, our feet on the bench below. We strolled along the bank holding hands as we walked.

"I had fun today," I told him.

He looked at me quizzically.

"You did?"

"Yes."

"I thought I'd frustrated you all day."

"You did."

"How's that fun?"

"I had fun being with you," I said as I looked into his eyes.

His hand rose, and I could feel the warmth of his fingers against the coolness of my cheek. I felt just the slightest pressure as he pulled into me. I felt the graze of his lips against mine and that familiar tingle I so often felt when we touched. His lips were warm and dry against mine, brushing first across the surface of my skin. I felt the coolness of his nose against mine as the effects of the cool fall evening left their mark upon us. The contrast of his warm breath mingling with mine sent a balminess radiating through me.

His kisses trailed over my mouth from one corner to the next, igniting an intensity. I touched my tongue against his lips, passing lightly over them, wetting the surface between us. I felt his touch against mine, beckoning me with his teasing. Placing my hand against the back of his head, I pulled him into me, pressing our lips together. His warm, hard chest pressed into mine, and I could feel myself react, knowing he could feel my body pressing back into his.

I felt his palms as they slid down my back to my hips, his fingers taking me in his grip and drawing me into him. My arms moved around his sides, and my fingertips pressed into his back tugging at him, desperate to remove the space between us, heat rising up within me.

My body melted as his lips left mine and trailed over to the space just under my ear then down to my neck. I felt the coolness in the air as it touched the places where his lips left moisture on my skin. His kisses trailed on down my neck, along my collar bone.

It was intense and demanding. The park was deserted; we had it to ourselves. There was nothing to stop us from allowing our feelings to take their course; nothing except me and the integrity of my guy.

He pulled away, pressing his forehead against mine. He rubbed his nose against mine and smiled an uncomfortable smile.

"I'm sorry," he whispered.

"I'm not."

His smile turned from forced to mischievous.

"Okay, I'm not either, but we need to stop before I am."

"Okay," I whispered and then kissed him lightly on the lips before taking his hand and turning toward the truck.

"You're getting better at this."

"I got what I wanted."

"What was that?"

"I got under your skin."

"Oh! Way under my skin!" he assured me.

"After all the arguing today, I wasn't sure."

"We didn't argue. We differed in opinion," he corrected.

"Okay, after all the differing, I wasn't sure."

"I don't give up that easy."

"Oh, I know that. Well, at least not on some things," I said poking him in the ribs.

He looked around us. The sun was growing low on the horizon and under the canopy of trees at the lake it was becoming quite dark.

"I better get you home. Your folks will be wondering where you've been and what you've been up to all day."

"My folks know I'm with you, and they know they can trust you," I said squeezing his hand.

"I do too," I added laying my head on his shoulder.

The trip home was quiet. I was still swimming in the emotions that had been sparked down by the lake. I had a feeling he was too. I hardly realized we were home when he pulled up in front of my house.

"What are you doing tomorrow?" I asked.

"Going to church, then work. I really need to work tomorrow."

"Come by after work?"

"Sure."

"Want to go to church with me?"

"Um, I don't know. I'm not sure."

"Alright. Let me know if you do. Otherwise, I'll see you tomorrow evening."

I leaned forward placing my hand against his cheek, kissing him lightly.

"Thanks for a beautiful day."

"You're welcome. I'm glad we could share it."

My hand trailed from his cheek down his chest and across his arm. Then I turned and opened the door to the truck. I paused and turned to him, pulling him to me and pressed my lips against his in a deep kiss. Pulling away quickly, I exited the truck and waved before turning to go into the house. He waited until I closed the door before pulling away. I watched as he slowly idled down the road. Then I leaned with my back against the door, thinking about what might be going on in his mind, and smiling at the possibilities.

Chapter Sixteen

On a beautiful April evening, Cole and I sat in the bleachers of the softball field. There was just a slight breeze. It was enough to muss up the hours spent in beauty shops and sway the long gowns of the girls as they made their way arm in arm with the beau of their choice through the promenade.

"Oooh. There's Jaima Sanchez dressed in a black silk gown cleverly concealing the black ooze which flows from her soul," Cole announced with sarcasm as he imitated the voice of Mrs. Whann.

"And I do believe she is being escorted by the extremely intelligent Tate Jordan. Strange, it appears Tate must be suffering from some type serious neck injury. I'm not sure how much this will impact his notorious his hair flip and thus his ability to compete," I said trying not to giggle through my part.

"Yes, Sasha. I believe you're right. It's been at least three minutes since the last hair flip; a definite indication that Tate is suffering an injury in tonight's competition," he continued as he spoke into the invisible microphone in his hand.

"And now we can see the charming Leza Wilson making her way up the promenade. Oh! Oh my! It appears Leza is throwing Jaima a curve. She too is dressed in a black silk gown. This little number is going to cause a major distraction for the titleholder," he said trying his best to sound over-the-top.

"True. True. There are distinct rules against minions trying to upstage their mentors,' I admitted in support.

"I certainly hope this doesn't cause a disturbance within the social network."

"Leza is being escorted by the handsome Garrett Riley," I oozed with a sexy sweetness in my voice.

"Judging by his body language, Garrett seems to be at ease with his position in the social hierarchy."

"Yes, no power struggle there. Notice even the tail of his coat seems shorter than Tate's." I pointed out.

"Ah, it appears size does matter."

I turned to Cole startled at his comment. I could feel the blush moving into my cheeks.

Cole looked at me with an amused look on his face.

"I can't believe you said that."

"What?" he asked overdoing the innocent look. "Oh, Sophie, get your mind out of the gutter. I was talking about the tails of course."

I rolled my eyes and turned to stare up into the baby blue sky.

"You suppose they plan out who's wearing what ahead of time?" he asked.

"Probably. Who knows? However, I can't see Jaima taking a chance on coincidence where something like that's concerned. There's no way she would allow Leza or Stacy to show up there in anything, but a traction halo if she knew they had picked the same dress."

"Hmm. Maybe we'll see a catfight," he mused. "It might be worth it just for entertainment value."

"I don't know. I'm not sure anything would make it better."

"Aw, don't get on a downer."

I scrunched my nose. I just wasn't into this prom stuff. It wasn't like I was going to be the queen of the ball or anything.

"What if we went like this?" he suggested.

"They wouldn't let us past the front door dressed like this," I scoffed.

"It's our prom too," he defended.

"Yeah, but don't they have like a dress code or something?"

He laughed.

"What? You don't think we'd pass muster?"

I glanced at him. He was wearing blue jeans and a Bulldog shirt."

"You might, since you're at least wearing the team mascot."

"Oh, come on. You look great."

"I didn't even do my hair. I just pulled it back and put it in a ponytail."

"Well, it looks fine to me."

"You're not serious?"

He shrugged.

"Maybe."

"They'd die if we showed up on the promenade like this."

He smirked.

"It would definitely get someone's attention."

"Maybe we should spruce up a little."

I could see from the twisted way his mouth fell I was spoiling his fun.

"Kind of defeats the purpose, doesn't it?" he offered.

"So you just want to go over there and line up in the promenade and head into the banquet?"

"Sure. What's the worst that could happen? They tell us to leave?"

I rolled my eyes again and stood up.

"Okay, enough fantasy. We have to get ready," I said reaching down for his hand. "My mom will kill me if I don't wear the dress she bought."

"Aw, jeeze. It was fun while it lasted."

"So, did the tux fit okay?"

"Yeah, a little stiff around the collar."

"You're not going to wear that cowboy hat, are you?"

"What? You want me to leave the Hat of Glory behind?"

He was impossible.

"You're not are you? Leaving it behind?"

"Of course not, Little Lady. You don't expect me to show up lookin' like some kind of city slicker."

He dropped me by the house, and I spent the next hour under Geneva's creative influence. Between the makeup and the hairspray, I felt like I was encased in plastic. I made her leave the room as I finished dressing. I was uncomfortable enough being all dolled up like this; I didn't want her there trying to rearrange my boobs.

Still, when I saw myself in the full-length mirror with the blue sequined dress hugging my curves and flowing down to my four-inch heels, I could hardly believe I was looking at my reflection. I'd always kind of considered my chest to be less than spectacular, but after seeing how my average little mounds were lifted up in the front creating cleavage I'd never dreamed to possess, I was glad I'd picked the dress with straps. I'd always kind of had this fear of things falling out of place and becoming the center of attention by baring myself in front of the whole high school world.

I twirled cautiously around and watched how the alluring slit up to my thigh allowed a flash of flesh when I moved; teasing, but safe. I took a few tentative steps, unsure of how much control I had over the heels. I wasn't exactly used to walking on stilts. There was a little wobble in my walk, but I adjusted to it quickly. I took another glance in the mirror before moving toward the bedroom door.

"Definitely more daring than the normal Sophie," I thought.

I slowly opened the doorway, my head hanging with a slight pang of embarrassment. I glanced up at Geneva and registered her amazement; her fingers pressed to her lips; her mouth agape. It wasn't often I'd seen her speechless.

"Well? What do you think?"

I saw the tears pooling in her eyes before they started to slide down from the corners.

"Mom! Do I look that bad?"

Her hand slid slowly down from her lips, and her voice was just over a whisper.

"Beautiful. Simply beautiful."

"Really?"

She nodded approvingly.

I reached out and pulled her to me, feeling the tears well up in my own eyes. We hugged for a moment and then she pushed me away.

"You'll mess up your makeup," she said as she took my hand. "Let's go show your father."

Will was reclined in his chair, his eyes glued to the television, when I entered the living room. I stood for a moment before Geneva finally cleared her throat. He glanced up and back to the tube, then he did a double take before popping up out of his chair.

"You are not going out like that," he announced.

I stood there stunned at his reaction.

Then he smiled.

"As much as I like him, Cole doesn't deserve to be seen with a girl this gorgeous."

I jumped at him and threw my arms around him.

"You scared me to death," I whispered into his ear.

He stepped back from me, and I twirled around.

"Hmm. I don't know. I think this is just too much for the kid to handle."

"Oh, Daddy!" I said punching him in the arm.

I could hear Cole's truck before I saw it pull up out in front of the house.

"Go back to your room," my dad said. "I'll get the door."

I pointed my finger at him.

"Don't give Cole a hard time."

"I won't," he said and then mumbled. "Not too hard anyway."

I waited in my room until Geneva called me into the living room.

It's a good thing my mother was using her camera to record the moment. I missed the look on his face when he saw me. I was still trying to get over how handsome he looked in his tux. The tuxedo was black with a long cut coat, almost like a western frock coat. The cummerbund wrapped around his tight abs and the bow tie at his neck were royal blue; the perfect match for my dress. His muscled chest filled out the crisp wing-collared white shirt. His bright blue eyes seemed to glisten in the light of the room. Even with that crazy cowboy hat on, he was absolutely incredible.

When I glanced up into his eyes, the look sent chills over my body, and I could feel the little goose bumps forming on my skin. The look of adoration nearly swept me away. His face slowly transformed from stunned to stunning; his grin lifting his cheeks high, showing his white teeth.

"Talk about wow factor," he said.

"Do I look okay?" I asked fishing for more.

"No," he said straight-faced. "You don't." He continued shaking his head. "Okay isn't even close. You look incredible," he encouraged as he stepped toward me, reaching out to take my hand.

He set the little box he had been holding down on the television stand. Gently removing the corsage from the box, he turned my hand; my fingers grazed against his warm palm as he slid the

flower arrangement over my wrist. Then he turned
me to face my parents and slipped my arm over his.

"Mr. and Mrs. Carter, thank you for allowing
me the opportunity to escort this beautiful young
woman to the prom. I promise I will take good
care of her and bring her home on time."

For once, Geneva and Will looked like normal,
everyday, caring parents. The sense of pride and
satisfaction emanating from my parents' eyes was
warming.

"I know you will, Cole," Will offered.

Geneva took a few more pictures before we
left, trying hard not to overdo it or embarrass me. I
held my patience, understanding how important
this night was to her.

Cole walked me to the passenger side, opening
the door for me. After he'd slid into his seat, he
gave me another once over and took a deep breath
before putting the truck in gear. We lined up in the
promenade and waited our turn. The promenade
worked kind of like valet parking at a ritzy
restaurant, with our fathers working the line and
taking the cars to park them while we made our big
entrance. When he had pulled the truck to a stop in
front of the building, Cole gave me a quick look.

"Don't move," he said before hopping out.

In a second, he was at my side, opening the
door. He reached for my hand and when I stepped
out I almost thought I heard the crowd take a
breath. Maybe it was my imagination, or maybe I
just heard my breath being sucked into my lungs,
but I can tell you I felt incredible. Walking up to
the community building with my arm hooked
around Cole's, I was a little nervous or self-
conscious, but not enough to overshadow the

moment. I didn't even worry about falling off those four-inch heels.

It wasn't so bad. Really. I had a good time. Cole and I danced nearly every dance together. He got cut in on a couple of times, but for the most part, I was there for him, and I wanted him to get every moment of the night I could offer.

Even the Wicked Girls seemed to be on their best behavior. Although, Jaima did look a little miffed. It seems that Leza actually did get a dress almost exactly like hers.

"Looks like there is going to be trouble in the social network after all," I whispered in Cole's ear.

"We'll feel pretty prophetic if we see Leza in a neck brace and halo on Monday," he added with a chuckle.

With all the bodies moving and crowded together, the room had been growing warmer throughout the evening. When we got to the last dance of the night, I was starting to feel a little flushed.

The music started to play a slow romantic tune, and I moved into Cole as he slid his arms around me. My head rested on his shoulder as we swayed back and forth in time with the beat. I felt his hands against my flesh as his fingers caressed the spot just above where the dress dipped in the back. Tingles rolled through me at his touch.

His hands moved, sliding down on either side of me and through the thin, cling of the dress it felt almost as if I was naked beneath his touch. His hands stopped at my hips, and I felt the grip of them as he held me, our bodies shifting together. His body was warm against me; my chest pressed into his. I felt his breath against the back of my neck, and I nuzzled further into his shoulder.

As arousing as it may have been to feel Cole's body pressed up against mine, the sensuousness of the moment was overcome by the balmy, lazy, comfortable feeling which had enveloped me. It lulled me into a peaceful state. Against him was the only place I wanted to be.

We swayed for a few moments together after the music ended. Neither of us seemed to be eager to let the evening die. When we finally stopped moving together, we pulled apart slowly, our foreheads resting together. I felt his head rise away from me, and he placed a kiss against the top of my head.

"We better go before they run us out of here," he whispered.

My fingers trailed down his arm to find his, and we made our way out of the building hand in hand.

"Well, was it so bad?" He quizzed as we walked out to the car.

"Okay, I have to admit it. I had a really good time, but it was only because I was with you."

"Is that so bad?"

"No, that's not bad at all," I whispered leaning my head against his shoulder as we walked along.

"What time do you have to be home?"

"You know my parents. They didn't give me a curfew."

"Okay, what time should you go home?"

"We can stay out a little while."

He opened the door for me and held my hand as I slid into the seat. After he had settled in behind the wheel, he cranked on the ignition and the truck rumbled to a start.

"Do you want to go home and change?" I asked.

"Not really. I had something else in mind."

I'd learned with Cole there was no end to his surprises, so there was simply no reason for me to ask what he was up to. I knew he wouldn't tell me until we were there.

"Okay."

"Okay? No twenty questions?"

"Would you tell me if I asked?"

"No."

"Then I guess there is no point in asking. Whatever it is you have in mind, I trust you."

He raised his eyebrows.

"That leaves me an awful lot of leeway."

I giggled.

"Don't go getting any big ideas, trust only goes so far."

He smiled and flicked on the headlights. The sound of the truck seemed to lull me back into that lazy state I had been in earlier. I was almost drowsy as we rolled out of town and turned down a dirt road. A few miles out of town, Cole pulled into a drive. The rumble of the truck as it rolled over the cattle guard got my attention and my curiosity. The trail road we were on rose over a hill, and when we dropped down over the other side, the lights of the town disappeared behind it.

He pulled the truck to a stop near what appeared to be an abandon homestead and turned off the ignition. There seemed to be nothing left except the foundation.

"Uh, Cole? What are we doing out in the middle of a pasture in formal dress?"

He looked at me.

"You trust me, right?" he whispered.

The sound of his voice in the sudden quiet of the cab brought back the emotions I'd felt earlier. I was there with him, alone in a little hidden spot three or four miles away from everyone else. The thoughts of what he might have in mind mingled and stirred within me creating a sort of confusion as to what I hoped and what I feared it might mean. The emotions stirred within me -- like butterflies flitting along, their soft, tissue-thin wings dancing and toying with the nerve endings of the most sensitive spots within me or a feather being slowly drawn against my skin.

"Yes." I whispered back to him, eliciting a mischievous smile from him in return.

He leaned forward slowly, his cheek grazing lightly against mine. I felt his heated breath against my ear. His hand slowly moved up my arm, and I could hear my heart beating in my chest as my pulse began to race. I felt the moisture of his lips against my ear. His hand gripped my arm pulling me toward him. I was putty in his hands.

"Okay, then. Let's go." He said as he turned to open the door of the truck and pulled me along behind him.

For a moment, I was dead weight. It felt as if my body had melted into the seat, and his tug against my arm met with solid resistance.

"Come on." He said as he tugged again.

I shook my head trying to make sense of it all.

"Out there?" I quizzed.

He smiled.

"Well, we can't do it very well in here."

"Cole?"

A sly grin formed on his face, and his eyebrows arched once again.

"You trust me, right?"

I slid across the seat to the driver's side. He stood and reached for my waist, helping to lift me off the seat and to allow me to slide over the edge. I could feel the dress bunching up at my bottom as my heels sunk into the dirt just outside the pickup.

"My heels are sinking."

Cole bent and scooped me up into his arms. He carried me over to the foundation where there was a slab of concrete, and he set me on my feet.

"Just a minute," he said before turning and stepping back over to the truck.

A moment later I heard the sound of the CD player as he turned up the volume. He rolled down the window on the truck and closed the door behind him. Stepping back over to me, he reached for my arms and lifted them up placing them over his shoulders. Then he pulled me to him once again.

I looked at him quizzically, and he shrugged his shoulders.

"I was enjoying the feeling of you in my arms. I just thought maybe the dance ended a little too early."

I smiled at him and laid my head against his shoulder all the while think about how lucky I was to have him in my life. As we moved together, I stared off into the black night sky. I remembered the first night he took me down to the river and how amazing it was to see the multitudes of stars twinkling back at me from millions of light-years

away. More stars than I'd ever seen in my life.
They were all up there looking down on us now as
we swayed together, moving in a slow circle as
they passed across my line of sight.

I felt that comfortable feeling return to me
once again, and I closed my eyes while
contentment filled me beyond full. His scent lifted,
and I breathed it in. His warmth radiated, and I
took it in. His touch once again caressed my flesh
along the spot where my dress dipped in the back,
and I allowed it to flutter down into my soul.

The confusion was gone. Although I knew
there might be something better, a state which
would lift me beyond this comfortable, contented
moment; I knew it wasn't for now and I was good
with that. This simple moment was what I wanted.
It was what I needed. And I was with a guy who
knew and respected that this was all I needed.

We danced together out there in the middle of
nowhere in particular for nearly an hour. The
coolness of the night air fell over my bare skin, and
as he ran his warm hands over my shoulders, he
knew it was time to go. He pulled away and
slipped out of the tuxedo jacket, placing it over me.

"We better go," he whispered.

I looked up into his eyes. My hand moved up
to his chin pulling him closer. I felt his warm lips
against mine as I touched lightly against him.

"Thank you," I whispered back at him.

He smiled.

"My pleasure."

He wrapped me in his arms, pulling me close
and then he bent and scooped me back up into his
arms, carrying me over to the pickup. I stared into

his eyes as I floated above the ground in his arms. My hand touched his cheek, and I kissed his neck.

There was a moment of awkwardness as he tried to open the door without setting me down.

"It's okay. I can stand here."

He placed me on my feet and opened the door for me. I felt his hands on my hips as he lifted me up onto the seat. He stood there a moment, his hands lingering along my hips, his fingers moving lightly over the sequined fabric of my dress, his body against mine. I pulled him to me once again and kissed him deeply, pressing my lips against his, my fingers combing through his hair.

He pulled away from me and took a deep breath, allowing it to exit slowly through his lips.

"We better go," he said more urgently.

I smiled at him.

"Yeah, we probably better," I said twisting into the seat and scooting back to the middle. "I'm kind of hungry."

"Subway?"

"Sounds good."

We drove to Spring Creek and grabbed a couple of meatball subs. Then we went back to town and sat in my driveway while we ate.

"Oh, this is so good. I was starving," I swooned.

"Me, too," he agreed.

It was after two in the morning when he walked me to the door.

"Will your parents be waiting for you?"

"Hmm. Maybe. They don't wait up very often, but this is kind of a special night, so I'm guessing Geneva will want a recap."

"Maybe I shouldn't have kept you out so late then," he suggested.

"No, it's okay. My parents think the world of you and most importantly, they trust you."

He turned to face me.

"Sophie, I don't want to ever do anything to damage that."

I could hear the message he was trying to send. I offered him a confident smile.

"I know. You won't."

"Thanks," he said, understanding my message.

"See you tomorrow?" he asked.

"Yeah, but don't go thinking about an early fishing trip or anything. I won't be up until after noon."

"Don't worry. I have no intention of getting my butt out of bed before lunch time."

I turned from him and reached for the doorknob, then paused and turned back to him.

"Cole, I had a great time. Thanks for taking me."

"Aww, shucks Ma'am. It was my pleasure," he said with a goofy accent.

"You dork. You really know how to kill the moment."

He took my hand.

"And you really know how to make one."

He leaned over and kissed my forehead.

"Goodnight Sophie."

"Goodnight Cole."

I went inside and did as I did so often after leaving Cole's side at the end of the day. With my forehead pressed against the door, and my eyes closed I listened for the sound of his truck starting up and driving away. Juliet's words filled my mind. "Parting is such sweet sorrow."

I don't know how long I stood there, probably only a few seconds. It seemed like longer as I tried to condense all the emotions I'd experienced throughout the night into one small little package I could bury into my heart and hold keep as a memento. When I did open my eyes, the first thing I saw was my mother standing there grinning like the cat who ate the canary.

Okay, so maybe I wouldn't be waking up until sometime mid-afternoon.

Chapter Seventeen

It was finally our senior year, and Cole was pumped. He had been itching for that opening kickoff since the last season. When it finally came, he was more than ready. It was looking like he had good reason to be excited. The Bulldogs were having a great season and Cole was having the best time of his life. He had worked so hard, and all that work was paying off. He was gaining yardage which was surely going to put him on track for a school record, and he just might have a chance for some recognition on the state level.

Home games were the most exciting of all. The Grumpy Dawg had started hosting the fifth quarters after the game with a pizza night. It was all you can eat with just a door charge. Even the visiting teams participated. We had a great time with each other, and we were meeting new people. Things were looking bright, and Cole was riding high, excited as ever, but he was still that humble, likeable guy. As I watched him work the crowd, talking to the other players, and laughing, it warmed me inside. He was an incredible guy. Yep, things were looking up for both Cole and

Sophie. Then came the game that would change it all.

It was late in the season. So far it had been a perfect season as the Bulldogs held on to their winning record. There were just three more games until the playoffs. Cole was confident.

"We win this one and we are in the playoffs no matter how the rest of the season plays out."

"Do you think it's going to change anyone's outlook if you win it?"

"What do you mean?"

"Well, if they know they're going to the playoffs even if they lose the next two games, will they play just as hard?"

"Yeah, I think so. Everyone wants that first place district patch on their jacket, almost as bad as they want the state champ patch. And who wants to ditch a perfect season just because we got a little lazy?"

It was a chilly October night. I was bundled up with Tisha under two blankets. Neither of us wanted to leave the warmth of our fluffy fort to venture to the concession stand for hot chocolate. Across the stands, vapors of carbon dioxide lifted like fog from the faces of fans. Others retreated to their cars to watch from behind their windshield where they could stay warm and comfortable. Horns honked around the field as the Bulldogs worked their magic on the brown grass.

We started out strong, marching quickly down the field to score within the first two minutes of the game. Then we held them on the return. Stuck at the twenty, they had to punt. Cole was back to receive. He caught the ball as it dropped and headed up the center of the field. He shot toward a hole along the sideline, stiff-armed a defender, and broke into the open. We were up by fourteen just three and a half minutes into the game.

By halftime, we had rung up another twenty-one points to bring the total to thirty-five while the Cats still had a goose egg on their side of the board. Tisha mounted her courage.

"I'm making a break for it. You want some hot chocolate."

"Sure," I said holding back the chatter in my teeth.

"Well, then keep the blankets warm while I'm gone."

After standing in line, she returned with two cups and handed them to me.

"Hold these."

She slid back under the cover of fleece, and once again we huddled together.

"I don't know how those guys find this to be fun," she stated. "I'm glad Duane plays his games in a nice warm gym."

"Yeah, I don't get it either. Is Duane still running the chains?"

She nodded as she sipped her hot chocolate.

"Yep, he's hoping we get enough of a lead to end the game early."

We had to abandon our warmth a few moments later, when the spirit line began to form as the Bulldogs prepared to come back onto the field. Though we all clapped and cheered to show our spirit, we were also trying to keep our blood moving. As soon as the players broke through the line, we all rushed back to the stands.

The Bulldogs kicked-off and just a few plays later had taken over the ball from the Cats. Two more plays and we were in the end zone once again. With the score standing at forty-two to nothing, we only needed one more touchdown to end this thing and send everyone home to warm up. We kicked the ball away and headed down the field. One of the Cats slipped up on the return, and the ball went bouncing across the field. I watched as Cole flew across the field to pounce upon the loose ball. He landed on the ball, and we were back in possession.

With the first two plays, the Bulldogs moved the ball nine yards. On the third play, Cole weaved through a hole and was just about to break into the open when a Wildcat flew into his range from the side. Another was rushing in from behind. The next few seconds of the game etched their way into my mind in slow replay. I've never seen it at full speed -- no matter how many times I've relived it within the confines of my mind. It is a moment I'll never forget.

As his image continued to race for the goal line, time seemed to slow down. I watched in horror as one the Wildcat's helmet met Cole's facemask, thrusting his head back and whipping him off his feet. At the same time, the other Wildcat player crashed into him from behind. His body scrunched between them. The ball popped out from his hands and shot out of bounds. His body took on the look of a ragdoll. It went limp as it seemed to bounce, almost ricocheting from the collision. Then he fell into a crumpled heap before rolling over onto his back on the brown grass. I waited, holding my breath. He didn't rise; in fact, he didn't move. The seconds ticked away, and players slowly made their way to where Cole's still body lay sprawled on the ground.

There was a collective gasp as fans put their hands to their mouths. Then the stadium went silent; the only sound was that of the American flag whipping in the wind from the far end of the field. Apprehension hung in the air as our coaches rushed out onto the field. Players on the other side took to their knees and removed their helmets as their coaches made their way out onto the field. After a few agonizing seconds, our hearts dropped even lower when they motioned for the ambulance to move out onto the field. I watched as Cole's parents rushed out of the stands, clearly shaken. And before I even realized what I was doing, I found myself following them, tears streaming down my face.

There was no movement from him at all. Not even a flicker from his eye lids. I kept staring at him, willing him in my mind.

"Cole, get up. Please, get up," I mentally urged.

I watched as the EMTs worked cautiously and efficiently. I gasped when they put a bag over his face to squeeze air into his lungs. My heart dropped even further when they placed the brace around his neck and slid the backboard beneath him. There was no outside sign of life, and he didn't show as much as a flinch when they loaded him in the back of the ambulance. His mother rode with him while his father rushed out of the stadium to their car. The air was eerily silent as the flashing lights of the ambulance moved across the field and exited the stadium.

I can't imagine the feelings of the players as they realized they still had a game to finish. I didn't stay. I felt a hand take hold of each of my arms and when I glanced around I realized Tisha was at one side, and Duane was at the other. They led me off the field; my eyes blurred by the tears that both filled and overflowed from them. I was numb with no thoughts in my mind, except the image of that moment replaying over and over. I didn't even realize we were at the hospital until I felt Tisha touch my arm.

We were there only moments; not even long enough to see him. They had already made the decision to move him to Oklahoma City, and the air flight team was on its way. Duane called home and cleared it with his parents. Then he called Will and Geneva, to explain what had happened. The three of us were going to Oklahoma City as well. Our parents offered no protest.

It was a quiet trip. Duane drove the whole way and we only stopped for gas. Cole had arrived by air hours before us. His parents made it just ahead of us.

When we reached the hospital, he was in ICU. It was hours before we were allowed to see him, and even then they only allowed us to go in one at a time, for just a few minutes. He had still not regained consciousness.

I entered the dimly lit room; the machines beeping, buzzing, and humming around him. The tubes and lines to monitors nearly hid him from my view. I found his hand and touched his fingers; they were cool and limp. The rise of his chest and the pulse registering on the monitor were the only signs to indicate any sense of life. I suddenly realized how much a part of my life, this young man owned. He was nearly everything to me. He was my friend, my confidant, the echo to my thoughts, the life in my day, the laughter in my life, and one of the reasons I found for waking each day. And as scared as either of us may have been to admit it, he was my love.

It was in that stale, lonely moment, I finally recognized that love was indeed much deeper than an emotion. What would I do without him? There was an ache within me; an emptiness. I likened it to the phantom pain an amputee feels when a limb is lost. More than a physical attachment or connection had taken place.

Of course, people go on, but I now understood if anything happened to him, a part of me would literally disappear. There was a connection between us which I could not explain, but existed none the less. Was this what Cole meant when he talked about being connected by something deeper? It was almost as if our energy had somehow combined, fusing together, and if that bond were to be broken... if it were severed... surely a part of me would die as well. I had questions I couldn't explain.

Science believes that consciousness is simply a neurological response to electrical and chemical changes in the brain. It doesn't account for why my consciousness can't be replicated in another person or a computer. Love can be explained in the physical sense by attraction, attachment, and of course the chemical responses in the body which occur or contribute to how two people come together, choose to partner, and copulate. But these physical explanations don't account for that deeper bond which connects two people as true as the word "and" connects two parts of a sentence.

And now I faced another issue with my world view. I had no doubt I would will Cole to fight back against this separation. I couldn't accept the possibility he might not make it. He had to make it. And I knew if he were able to talk to me at that moment, I would have had to explain this intense desire for him to fight to come back to me.

"After all, we're all going to die, right? No, big deal." I could almost hear him mocking me.

I whispered into the darkened room.

"Okay, you were right. I know that now. Stay with me Cole."

Chapter Eighteen

Snowflakes snaked down the road, gathering along the edges like piles of sand driven by the stinging winter wind. As they grew in size, they spread a white blanket over the surface of the earth. A pale gray sky casts its gloomy shadows over the world around me. As winter did her best to drive away the hope of the coming spring, the battle for life and death continued.

I stared out the window of the waiting room at the white tops of the buildings below, contemplating these struggles and their meanings. The cold world outside could be felt radiating through the pane of glass in front of me. The sound of the wind whipping around the edges of the building had a slight roar to it, a high pitched whistle sounding as it reached its crescendo in gusts.

I felt a hand touch my elbow, and I turned to look into the warm eyes of my mother. My father stood by her side, and I had never sensed as much compassion from either of them as I did at that moment. I fell into her embrace as her arms wrapped around me. Dad stood by encouragingly, his hands upon both our shoulders.

She held me as I wept; something that had rarely occurred since I was a small girl. I felt a flood of warmth and comfort which had been eluding me for a long while. We, she and I, had not known this kind of relationship, and I suddenly wondered why. Had I become so sterile I could not even share emotion with my mother?

Cole would have had a field day with that situation. He'd been riding me to tap into my emotions since the day we met. So full of vitality, he couldn't understand how a person could move through life never experiencing its touch. It was amazing it had taken his accident to make me see how much of life is worth trying to hang onto.

She stood back holding me at arm's length.

"How's he doing?"

"He's hanging on."

"Has there been any change?"

I shook my head.

"He'll be okay," she said encouragingly.

I nodded. Of course, she didn't know. No one knew at that point.

"Have you eaten?"

"I'm not hungry."

"Sophie, you have to keep up your strength. You won't be any good to Cole if you don't."

"I know. I just don't feel like eating right now." I paused. "I will. I promise."

"Can we see him?" Dad asked.

Again I nodded. Then I led them to the nurse's desk.

As the nurse took them into his room, I waited there by the window, watching the world change before me. The same wind which piled the snow in mounding drifts had begun to shape it into sleek aerodynamic sculptures, concaves and peaks, smooth and sleek. Spindly, bare limbs of trees sprung up from the white landscape, stooped and bending from the weight of the ice coats they wore, swaying heavily from the gusts.

In the hazy, gloomy, cold world around me, I tried desperately to hold on to warm flickers of hope. I replayed conversations and images from the time since I had made this transformation from city girl to country bumpkin. All along the way there was one, kind, loving force that had helped me to assimilate into my new world. Quite honestly, I'd come to be so comfortable in this new home the city life felt far from ideal.

My cell phone chirped in my pocket, and I pulled it out and glanced at the screen. I didn't recognize the number.

"Hello."

There was a slight pause.

"Hey."

"Who is this?"

"It's Jaima."

"Jaima?"

"Yeah, I just wanted to check on Cole."

That was a conversation I had never expected. I didn't even know she knew my number.

"He's about the same. Not really any change."

Another silent pause.

"Look, Sophie. I'm sorry. I know I've given you a lot of crap and to be honest; you took it pretty well. I just want you to know that I'm not such a bitch that I don't care. I like Cole."

I had to choke back the lump in my throat to reply.

"Thanks, Jaima.   It means a lot that you called."

"Hey, save my number, okay. Let me know if things change."

"Okay. I will."

"And, Sophie…"

"Yeah?"

"Call me if you just need to talk."

"Thanks," I said, pushing the end button before I broke down.

The idea that Jaima Sanchez would call me, just to talk, was something that never would have entered my head. Only Cole could affect people like that.

After a short while, I felt mom place her arms around me.

"I'm so sorry, Sophie."

I turned to her.

"He looks bad, doesn't he? He has so many tubes in him."

"He looks hurt, Sophie. The tubes are there to help him."

"I know. He just looks so helpless. I wish he'd wake up."

"Are they keeping him sedated?"

"Yeah, I guess so. They said he had swelling in the brain."

"Is there anything else?"

"They don't know for sure how bad it is, but they think he may be partially paralyzed."

She looked away. I know she didn't want me to see the fear in her eyes.

She turned back to me.

"Well, let's just pray for the best."

"Pray?"

She nodded.

"Pray."

Those were confusing words coming from my mother.

"When you don't know anything else to do, Sophie, you pray."

"But you and dad, you never pray."

"Sophie, we covered this. There are a lot of things in this world I can't explain, but if you have nowhere else to turn, there is no reason not to pray. And I do pray, every time you leave the house."

Later, after they had left to go get a motel room, I found myself wondering slowly down the hallway toward the chapel. A strange feeling fell over me as my eyes took in the ornately decorated room. It felt so solemn and humbling to be there. The only sound came from the sound of my shoes as I walked up the aisle toward the front of the room. In the center of the wall, a large crucifix hung. I studied its image. I'd learned to look at the man on the cross, much as I would images of Zeus or Apollo. It was part of the Christian Mythology. However, this time it was different. Instead of a Christian legend, I saw the image of a man; a man beaten and torn, bloody and bruised. His body hung forward from the nails in his hands; his head languished, his eyes filled with pain and sorrow. If the legend were to be believed, it would surely take a man of great love and compassion to endure this type of death for others.

When I could finally pry my eyes away from the image of Christ, I stepped to the wooden rail and eased myself down to my knees. I had no idea what I should say or do.

"God, if you're there, we've never met. You may know me, but I certainly don't know you. I won't try to make myself out to be something I'm not. If you're really there, then you know my heart, and you know there has never been a place for you in it. I'd like to believe you're there. It would make life more comfortable to know. I have a friend…"

I corrected myself.

"Well, he's so much more than a friend, but if you're there then you already know that. Cole believes you're there, and he needs your help. He had a terrible accident, and I don't know if he will make it, but I'm hoping you can help with that. Please, if you're there, please take care of him and bring him back to me. I just don't know what I'd do without him."

I bowed my head down against my hands. Even with the heaviness of Cole's condition weighing upon me, I could feel the comfort of that place. I heard footsteps as they moved across the tile floor, and when I glanced in their direction, I saw Jenna, Cole's mom. I felt her hand on my back as she knelt beside me. She leaned her head against my shoulder as her arm around me drew us closer. Then she lifted her head to look me in the eyes. I could see the strain of what she was going through in them.

"I'm so glad Cole has you in his life. You're his inspiration you know."

I'm sure she could see the surprise in my reaction. Me? An inspiration? Cole was the one with the amazing outlook on life.

She smiled.

"Don't be so surprised. He hasn't always been so gregarious. Oh, he's always been funny, but he never had as much confidence before you came along."

"But he's the inspiration."

She nodded.

"For you and for me, but you are his inspiration. He wakes up every day looking forward to seeing you."

I took a few minutes to absorb her words.

"How long will they keep him sedated?"

"Until the swelling improves."

"I miss his voice."

I could see the tears in her eyes.

"I do too, Sophie."

"Has he told you much about me? I mean, about my philosophy on life?"

She smiled again.

"You mean like why it would be strange for you to be here in the chapel?"

"He told you. Do you think badly about me?"

She brushed a lock of hair out of my eyes.

"No, Sweetie. We all have to figure out what we believe on our own. You're a wonderful person, Sophie. My son wouldn't be so crazy about you if you weren't. Has he ever told you what he wants to do when he graduates?"

I shook my head.

"No, we've never talked about it. He spends most of his time trying to debate me."

"He wants to be a youth minister."

"Really?"

"He has for a long time."

"He'd be good at it. He is so funny, and he has such a good heart."

"Yes, and he knows when he sees someone who is searching for answers."

"Is that why he debates my philosophy so much? He thinks I'm looking for answers?"

"No, he debates you so much because he enjoys it and because he wants to know if you believe what you're saying."

"I don't know what to believe anymore. My mother suggested I pray for him. She's never done that before. We don't even talk about religion."

"Don't let it confuse you. She's just telling you she doesn't have all the answers."

"I've always been raised to believe science was the answer. You break it down and figure it out."

"Science has provided us with mountains of information and great understanding of our world. We've found cures for diseases and explored places throughout the universe, but science can't explain everything. For every question science answers, it creates another question. And at some point, we have to realize there are some things that are beyond our understanding. That's where faith comes in."

"Faith?"

"Yes, faith. Faith is the substance of things hoped for, the evidence of things not seen."

"What's that mean?"

"It means you believe without asking for any proof. If you wait to gather evidence to support the truth, you aren't acting in faith. Faith in God, faith in people...it doesn't wait for the evidence; it is a pure and simple trust that they are true."

"That doesn't fit well with science."

"Well, no, it doesn't, but lots of things don't fit with science. I don't think that science and religion have to be at odds. Science gives us amazing understanding of how our world works, but it doesn't explain why it exists. It can tell us the chemical makeup of our bodies. It explains how our nervous system works, but it can't explain what makes you who you are. It can't tell us how the human brain, which is just a glob of flesh, can make decisions that stump a supercomputer the size of a semi-trailer. Science falls short of having all the answers."

"Well, I certainly see where Cole gets it. You sound just like him."

"Cole is his own guy. He thinks this stuff out for himself. In fact, I think he wants you to do the same thing."

"I'd grown a little weary of the constant debate, but I'd give anything if he were able to quiz me right now."

She kissed me on the check and gave me a hug.

"Me too, sweetheart."

"I'm going to go back to the waiting room. My folks should be back soon."

"Why don't you leave with them for a while? It would do you good to get away for a little while."

"I just don't want to be away from him."

"He'll be okay. He'd want you to."

"Are you staying here?"

"For a little while."

I hugged her again and rose to my feet.

When I looked back, I could tell she was praying. And, I had this strange admiration for her ability to do that; to be so at peace when her world, her very soul was hanging, dangling on the edge of a precipice. Inside of me there was a distinct desire to feel what she felt. How ironic that my evolution was being fueled by something science chose to discount. I still had a lot to figure out.

Chapter Nineteen

Three weeks had passed since the accident. I'd spent almost every waking moment willing Cole to hang on, praying he would survive, and finally realizing why people fought so hard to live or to encourage others to live. He was the world to me. I couldn't bear the thought of being without him. It's somewhat selfish, I guess, but our connection was such that it left me feeling half alive without him near. Simple things didn't share the same depth or meaning.

Though the swelling improved and his vitals had stabilized, he'd yet to show any outward signs of life other than the occasional muscle spasm. We'd endured a long, agonizing vigil. Although it aggravated me to have to leave him each week, Geneva and Jenna both insisted I go back to school through the week. It was tough to keep my mind on things that seemed so trivial when my heart and mind wanted to be near Cole.

I wondered around in a fog the first week I was back. It was strange being at school without him around. After the first week, it became a little easier to fall back into the groove, but the feeling I should be near him didn't go away. I continued to make my treks down to Oklahoma City to see him on the weekends. Some weekends I went down with Duane and Tisha and other times my mother and father took me.

As one would expect, the other kids in school were always on the lookout for more information about how Cole was doing, and I spent much of my days explaining his condition. It seemed Cole's tragedy might have produced a miracle of sorts, bringing people together who would otherwise never consider the thought.

"So, how's he doing?" Jaima asked one day after history.

Her voice displayed her sincerity.

"He's holding his own."

"Is he awake yet?"

"No. He's still out. The swelling has improved, but he's not coming around yet."

"Well, I'm sure he'll be okay, Sophie. He's a strong person."

"I hope you're right."

She leaned forward and hugged me. It was a move I would never have expected from either her or her friends. There was a definite change in the dynamics of our social norm. All around us there was a mixture of emotions. Although the school was in turmoil over the accident, the Bulldogs were on their way to a state championship fight. They had plowed their way through their regular season opponents and taken the first two games of the playoffs.

On the following Friday, the Bulldogs were heading to Woodward, Oklahoma for the State

Semi-Final game. They were to practice that evening and play the next day. I was torn. I wanted so desperately to spend the weekend with Cole, but I knew where he would want me to be. I finally settled on going to see Cole after the game on Saturday afternoon. We wouldn't have as much time together, but I knew that's how he would want it.

For a late fall day, the weather was mild. The game started under a light mist. As it continued, the weather improved, the sun burning off the cloud cover. The Bulldogs struck first tacking up six points on the scoreboard, but the Tigers replied with six of their own. At half time, it was tied at twelve all. It was a back and forth battle, but with seconds to go in the final quarter, the Bulldogs pulled it off with a twenty-four to twenty win. They were headed to the Championship game.

When we arrived at the hospital, our spirits lifted. Cole was awake; not the awake we expect from watching movies; disoriented, groggy, not quite completely with it, in and out for only moments at a time. The excitement at seeing his eyes open was short-lived, however. Moments later Jenna took me aside.

"I need to tell you something. It's going to be hard to hear, but it's going to be harder for Cole."

She let her words sink in.

"Cole is paralyzed. He doesn't know yet."

I felt the air being knocked out of me like I'd been punched in the gut.

"How bad is it?"

"He's at the C8 level, but they don't know yet if it is complete or incomplete."

"What's that mean?"

She placed her hands on my shoulders.

"It means he can move his arms and elbows. He'll have some finger movement. It depends on whether the level of paralysis moves down or not."

"So what does complete or incomplete mean?"

"If it is complete, it is permanent. If it is incomplete, he may recover some or all of his feeling below that level. They're still trying to determine that."

I looked back over at Cole. He was out again. They had not removed the tubes from his chest, and I could still hear the drone and hiss of the machine moving air in and out of his lungs.

"He's going to ask me questions as soon as they take out that the tube and I can't lie to him. He'd know in a second whether or not I'm telling the truth. What do I say?"

"Just tell him we have to wait for the doctors to finish their tests," she cautioned.

"He's too smart for his own good. He'll probably figure this out before they can tell him what's happening."

"We still have hope."

I closed my eyes and offered up a short prayer of hope. I was still new to this and wasn't sure I was saying the right things, but I could try.

"When are they taking the tubes out?"

"As soon as they're sure he can breathe on his own; possibly this afternoon."

I nodded. Then I made my way to his side and took his hand. With my best effort, I tried to look on the bright side of things. He was on his way back to being fully awake, and he was alive. It was another hour before he stirred once again.

"Hey Sleepyhead. It's good to see those big brown eyes. I've missed you."

I felt his fingers move slightly within the palm of my hand, and I could tell he was trying to squeeze back. And then he was gone again. He had lingering periods of wakefulness throughout the rest of the day. At one point, I was standing by his side when he opened his eyes.

"I love you, Cole."

It came out on its own, and it was the first time I'd said it out loud. I'd thought it over and over for the past few weeks. There was a time when I would have been afraid of making that statement. I'd lived in fear of crossing some invisible line between us. We'd both been afraid such an admission would somehow risk our friendship, but I was past that. I'd almost lost him, and the fear I felt at never having told him how I felt was greater than any imaginary barrier.

I could see the surprise in his eyes.

"I know. You didn't expect that did you?"

I lifted his hand and kissed his fingers.

"I've had a lot of time to think about it, and I worried I might not get a chance to tell you. Now, you're here, and I want you to know. It doesn't matter what happens. I don't care if you can't say the same thing to me. I just want you to know that's how I feel about you."

He slowly removed his hand from mine and placed it on his chest. Tears filled my eyes as I watched him struggled to point his fingers at me and somehow I knew exactly what he was saying.

I smiled as the tears trailed down my cheeks.

"You always know just what to say, don't you?"

Shortly after that we were ushered out of the room as the doctor came in to see Cole.

"We'll let you know when you can come in to see him again." The nurse advised.

It was a long wait. As I stared at the clock on the waiting room wall, I watched the second hand tick slowly along.

Jenna rose and took my hand.

"Let's go get a soda," she said.

We took the elevator down to the cafeteria. After we had visited the soda fountain, we took seats across from each other at one of the smaller tables.

"He's still got a long road ahead of him," she stated.

"I know."

She had something else on her mind.

"Are you sure you're up for it?" I could hear the caution in her voice.

"What do you mean?"

"I just don't want you to feel trapped? If the damage is permanent, the last thing he needs is pity."

Her words stung.

"I'm not sure I understand."

"Sophie, I heard you tell him you love him. I just don't want you to say that out of pity or guilt."

"I told him I love him because I do. Jenna, I've spent the last three weeks wishing I'd said that before the accident. I had no idea whether he was going to live or die. I just didn't want to miss the opportunity to tell him how I feel about him."

She patted my hand.

"Don't be angry with me. I just want you to be sure. If the news doesn't go our way, his life is going to change forever, and if you love him, your life will change as well."

"You keep talking about this like you are expecting the worst. What happened to 'holding on to hope?'"

"I am holding on to hope, but I don't want either of you to get hurt if we don't get the news we're hoping for."

"I believe we're experiencing a life changing event, no matter how this turns out. Even if he gets up and walks out of here, some things will never be the same. I once told him I didn't understand why people fought so hard to live. Now, I know. I couldn't stand the thought of losing him. I felt as if a part of me was lying in that bed, and I finally understood what it means to love someone. Jenna, I'm not the same person I was before this happened, and I don't expect Cole to be the same either."

"He stumbled on a good thing with you Sophie."

"I could say the same about him."

She stood and took my hand, helping me to my feet. We embraced.

"Let's keep thinking positive thoughts. Okay?"

When we got back to the room, he was out again.

Late that afternoon they came in and removed the tubes. He wasn't allowed to talk for twenty-four hours afterward. It was good he slept off and on through most of that time. I'm sure it would have been a struggle for him otherwise.

I feared for the moment when he would start asking me questions. The doctor had yet to come in to offer his findings, and I had no idea whether or not he would believe me if I told him we didn't really know anything. Although, I wanted to hear his voice, I was thankful he wasn't prepared to carry on a conversation.

Sunday morning he received a completely unexpected visit. I'm sure he was as surprised as the rest of us when four football players appeared at the doorway. The two Bulldog captains, accompanied by the two rival Tiger captains, entered the room wearing their football jerseys. In their hands, they carried a special gift; it was the game ball, signed by the players of each team. It was such a touching event it brought tears to my eyes. Though he couldn't speak, I could see Cole was moved as well.

The visit from his football friends got cut short when Cole's doctor arrived. The doctor attempted to have us all leave the room, but Cole wouldn't have it. He shook his head and rasped out an insistent "No." The doctor relented.

The apprehension in the air was stifling. Although he was compassionate, his words cut like a knife, and they were completely unexpected. The tests were finished; the spinal injury was not complete. Cole had a very good chance of walking out of the hospital, when he finally got the opportunity. The problem was Cole had several huge hurdles to overcome before that could be a possibility; one of those being the damage to his spinal cord and the physical therapy he would have to endure. The biggest challenge came from out in left field, and it had the ability to stop every heart in the room.

"Cole, we had to wait for the swelling from your head injury to subside to be sure. But all indications are that you have an intracranial solid neoplasm; a tumor. Of course, we'll have to do some more tests. Perhaps a biopsy to determine what's going on in there for sure, but I feel it is safe to say there is a probability we are looking at an anaplastic astrocytoma; a grade three tumor. It is harder to get rid of, but since you've yet to experience any of its symptoms, we feel fairly certain we have caught it in its early stages."

Even in our stunned silence, we all knew Cole would not be walking out of the hospital anytime soon

Chapter Twenty

I don't know how long it was before I took my next breath. As I glanced at Cole's parents, I could see they were as shocked as I had been. The only one, besides his doctor, who didn't seem to be totally at a loss for words was Cole. I heard his raspy voice.

"So the rough tackle may have saved my life?" he questioned.

"It would appear to be a distinct possibility, but I have to warn you, a grade three tumor is serious and the prognosis will be mixed."

The doctor turned to face his parents.

"We'll set Cole up with Dr. Hsieh. She is an excellent oncologist. In the meantime, we still have work to do to get those spinal cells past the inflammation which is causing a temporary paralysis. When the swelling and pressure are relieved the nervous system functionality should return, however the improvement isn't likely to be instantaneous. There is a high probability we will only see the kind of progress we need with physical therapy."

I left Cole alone with his parents after the doctor left the room. As amazing as I felt when we learned the paralysis was temporary, I felt I'd fallen into an abyss when the word "tumor" was mentioned. I know it sound weird, but in some ways, the paralysis seemed easier to deal with. His functions would have been limited; life would certainly change for him, but he would be alive. A tumor threatened to steal that life from him. It placed a shadow on his future, something that seemed suddenly more immense than dealing with accommodations or ergonomic accessibility devices.

It was a scary situation. I'd looked it up on my phone as soon as I left the room. The prognosis wasn't good. Median survival rates for adults with standard treatment were two to three years. About ten percent of adults had a survival rate of five years, or more and children fared a little better with twenty-five percent surviving the five years or more rate.

As I wondered the halls of the hospital, I found my mind swimming over the looming dangers. Surgery, radiation, chemotherapy, a weakened immune system, any those things could pull him out of my life permanently. Yes, I'd already faced that possibility when he was lifted out of my world and into this sterile environment, but we'd moved past that moment and I'd adjusted to the probability he would be there but in a different way. Now this darkness hung in the air and swallowed me up in its emptiness.

He was facing the very situation he'd described to me when our relationship was in its infancy. He was fighting for life, and I'd told him

life wasn't worth the fight. Was it? Was life worth
what he was going to go through? Is it just a blip
on the screen of existence? Do we serve a purpose
or are we just marking time?

Certainly, for me, Cole was more than a mark
in time. He was special. He gave my life the spark
that allowed it to hold a deeper meaning. He gave
me a reason to look forward to each day. Most of
my life had been spent in monotony; going through
the motions; memorizing facts, and analyzing
results. There'd been no room for fun,
refreshment, or those little details which make one
life different from the next.

Cole changed all that. He brought the wonder
of the world into focus, not under a microscope,
but within me. Little things like the tug of his
smile upon my heart. My heart? An un-scientific
idea if there ever was one. Any good science
student knows the heart doesn't do any more than
serve as a processing plant for oxygen distribution.
It can't hold on to feelings or emotions. Those are
simply phantasms created within the walls of the
mind. They don't exist as factual substance, and
yet they were there. Certainly they were there, and
they were there because of Cole Allen.

How had this guy been able to impact me in
such a way? How had he reached into me; to a
place where no one else could find? How had he
found a way to place something substantial within
the vacuum? Through the simple process of living,
he'd successfully distorted my view of life and its
depth. I no longer lived on the surface. There was
no longer that clear cut vision of life as a series of
chemical reactions. It had somehow been replaced
by this girl who longed for love and life, and the

chance to experience the things she'd always tried
to avoid.

So, Cole meant more to me that just incidental
contact as a result of life. The question was: did I
think this deeper vision of life warranted the
struggles he would endure to hang onto it? Based
on Cole's example, I'd given every indication to
him I didn't believe it was. Now, with his life
hanging in the balance, I found myself wishing I'd
never expressed those feelings. I questioned why I
would have allowed them to exist in the first place.
Had I become that callused and cold? Prior to
meeting Cole Allen, the answer to that question
would have been an unquestionable "yes."

I felt Jenna's hand on my shoulder.

"He wants to see you."

"I'm not sure I can face him."

Her face softened with understanding.

"Sweetheart, he thinks the world of you and no
matter what you may be feeling right now, he
needs to know you are going to be with him on this
journey."

"What if I'm not strong enough? What if I let
him down? I told him one time I didn't understand
why people fight to live. What if my thoughts
cause him to give up?"

Jenna smiled.

"Sophie, if there is one thing I know about
Cole, it's that it'll take more than a disease to pull
him away from you."

I made my way down the hall toward Cole's
room. Even the shiny surface of the wax over the
bright white tile seemed to darken as I moved
forward. Feeling as though I was headed down a
tunnel I inched closer to him. My hand slid down

on the elongated door handle familiar to most hospital room doors. It was cool against my fingers.

Despite the news he'd been delivered and the weakness he was still feeling, I was met with that wonderful smile as I opened the door and stepped into the room. I couldn't help but smile back.

"Hi," he creaked in his broken voice. The sound was just above a whisper.

"Hi," I said back timidly.

"Missed you."

"I missed you, too."

He patted the side of the bed, and I moved over next to him, careful not to disturb him or to make him uncomfortable as I sat down.

"So, what are you thinking?" He got straight to the point.

I wasn't sure exactly what he was expecting to hear.

"I don't know. What do you think?"

He shook his head slowly.

"Not fair. I asked first."

"I think I'm scared."

"Me too."

"You don't look scared," I said. "You look like you're just happy to be here."

He shrugged his shoulders.

"Well, I am happy to be here, but that doesn't mean I'm not scared, too. This is kind of a big deal." His voice wavered uncharacteristically.

I reached over and pushed back a lock of his hair, running my fingers gently over his skin. The touch sent tingles through me, and I knew in an instant, I would be rooting for him every second of the fight.

"You'll do okay," I whispered as I tried to erase every ounce of negativity.

"You really think so or are you just saying that?"

I closed my eyes and smiled as I nodded at him.

"Yes. Yes, I do."

"What makes you so sure?"

I paused. I couldn't explain it. The Sophie I used to know would have steered away from making any such proclamations for fear of giving false hopes.

"Just a feeling I have."

His eyebrows rose.

"A feeling?"

I giggled.

"Yeah, a feeling."

"What's happened to you?"

I leaned over and kissed his lips, my hand caressing his cheek.

"You," I whispered.

Chapter Twenty-One

There are moments in time which seem to freeze. Captured in our minds, they almost seem like photographs; still and unmoving. The moment of impact; his still body lying on the ground; the slamming shut of the ambulance door; the first time I saw his body tethered to machines with tubes; and the look on his face when he found out the extent of his condition. They all flashed through my mind like a slide show; each of them taking place while I held my breath waiting for the world to start spinning again.

The room, in which we'd spent so much time, suddenly seemed so unfamiliar, so distant. It was as if I'd left my body for a moment and was hovering above it; there, but not a part of it. And yet I was a part of it. I'd traveled along with him through it all, but for a solitary, agonizing moment this journey was his alone. I could not genuinely understand what he felt at that moment. I could imagine how I'd feel. I could stand on my side of the abyss and stare across the void at him. I could pretend to know, but I couldn't grasp the reality of what it was like to be him.

I heard her words echoing in my mind.

"This type of tumor is difficult to remove. It has fingers which spread out in a butterfly effect. We'll try to get as much of it as possible."

"What if you can't get it all?" he quizzed.

"We'll do our best." She paused. "Near complete removal of the tumor results in about a forty percent chance of a five-year survival rate."

He swallowed.

"You mean at best I only have five years?"

She shook her head.

"No. No one can tell you how many years you have. We're speaking statistics only. It largely depends upon the success of the surgery. With all or at least most of the tumor removed your chance of surviving the next five years is forty percent. That doesn't mean that you will survive five years, but it also doesn't mean you won't go on to live a long and productive life. Our best chance is to get as much of the tumor as possible. And the success of the surgery will depend on how deep the fingers have dug into the cerebral hemisphere of the brain. You're fortunate; we discovered this tumor before you started experiencing the symptoms of the tumor. Most of my patients don't know they have a tumor until they experience the effects of the tumor; until it has grown enough to send out the signs of its existence."

She moved around near the side of the bed and took his hand. I instantly liked her. She wasn't so clinical that she couldn't interact with her patients.

"Cole, I can't give you any guarantees. No one can. However, I can tell you that you are at an advantage to most of the patients I see."

She patted the top of his hand with her right hand while holding it in the palm of her left hand.

"We'll take it one day at a time. Every step will be based on what we think is the best course for treatment."

"How's this going to affect my physical therapy?"

She shook her head.

"Not at all. Other than some weakness from the procedure, which would be completely normal, you should be able to continue therapy as directed. Now, that doesn't mean that the other steps of treatment which we may choose to pursue won't cause you some difficulty. Radiation and chemotherapy impact each patient differently."

"So when do we get started?"

"Surgery on Monday. That gives you a few days to get started on physical therapy. We don't want to postpone that. The sooner we get that spine back in shape, the better. You'll also be getting some steroid shots into the inflamed area to help reduce the swelling. Dr. Anderson will fill you in on that course of treatment."

She paused once again.

"Cole, I'm not going to tell you this is going to be easy. The physical therapy alone will be grueling enough. Physical therapy, while you are undergoing treatment for a brain tumor, is going to be exhausting."

After she had left, he seemed to be drained of his normal positive outlook. He was quiet and reflective.

People are different. There are so many different ways in which they react to changing situations. Cole's initial reaction was completely as one would expect. Anger, bitterness, denial, hopelessness; these were the emotions that surfaced either in his comments or his disposition. It was a part of him I'd never seen before and in many ways it was uncomfortable. But then again, it wasn't really him; it was the situation in which he found himself. I still believed the real Cole would win out in the end.

"You know you don't have to be here." He said after a few minutes of uncomfortable silence.

"I know I don't have to be here. I want to be here. Why? Do you want me to leave?"

"No, I'm just saying you don't have to be here."

"Cole, I'm here because I want to be with you, but if you don't want me around, I'll leave."

"Whatever you want to do."

"No, Cole. What do you want? Do you want me here? Do you want my support?"

"Look, I don't need your support. There isn't anything you can do. Okay. I don't need you hanging around because you feel sorry for me."

That stung and I struggled to keep from showing it.

"I am not here because I feel sorry for you. I'm here because I love you and want to be with you."

He sat silently for a few minutes; his face displaying the chastisement he was heaping upon himself.

"I guess that was a pretty self-centered outburst, wasn't it?"

"Who am I to judge?"

"Don't let me off that easy. You'll just reinforce the idea you're feeling sorry for me. Be truthful with me."

"Okay, I don't know if it was self-centered or not, but it was certainly unfair of you to assume I'm here out of sympathy. You know I'd want to be with you no matter where you were."

"I know."

"So, do you want me here?"

"Of course I do. I can't imagine what this would be like without you there to encourage me. I just don't want you to feel trapped. I don't want you to be here because you feel you have to be here."

"I do have to be here; my heart wouldn't let me be anywhere else."

He winked.

"There's those darn feelings cropping up again."

I threw a pillow at him.

"Oh, leave me alone before I start blaming it on hormones or something."

His bouts with self-reproach didn't end that day, but his fight to control them continuously improved. As he moved on through physical therapy and rehabilitation, he faced enormous challenges.

In the beginning, physical therapy consisted of manipulating his seemingly lifeless limbs from his bed. It didn't seem too demanding before surgery. In fact, it almost seemed a refreshing change for Cole from the time spent lying still in his room. The next day they helped him into a wheelchair, and we were able to move about on his floor. We snuck some snacks from the vending machine back to the room and between mouthfuls of Cheetos Cole tried to carry on a conversation.

"Have you read up on this stuff?"

I nodded my head.

"Briefly. I haven't had the opportunity to read a lot about it."

"There are some pamphlets the nurse brought over on my tray table."

He munched on his Cheetos with what appeared indifference. I was caught off guard when he continued the conversation.

"You know this thing can cause seizures, vomiting, headaches and mood changes?"

"Um. No, I didn't, but I guess it makes sense. As it grows, it would put pressure on the brain."

"Strange thing is the side effects of the treatment are the same as the symptoms."

He continued shoveling the crunchy orange sticks into his mouth.

"Did you know the outlook for this cancer is poor? Most of the time they can't remove the whole thing and without complete removal a survival rate for five years is twenty percent."

My mouth went dry, and I swallowed hard trying to keep my voice from sticking in my throat.

"But that doesn't mean you can't be in the twenty percent."

He smiled weakly.

"No, Sophie, it doesn't. But if we were in Vegas, I wouldn't be pulling good odds."

I walked over and took his hand.

"Maybe not, but we're not in Vegas, and I don't care what the odds are; I'm betting on you."

His face scrunched.

"Come on, Sophie. You're the scientist. The outlook isn't good."

I could see the look in his eyes. He wanted me to be honest, not coddling.

My hands moved to his shoulders; arms extended, eyes direct.

"No, Cole. The outlook isn't good. It's scary, in fact. It's scary enough that it makes a person want to run away from it. If you're looking at the facts, the statistics, then you're looking at a lot of gloom and doom. But that's not the Cole I know. The Cole I know has faith. He believes if this is his path; then he must follow and trust the outcome. The Cole I know believes in the miracles of the twenty percent. He doesn't allow himself to mull over the negatives, and he doesn't let the odds dictate to him. He believes in a Higher Power, and he knows there is a plan for his life. He won't give in until his last breath is spent trying to fight this thing."

I could see the tears welling up in his eyes.

"What do you believe, Sophie?"

I felt like I'd just taken a baseball bat in the chest. His question had knocked the air from me, and I felt my head swimming in the lack of oxygen.

He closed his eyes, and a tear rolled down his cheek.

"It's okay. You don't have to tell me." He admitted, clearly believing my silence had given him the answer in my heart.

"No, I want to tell you. I'm not sure, Cole. I want to believe and trust it will all work out, but there is a part of me that just keeps running the numbers. I guess I'm hoping you'll help me realize science and numbers aren't the only controlling forces in the universe. I know that sounds selfish. I should be the one encouraging you, believing in the possibility of miracles and the strength of the individual, but the truth is: I'm still weak in that area. So, you see, you have to make it Cole. You have to make it, so you can finish saving me. I guess if I were to believe in a plan for life, then I'd have to believe the plan for your life is to help me save my life. If that's true, then you can't go; you have to fight it. Because, Cole, if I lose you, I'm not sure I'll have the possibility of believing ever again."

"As flattering as all that sounds, Sophie, you have to believe on your own. I can't do it for you."

"No, you can't. But if God were to allow someone as terrific as you to die, I don't know how I could ever believe He exists."

"God didn't do this to me, Sophie. In all probability, He's most likely the reason we found it early."

Losing control of my emotions and allowing them to be expressed in a way I would later regret, I snapped back at him.

"Oh, so now you're saying he caused you to experience a near death accident so that He could save you from a near death disease?"

"No, I'm saying He used a tragedy that is just part of life on this planet to let the doctors know there was something else wrong with me."

He paused.

"I told you before. God didn't put the bad stuff here. It is part of the world in which we live."

"According to you, God made this world. If he didn't put the bad stuff there, then how'd it get there?"

"Do you really want a theology lesson right now?"

His reply slapped me across the face and made me realize I wasn't helping him at all.

"I'm sorry. You don't need this right now."

He shrugged.

"Maybe I do. You pulled me out of my slump; made me think this out so I could respond. Maybe it was exactly what I needed, and maybe God knew that too."

Despite the intensity of the conversation, I laughed.

"See, you don't give up."

"You're right," he conceded.

I shook my head.

"I hope you are."

The morning of his surgery was filled with anxiousness. Of course, Coles parents were there, and mine had come down for the surgery. They had tried to get me to come home for a few days to catch up on some schoolwork. I'd missed nearly a week of school, but I had no intention of leaving. It didn't matter if I had to take the whole year over; I was going to be with Cole. Fortunately, fall break was just around the corner and would offer me some time off without the cost of falling further behind.

Cole went in at seven in the morning. I saw him before he went in, and though I could see the angst in his eyes, he displayed a confident smile. I kissed his cheek before they wheeled him away.

"Do me a favor?"

"Anything."

"Pray for me."

"I will."

The morning was filled with the smell of stale coffee, old magazine articles, and the steady stream of cable news. Though the seats started out feeling comfortable, it didn't take long before I was pacing the floor. The hands on the clock crept along in a slow, lazy, monotonous circle. At lunch time Geneva, Jenna, and I went down to the cafeteria while Craig and Will waited for any updates. Though my mother did her best to engage me in small talk, I just couldn't seem to find my way into it. My thoughts were constantly with Cole.

We received a couple of updates throughout the day, but we didn't get confirmation that the operation was complete until six o'clock that evening. Outside of the night they flew Cole into the hospital which now seemed to be almost a blur; it was the most stressful day of my life. I couldn't imagine the depth of emotions Jenna and Craig had been going through.

"He's doing fine," Dr. Hsieh assured us. "Dr. Anderson preformed a stereotactic laser surgery and removed as much of the tumor as he could. The fingers of the tumor didn't protrude deeply into the white matter. Of course, we won't know for sure until we follow up with the post-operative MRI. Due to the swelling, he has a temporary stent and will be in ICU for at least twenty-four hours."

"So you don't know if you got it all?" Jenna asked.

"The stereotactic surgery is guided by a three-dimensional image produced of the brain. The surgeon has a very good look at the tumor and its fingers. There is always the possibility that portions of the tumor get left behind, but the surgery looked good."

"What's next?" It was Craig this time.

"Well, of course, we have to keep him stable and get him out of ICU. Normally, patients stay about a week after they come out of ICU. Of course, each case and each patient is different. We'll determine what the circumstance calls for. Cole's case is rather unique. He was undergoing therapy due to his injury. Depending upon what skills or motor movements are affected by the removal of the tumor, he will have some degree of therapy. Some of that will be here while some of it will continue at home."

"So what can we expect as far as results?" Craig continued.

"I can't tell you specifically. Again, each patient and each case is different. Cole is young and healthy. He has experienced trauma to his nervous system, which has caused him to loose lower motor movement. This surgery may not cause him any additional complications, but he does have that against him. If you are asking about a prognosis for the tumor, the only one I can give you at this point is the one you were given prior to the surgery. He will need to undergo additional treatment. We'll determine the course after we examine the results of the post-op MRI."

After a long day, I think we were all drained. We sat in silence for a few minutes.

"Can we see him?" I asked.

"Just for a few minutes. One at a time."

Jenna went first. When she came back, Craig motioned to me to go ahead.

It was much like seeing him after the accident. His body was connected to tubes and monitors. Bags hung above him dripping fluids and medicine

into his body through the web of IV lines that
dangled from above. The familiar beeps and hums
of the equipment hooked up to him filled the air.
In the darkness of the room, the lights and displays
lit up like the cockpit of some science-fiction
spaceship.

It was sad seeing him go through this again.
My heart ached to have things back to normal. I
wished I could be by his side down at the river,
lying against his shoulder as we watched a movie,
or just sitting next to him as he drove his truck
down the road. I longed for the simplicity of being
with him; for the laughter in one of his stupid
jokes; or even one of our arguments about the
origins of life.

I thought back to the day I met him and his
answer to our test question. Despite the scene of
him lying broken before me, I chuckled at the
conversation. He always knew how to make me
laugh. He'd done it since that first conversation.

I took another look at his bandaged head and
ran my fingers over his cool skin before the nurse
told me it was time to go. When I returned to the
lobby, my eyes were overflowing with tears as they
made their way down my cheeks and left their taste
upon my lips. I saw Geneva through my blurred
eyesight and felt her arms as they wrapped around
me.

I don't know how long I wept, with my face
buried in my mother's shoulder. I'm not sure how
long we stood before Will took my arm and led me
away. I don't remember much of the ride to the
motel or what it looked like when we stepped
through the door. I don't remember taking a
shower or my mother helping me into the bed, but I

remember to this day the image of the most wonderful guy I know lying motionless in that room, surrounded by monitors, tubes, and the smell of antiseptic.

I remember that moment, standing there taking in his image, understanding what it would do to my soul if I lost him. Yes, my soul; that me buried deep beneath the skin and muscle; the me which coursed along with each droplet of blood as it traveled through my body and each molecule of oxygen as it replenished every cell; the entity which inhabited this vessel of flesh and bone and hair. I knew it was there; she was there; existing as part of the universe, because I could feel the depth of her pain and the entirety of her love. I could feel the despair which gripped her at the thought of losing him, and how she knew without a doubt, such an impact would result in her losing the very soul she had just discovered.

I don't remember falling asleep, how long I slept, or what time Geneva's hand stirred me into wakefulness. I don't even remember the dreams, what they meant, or who filled in the supporting cast. I only know Cole Allen was the leading man.

Chapter Twenty-Two

Coach Curtis looked up as the door to his office opened. Taylor Jordan, Tate Jordan's younger brother, peeked inside.

"Coach, you got a minute?"

Coach Curtis put down the papers in his hands.

"Sure."

He watched as his team filed into the small room; everyone from the starters to the scrubs.

Taylor stepped to the front.

"Coach, we had a little team meeting and we want to talk to you about something. It has to do with Cole."

"Okay, what's on your mind?"

Taylor shifted awkwardly. He had a feeling the coach wasn't going to like what he was about to propose. He'd consider it foolish and a squander to their hopes and dreams.

"Well, you know how the Air Force has their missing man formation?"

"You mean where they fly in a formation, and one plan moves off alone to leave the others?"

"Yeah."

"Sure, I've seen it at a couple of air shows."

"Uh, me and the guys have been talking and we'd like to suggest something. You're probably going to think this is kind of crazy, but we feel Cole is an important part of the team. We'd like to honor him by doing something different."

The coach was intrigued.

"Go on."

"We'd like to play the championship game in a missing man formation."

"I'm not sure I understand."

"We want to play with a man missing."

"Are you saying you want to play eight-man football with seven players?"

"Yeah, we do," he said apprehensively. "UCLA did that for Nick Pasquale when he got killed."

"Yeah, but they did it for one play; the first play."

"But Coach, Cole's not dead. He's still alive, and he's missing, not gone."

Coach Curtis straightened in his chair. Though the thought disturbed him, he maintained his composure.

"Jordan, this is the State Championship." He said clearing his throat before continuing.

"I appreciate that you all want to do something special for Cole. You're right. He's an important part of this team, just as each of you are important to this team. What about Thompson? He's been working all year to step into Cole's position. Don't you think he deserves a shot?"

"Uh, Coach, I'm with the rest of the guys. It's Cole's position. I wouldn't feel right about taking it this way." Steve Thompson spoke up.

"You wouldn't be taking Cole's position away, Thompson. You would be helping your team win a championship."

"Coach, this is important to us," Jordon urged.

"Why can't you just dedicate the game to him? We can see if they will announce it over the loudspeaker, let all the fans know you are playing for your teammate."

"It isn't the same. He's missing. He isn't here. He's our missing man and we want to play in a way that shows how important he is to us."

"Let me get this straight, Taylor. You guys want to play one man short for the entire game during the state championship?"

Taylor smiled as the others nodded.

"Kinda crazy, huh?" Taylor suggested.

"Yes, it is. You realize you will probably lose this game."

"We don't think it means we will lose. We think it means we'll have to play harder, which is what we'll have to do without Cole anyway. We want to make a statement coach. We want Cole to know how important he is to us."

"I don't think you guys realize what you're talking about here. This isn't something you should just go into with a head full of emotions. This is it; the big game. It's what we've been working for all year; some of you for four years. All of you have worked hard for this, especially Cole. Don't you think he would want you to do everything you can to win?"

"And we will. We'll work as hard as we need to. We'll practice all the extra hours you want us to practice. We'll put our heart and soul into it, not just for Cole, but for us too."

"You don't think it would be enough just to do this on the opening kickoff or maybe the first couple of downs? You really think you have to do this the whole game?"

"Coach, it's what we want to do. If you can't support us on this, then we understand. You're the coach, and we'll do what you say we have to do, but this is what we really want to do; as a team. The vote was unanimous."

Coach Curtis took off his hat and rubbed his hand through his hair. They knew this game was as important to him as it was to them. It had been almost forty years since the Bulldogs had been in a state championship game. Coach Curtis didn't have a state title, and he wanted it nearly as bad as his team.

"What about the people in town? This is their championship too. Have you given any consideration to what it would mean to them if you lost because you were playing one man short?"

"They've supported us all year, Coach; even when other people weren't taking us seriously. We think they'll support us on this."

Curtis shook his head.

"I'll have to make some phone calls. I'm not sure they'll let us do that if we have the kids on the sideline to fill the position. After all, it is eight-man football."

Taylor nodded in acceptance and Coach Curtis watched as his team filed slowly out of his office.

Word spread quickly. The coach was soon deluged by calls from concerned parents and fans; some of them supported the team's request and while others clearly didn't. In the age of Facebook and Twitter, it didn't take long for the Tigers to catch wind of it as well.

As much as he didn't want to see his team lose the state championship, Curtis knew this was important to them.

"Look, the OSSA says we can play that way if we want, but I don't want to see you throw your chances at a championship away. I'm sure Cole wouldn't either. I'll support you on this if you'll just go the first kickoff and the first series of downs."

Taylor Jordan spoke for the team.

"If that's how you want it coach, then we'll follow your orders. It's not what we wanted to do, but it's better than nothing."

The game was set for the first Saturday in December. It was an afternoon game, and the weather was gorgeous. The stands on both sides filled with excited fans. All across the stadium, conversations buzzed with the news that the Bulldogs were starting the game off a man short. Some of the tiger fans felt it might give them just the edge they needed to get on the board early.

Just before kickoff, Coach Curtis was summoned to a meeting with the referees and Coach Carter, the Tiger coach.

"Curtis, your team has created quite a stir. My kids have been talking about this the whole week, and they had their own little meeting. They want to start the game a man short as well. It seems they don't want to walk out of here thinking they beat your team on a fluke. So, if you're in agreement, we're going to play seven men as long as you're playing seven men."

Coach Curtis shook his head in amazement.

"Amazing. I never figured it'd go this far."

"Yeah, they can be pretty headstrong sometimes." Coach Carter agreed.

"So, whoever wins the toss, we start off with seven men on both sides?"

"We'll go along with it as long as you do. We don't want an unfair advantage. Let's say we play the first quarter this way. That way the advantage doesn't go to whoever wins the toss."

"We're going to start an eight-man football state championship game playing seven-man football? You know this is going to make history."

Coach Carter smiled.

"Yeah, I guess it is."

The two men shook hands.

"Tell your boys thanks. See you on the field, Coach." Curtis said as he headed back to talk to his team.

I stood with the rest of the fans when it was time for the National Anthem. Cole insisted that I represent him at the game. As much as I wanted to support him by being there, my heart wasn't really in it. I would rather have been by his side watching the game on television. It was being broadcast by a local channel in Oklahoma City. I was glad he was getting to see it.

Just after the band finished playing, the announcer's voice boomed over the loudspeakers.

"Ladies and gentlemen, welcome to the OSSA Eight-Man Class C State Championship between the Terry Tigers and the Prairie Blossom Bulldogs. Today's game pits the two best teams in Oklahoma Class C football. We have a special announcement to make at this time. Both teams have asked that this game be dedicated to Cole Allen a member of the Prairie Blossom Bulldog team who recently suffered a severe injury. In honor of Cole, both teams have requested to play the first quarter in a missing man formation. This eight-man game will begin with just seven men on each team. We hope the fans will respect the request of the team members and keep Cole in your thoughts during this first quarter of play."

I felt a lump in my throat and was nearly overwhelmed with tears, when I felt a hand touch my arm.

"That's an incredible thing they just did. Wasn't it?" Tisha commented, the emotion filling her voice.

"I can't believe they're doing it," I said as I wiped at the corner of my eye. "And even the opposing team is doing it."

"They must know what we know."

"What's that?" I asked, not quite sure what she was saying.

"That he's a really special guy."

I hugged Tisha's neck.

"I just hope he does okay."

"We have to keep the faith, Sophie," Tisha encouraged.

"Keep the faith." I'd heard that a lot lately, and I was trying to understand. It just seemed faith wasn't what Cole was going to need to beat what he was facing.

I smiled weakly trying not to let my skepticism show. We took our seats and watched as the teams lined up for the kickoff. Terry had won the toss and elected to kickoff. I couldn't help but count the number of players on the field. Sure enough, only seven white jerseys and seven black jerseys.

We scored quickly, just minutes into the game. Terry returned the favor and scored shortly before the quarter ended. The score was even at six points each. The second quarter both teams went back to eight-man play. We moved ahead, and at half time the score was twelve to six in our favor.

While we waited through halftime, Tisha kept me company.

"So, how's he doing? I haven't seen him for a couple weeks."

"He's keeping his spirits up. Probably better than would be expected from anyone but Cole."

"He's pretty strong willed you know."

I smiled and nodded.

"Don't I know it? He let me have it one day because he didn't think I was shooting straight with him. He said I was letting him off easy. He was right."

"I think Cole is the kind of guy who would rather be told what he's up against than to have it sugar coated."

She was right. Cole didn't want the sympathy vote. He wanted to know exactly what he was up against and who was on his side.

While we talked, I found myself absentmindedly running my fingers over the numbers of his jersey.

"You really care for him, don't you Sophie?"

"Like I've never cared for anyone in my life."

"I think he feels the same about you."

I knew she was probably right, but somehow with what he was facing, I seemed rather insignificant in his life.

"He's got bigger things to think about right now."

"It doesn't matter what he has to think about; you're still going to be on his mind."

"I wish he was out there. Because if he was out there, then he wouldn't be where he's at right now; he wouldn't be facing the obstacles he has in front of him."

I felt her hand run down my back and then she pulled me to her side.

"Keep the faith," she encouraged once again.

That time I couldn't help rolling my eyes. Such a simple thing to say and such a hard thing to do.

We kicked off to the Tigers. They had the wind and raced down the field using it to their advantage. Minutes into the second half, they were ahead fourteen to twelve. The rest of the game continued to go in the Tigers' favor. When it looked like there was no hope; Coach Curtis sent in the second string to give them the opportunity to play in the championship game.

When the smoke cleared, we were left holding the silver ball instead of the gold. The feeling of losing something that could never be recaptured hung heavy on our side of the field. As I stood there in the stands watching people file slowly onto the field, I realized silver balls are just as rare as the gold ones. Only one of each was awarded each year. Though it was a disappointment to come in second, they certainly didn't have anything of which to be ashamed.

After the game, Coach Curtis walked up to me.

"Can you take this to Cole for me? I'd take it myself, but we start basketball practice tomorrow."

It was a football signed by the players from both teams.

"It isn't the official one. That one goes in the trophy case, but this one was used in the game."

"Thank you, Coach. He'll love it."

"Tell him we're thinking of him."

"He watched the game on TV. After what you did that first quarter, he knows. That was an incredible thing to do."

"The team came up with that one on their own. I wasn't exactly one hundred percent behind it, but it worked out."

"It was a great gesture. Cole will like this, Coach. Thanks again," I said as he walked away.

I was right. The signed football almost erased the disappointment of losing the title. Almost. Cole was moved by the team's gesture in the first quarter.

"I can't believe they did that. It's crazy," Cole marveled.

"Yeah, but it was cool too. I almost cried when the announcer told us what they were doing."

"I wish they could have won. I bet they were even more disappointed than me."

"They were all pretty down. They probably would have come to visit you, but Coach Curtis had them start basketball practice the next day. I guess he wanted to get their attention on something else."

"Maybe, but the football playoffs put them behind on the basketball season. They would have started playing games last week."

"So, I guess Duane will be pretty occupied for the next couple of months."

"Yeah, this is his season."

"Maybe they'll win state in basketball," I suggested.

Cole sat staring at the ball in his hands.

"You're wishing you could have played, aren't you?"

"Is it that obvious?"

"I know how much football has meant to you. You worked your tail off to start."

"Well, it was going to end this year either way. I would have rather gone out in a different way."

"Cole, I'm sorry you couldn't be there."

"Sophie, don't say you're sorry for something you can't control. This isn't your fault."

"No, it isn't my fault, but that doesn't mean I can't feel sorrow at your disappointment. You know, you don't have to always brush off how other people feel. It's just like what those guys did for you. They share an emotional bond with you, and they wanted to do something to let you know. If I say I'm sorry, I'm just sharing my feelings."

"Isn't an emotional bond a bit beyond your life scope?"

"Just because I don't let emotions interfere with my sense of reason doesn't mean I don't have any. Don't paint me so sterile."

"Oooh. There's a new one. I believe you are the one who paints you as sterile. I'm not the one who tries to see life as black and white. I believe I've been the one to try to interject color into Sophie's portrait."

I smiled. He was right, of course. He'd injected color into my life from the moment I met him. Humor, appreciation, balance, hope, faith, peace – those were the colors Cole painted. He'd added a brush stroke here and there until he'd painted my world in a way I could never have expected. Cole painted the lives of everyone around him, just by being himself.

"Gotcha, didn't I?" he announced with both pride and amusement.

"Yeah. You got me." I said, adding, "in more ways than one" as an unspoken thought.

Chapter Twenty-Three

"I can't do this," he said as he faced the parallel bars.

"Yes, you can Cole," Sarah encouraged.

Sarah was his physical therapist.

"I'll be right here. I'm with you, but I can't do it for you."

"I'm not ready."

"Yes, you are. You're in great shape. We've worked on upper body, and you're ready. The only place you're not ready is in your head. Now, get your bottom out of that chair and lift," Sarah ordered.

He fought with the negativity inside of himself. Reaching for the bars, the toned muscles of his arms stretched and flexed. He took a deep breath and pulled himself forward, lifting his body above the bars. I could see his muscles straining under his weight, visibly trembling. With a determined look on his face he inched a gloved hand forward on the bar, his toes dragging beneath him. His face contorted; he swung his weight to his left arm, jerking his right arm forward.

Swinging his weight back to his right, he grabbed for the bar in front of his left hand. He continued, back and forth reaching the mid-point of the bars. His arms strained to keep his body aloft and just as he slumped back; Sarah stepped forward to catch him and slid him back into the chair.

"I can't finish it."

"Yes, you can."

"I'm played out."

"No, you're not. Now get back up there."

"You have no idea."

"You're wrong. I know. You have no idea how strong you are. You can do this."

"Can't we just call it a day?"

"Is that what you want to do, Cole? Do you want to be stuck in that chair? And if you are stuck in that chair, do you think you can just stop half way through something, and it's no big deal? It is a big deal."

"I thought this was temporary," he defended.

"Temporary can mean a few weeks to a few months."

She grabbed his arms.

"See these. These are your legs right now. They are your transportation, your tools. They have to be prepared to get you from A to B to Z. You have two choices. You either throw yourself on the mercy of everyone around you or you make yourself independent. Which do you want? And if it's temporary, the best way you can get your body ready to walk again is through therapy."

She was tough on him. She pushed him beyond every wall he set up, but she brought out the Cole I knew before the accident. Her energy and enthusiasm seemed to ignite the person he'd allowed to slip under the surface.

"Want to go for a ride?" He asked as we prepared to leave the workout area.

"Huh?"

"Come on. Sit in my lap."

"Cole, I don't want to hurt you?"

"Don't worry, I won't feel a thing. I probably won't even be able to tell how much you weigh."

"Cole, I don't think it's such a good idea."

"Just take a seat."

I eased into his lap, and he rolled us through the halls of the rehab center.

"One fifteen," he whispered in my ear.

"What?"

"You weigh one-fifteen."

I slugged him in the arm.

"You said you wouldn't know."

"Hey, I can't feel it, but I gotta roll it. And don't go damaging my tools. You might have to get out and push."

In between the physical therapy, there were the rounds of chemo. At first it was wretched, watching him struggle to keep foods down; seeing the drain in his face as he fought the effects of the drugs. His moods swung, and I knew he was struggling to control those as well. Though he tried his best to maintain his positive outlook, there were moments when he just couldn't help but strike out at anyone or anything that seemed to cross his path.

His mind seemed to wander and lose focus. He repeated things struggling to make himself clear, making his point over and over. He had trouble sleeping and longed just to rest.

"I wake up in the middle of the night. I have nightmares, and I wake up terrified. My heart races and I feel like my breath is being sucked out of me."

"It'll get better."

"How do you know?"

"I just know you. You're strong. You'll get past this."

"What if my brain is messed up? What if I'm like this all the time?"

"It's just the effects of the drugs."

"You don't understand. I'm so tired, and I just want to sleep, but I can't. I feel confused all the time."

"Your mind will clear. You'll get better."

"But what if I don't? What if it's growing in there? Sometimes it feels like it's growing. My head feels numb inside."

I took his hands in mine and looked deep into his eyes trying to get him to focus on mine.

"Cole, the MRIs have been good. The doctors say you are doing fine. It's the drugs. When you finish the drugs, and you get them all out of your system, you'll feel better."

"I'm just so tired."

"Could you sleep if I hold you?"

"I don't know."

"Let's try," I said, moving up beside him on the bed. I pulled him against my chest, allowing him to lie against the softness of my breast.

"Uh, Sophie, I don't know if this is going to help."

"Why?"

"I'm uh touching your uh.."

I smiled.

"Okay, that's the Cole I know. It's okay; just use me as a pillow."

"My pillow doesn't, usually, cause this reaction, unless I'm dreaming about you."

"You dream about me?"

"Sometimes; when I'm not having nightmares. That's when I sleep the best."

My hand stroked over his head, feeling the scar from his surgery under my hand.

"Shh. Just try to relax."

"Talk to me."

"What do you want me to talk about?"

"I don't care. I just want to hear your voice."

I paused for a moment trying to think of something to say. My mind went back to my first year of school after moving from California.

"I couldn't believe how different two parts of the country could be. I'd been around the ocean my whole life. Here I was in this place that seemed to be a time capsule from the past; some kind of throwback to the Wild West. Nothing seemed normal, and I didn't fit in, but then I met you and everything changed. As much as I miss the ocean, I couldn't imagine life without you in it. You took this dry, desolate place and filled it full of life."

"I'll never forget that first day I met you and that lame answer you gave on the science test. It was so funny, and I couldn't imagine giving an answer like that. If I didn't know the answer, I would have left it blank, but not you. You are so carefree and fearless. You do your best to make life interesting."

I looked down at him; his eyes closed, and his face relaxed. He was asleep. I leaned back and closed my eyes.

Though I felt comfortable with him against me, fear coursed through my veins. I'd never seen him so weak and fragile. His vulnerability was frightening. And what of the questions he raised? What if this did change his personality or his outlook? What if the cancer slipped up on us to steal his life away?

I wasn't ready to answer any of those questions; I wasn't even ready to acknowledge their existence. I was scared of them, and I pushed them away from me. As practical as I'd always imagined myself to be, I didn't want to deal with the practical aspects of the conversation.

"God, if you're there, please take care of Cole." I heard myself whisper. "Please give him strength and courage. Help his faith. If you want me to believe, then show me you're there. Show me that you are there for Cole."

"He is there Sophie. I know he is." I heard Cole whisper. I looked down at him, and his eyes were open, looking up at me.

"I know he is because he brought me you."

His comment made me smile. I brushed my hand against his cheek.

"That's sweet Cole, but I can't make you better."

"You've already made me better. You made me better than I was, just by being you."

"You're the special one here, Cole. Not me. I'm not the one with amazing faith or the charming personality."

"You are so much more than you ever give yourself credit. Those things you say about me, you bring those out. You're the reason I laugh and joke and smile. You make me want to be the kind of person I am. You gave me a reason to be courageous and laugh at life."

"How Cole?"

"I wanted you to like me. I wanted to be special to you."

"You are. You always have been. You've been special since the first day I met you."

"And you're special, too. You make me think and reason. You challenge me. You aren't some pushover. You're smart and witty and sarcastic. I have to think ahead and plan just to surprise you."

"Well, you do find your ways to surprise me." I giggled.

"It's my favorite thing to do."

I caressed his cheek with my hand.

"Shh. You need to sleep."

"You can't imagine how just those few minutes in your arms filled me. I feel like I've slept for hours. It's like touching you recharges me."

I leaned over and kissed his forehead.

"Close your eyes and recharge a little longer."

We laid there together in his bed. His head pressed against my chest. My hand gently moved over the arm he had draped across my belly. My cheek pressed against the top of his head as I thought and hoped for the future. Someday, we would hold each other like this again; it would be a sensuous, loving moment, free from fear and doubt. Someday, we would find ourselves lazing around near the river or lake, leaning back against a tree holding each other in a relaxing way just to enjoy being together.

It was on that thought I drifted off into a fitful sleep; fitful only because it was filled with the thoughts and dreams of Cole and all we'd do together.

Cole fought through the effects of the chemo learning how to help control the nausea and which foods seemed to trigger it. He still struggled with sleeping, but taking little naps throughout the day seemed to help. It seemed he slept best when his head was on my chest. I felt best when he was there as well.

After the first couple of weeks, they decided to let him go home. Armed with a tub full of pills and an enormity of instructions, he was released to continue his treatments and physical therapy at home. He had a physical therapist that would come to his house, and Sarah would be out to check on his progress every couple of weeks.

Though he hadn't regained use of his legs, there were hopeful signs. From time to time, he could feel some sensations.

In some ways, it seemed an eternity, in other ways it seemed like the time for him to come home came upon us too quickly. I feared he might not be ready. Of course, Cole was concerned at how the other kids would react.

"It'll be okay. They'll be awkward at first. They won't know what to say or how to treat you, but you'll just take it one day at a time, and they'll come around."

"Yeah, I guess. I'm getting kind of used to it here, but at home there will be all kinds of reminders of what I can't do or what I use to do."

"That's true. You'll have a lot of adjusting to do, but I think you'll be surprised at how well you'll adapt. You may be surprised at how well everyone else adapts, too. Besides, we're going to get you out of that chair sooner or later."

His parents had spent considerable time and money making the house more accessible while he'd been away. Ramps had been installed in the front of the house and on the deck out back. They'd widened his bedroom doorway and even lowered one end of the kitchen counter.

The school had been preparing for his return as well. His first day back at school was almost as exciting as the pep rally before the championship football game. He was the center of attention. But after the newness had worn off, Cole found himself faced with the awkwardness he'd expected all along.

"It's pretty unnerving to have a whole room full of people go quiet when you enter."

I smiled.

"Just think of them as rabbits."

"You'll never let that one go, will you?"

"It was good advice. They'll get more comfortable, and so will you."

Situations seemed to arise around every corner, but Cole soon learned how he reacted often affected the outcome. In normal Cole style, he reverted to humor when faced with an uncomfortable situation.

"Okay, everyone, line up like we practiced." Mrs. Sims directed in choir practice. "Cole, you stand over the...."

She covered her mouth at the slip.

"I'm so sorry, Cole."

The awkwardness hung thickly in the air.

"Tell you what. You just point, and I'll roll with it." Cole popped back with a wink and a smile.

Still stunned, she pointed at the end of the riser steps while the room erupted in laughter.

On another occasion, he happened upon Jaima and Leza as they debated whether or not his anatomy below the waist still worked as it should.

"Hey girls! What's up?" he tossed at them, and then laughed at their embarrassment.

He found it funny to watch them scampering off uncomfortably.

As they became more comfortable around him, he grew more comfortable as well. Though perhaps not what he'd been used to, the days began to fall into a routine. We spent most of our time outside school at Cole's house, just hanging out in his room. We found comfort in watching movies together and sometimes we read books together. I think we both longed for the days when we sat lazily along the river or took our afternoon adventures. And of course, we still hoped that we would, but it was winter, and we were better off staying indoors away from the stiff Oklahoma wind.

"Geez, you look out there, and it appears to be as warm as spring, but open the door, and that wind will cut right through you," I said entering the Allen house.

"That's no Oklahoma wind; it's a little puff." Cole chuckled at his remark.

"To you it's a breeze, I'm still hanging on to my California blood and I say it's a cold wind if ever I felt one."

"I thought you'd been here long enough to get over your sissy sensations."

"You go out there then."

"I stuck my foot out there. It didn't feel cold to me." He joked, and I rolled my eyes.

"That's not exactly an accurate way to determine the temperature."

"Works for me. What do you want to do?" He asked, changing the subject.

"I figured we'd watch a movie."

"I'm getting kind of tired of being cooped up inside. Why don't we go for a drive?"

"Uh, you can't drive."

"No, but you can," he suggested.

"I don't have a car."

"You can drive my truck."

I looked at him quizzically.

"Are you sure that's such a good idea? What if something happened? I wouldn't know what to do?"

"Like what? What's going to happen?"

I shrugged.

"I don't know; something; like an emergency or something."

Cole rolled his eyes.

"Sophie, nothing's going to happen. We're just taking a drive."

"I don't know if your parents would like that. They might not want to place the responsibility for your safety in my hands."

"You're not that bad a driver. Nothing's going to happen. Besides, I'm a big boy. I'm not your responsibility. Did your parents ever have a problem with you riding around when I drove?"

"No, but that's different. I'm not…"

He cut me off.

"Not what? Not paralyzed?"

I could hear the defensiveness in his voice, but he didn't understand what I meant.

"No, that's not what I was going to say. Why did you have to go there? I've never tried to limit you."

"Well, you said you weren't like me."

I put my hands on my hips.

"No, I didn't. You cut me off before I finished my sentence. Those were your words. I was trying to say I'm not used to it. You, usually, drive. I'm just nervous. It's just that, what if I had a wreck or something? What would I do?"

"What would you do if my legs worked?"

"Cole, give me a break here. I don't have a lot of experience driving other people around. I've spent so much time with you; I rarely go down to the convenience store on my own."

I could see in his eyes that he was sorry for taking the course he had taken.

"You know, I'm not everyone else. You don't have to assume that I have a problem with your mobility."

He nodded.

"I know. I'm sorry. I guess I just do it to myself. You know, sometimes I just want to go back to the way things used to be, and it makes me frustrated that I can't."

"It'll come back to you. You'll get better, and you're going to walk again."

"What if it doesn't?"

"It will; they've already told you there wasn't any permanent damage.

Surprisingly, Cole's parents thought it was a great idea.

"I think it would be a good change! You need to get out." Jenna's eagerness caught me off guard.

Cole loaded himself into the passenger side of the truck, and I put the chair in the back. We drove to Spring Creek and picked up a couple of Sub sandwiches and some sodas. Then we drove down by the lake and sat in the truck while we ate. There were some ducks down on the lake; stragglers I suppose since I'd heard most of them moving south months ago. It was relaxing watching the ducks swimming upon the lake with Cole by my side.

I glanced over at him. He looked at me with his head down as he took a bite of his sandwich, his eyes smiling a gentle smile. I could tell he was feeling it too; that old familiar comfort of being together; taking in the simple pleasures of everyday moments. He still had a long way to go. His treatments would continue, and he would have to undergo scans and tests to be sure he had beaten the disease. And of course, there was the obvious issue of his paralysis, but we could celebrate the little victories; like sitting by a lake, sharing lunch and being together. It was those little victories which offered the sustenance of life; filling me with value, and yes, even purpose.

Chapter Twenty-Four

Christmas break was coming up fast, and Jenna and Craig had planned a trip to the mountains for the holidays. Before Cole's accident, the trip was intended to be a ski trip, and I'd been invited to come along. Now I wasn't so sure about going.

"Are your parents still planning the trip?" I quizzed him one Saturday.

"Yeah, but I think they canceled my ski pass," he said without missing a beat. "You are still coming along, right?"

"Uh, I don't know, Cole. I'm not sure if I should."

"Why?"

"Don't you think it would be good if you spent the time with your parents?"

"I'll be with my parents, when they aren't out skiing. You could at least come along to keep me company. If you don't go, they'll just hang around the condo the whole time. I don't want them giving up their fun on my account."

248 | P a g e

"What are we going to do while they're skiing?"

"I was thinking snowboarding," he quipped.

"Cole, seriously."

"We can sit around a romantic fire and drink hot cocoa."

"Okay, that's one good idea," I agreed.

"We can sit in the lodge and read a good book. I'll let you sit on my lap."

"Ooo. Geez, how can a girl pass that one up?"

"Come on. We'll find a way to make it fun."

I reluctantly agreed. Little did I know just what he had up his sleeve.

We entertained ourselves on the way out. Cole and I shared his iPod, listening to music. We texted back and forth, even though we were sitting side by side. We oohed and ahh'd at the beautiful landscape; the trees and mountains covered in deep layers of snow; the dark blue of the river cutting its way through the white landscape.

When we got to the lodge, we settled into the handicap accessible condo his parents had rented. We were on the first level, which obviously made things more comfortable for Cole, but Jenna and Craig were able to ski out from the room to the lift.

"Hey, you kids need to get out there and get started," Cole encouraged them.

"Trying to get rid of us already?" Craig quizzed.

"I just want you to have a good time. You've had a rough couple of months."

"Look who's talking," Craig retorted.

"I have my own plans for the weekend," Cole said raising his eyebrows.

"Cole!" Jenna admonished.

"What? Sophie and I are taking snowboarding lessons. Then we might hit the hot tub."

"Snowboarding lessons?" Jenna quizzed.

"Yeah, I'm going to teach Sophie how to Ollie."

I rolled my eyes.

"Don't worry. I'll keep him in the lodge," I assured his parents.

"Hey, don't go spoiling my good time. I'm not going to be a firewatcher the whole holiday."

Jenna and Craig gathered their skis and told us goodbye, then slipped out the sliding glass door of the condo.

"Okay, they're gone. Go change."

"Change into what? Why?"

"Change into cold weather gear. We have a couple of appointments to keep."

"Cole, what have you been up to?"

"I told you, I'm not going to just sit around staring at flames the whole time we're here."

He rolled into the bedroom and closed the door. I had no idea what he had planned, but I knew better than to argue. It would serve me better to try to steer him once I found out what kind of crazy ideas were going through his head. I went into the other bedroom and changed. Then I went back into the living area to wait for him. When he came out, he had on a pair of ski pants and a sweatshirt.

"Get our coats."

I had no choice, but to follow his lead. He led the way down past the lodge and to the building at the end of the complex. As we neared the complex a man in a red parka began walking towards us.

"Sophie, this is Jim. He's with Adaptive Sports."

As Jim approached, he removed his gloves and stuck out his hand to Cole.

"Hey, Cole," he said with a confident smile. "Are you ready?"

"You betcha," Cole popped back.

"Ready for what, Cole?" I asked with suspicion in my voice.

"We're going snowmobiling."

"What? No. I promised your mom."

"You promised to keep me safe. Jim here is going to help you do that. Jim is an adaptive ambassador. He's going to ride with me, and his daughter, Shayla is going to ride with you."

"I don't think so."

"Okay, then I'll go by myself. You can wait in the lodge."

"I can't let you go by yourself. Your folks would kill me."

"Then let's go."

"Cole, what would your doctor say?"

"She said it was fine. In fact, I had to send Jim a release form from her before I could make the reservations."

I looked a Jim.

"Is this safe? I mean, could he get hurt worse?"

"Well, Sophie, the fact is no matter what you do, something can always go wrong. Just as any time we get in a car something can go wrong, but yeah, it's safe, as safe as any sport can be. You'll both be wearing protective gear, and I have lots of experience with handicap riders."

I was strangely excited at the idea, and it was great seeing the look on Cole's face. I hadn't seen him this energetic in ages. I felt myself giving in to the idea with very little influence from either of them.

"Okay, but your folks better not kick me out because of this."

"If they do, I'll rent another room."

"That's great, but I still have to get back home."

"It'll be all right."

I watched as Jim helped Cole get ready and loaded. While I watched, a young woman stepped up beside me.

"He's going to love this."

"I hope so."

"Are you worried about his safety?"

"Well, I guess I'm still a little protective."

"He's in good hands. Dad does this all the time. He's taken over a thousand rides with handicapped riders."

She turned to face me, reaching out her hand.

"By the way, I'm Shayla."

I took her hand.

"Sophie."

"What's your relationship to Cole?"

I had to think about that. We were obviously more than friends, but we'd never called what we had a relationship.

"I guess he's kind of my boyfriend."

Shayla smiled.

"Kind of?"

"It's kind of complicated."

"Aren't they all?" she said with a wink.

It was my turn to smile.

"Yeah, I guess they are."

"Well, Sophie, Cole is going to have a blast. And I hope you do too."

Jim turned to us.

"We're ready."

Shayla handed me a helmet and gave me a few instructions. Moments later, the building echoed with the roar of the engines. I glanced over at Cole, and he had a grin on his face like a kid in a candy store. Jim's machine took the lead as we pulled out into the snow.

Although there were concerns worming around in my head, it didn't take long for them evaporate in the exhilaration. With my arms clamped around Shayla's waist, I watched the machine in front of us spit snow out behind it. The snow swirled as it went past.

Trees stood up out of the mounds of powder like weird, white pillars rising from the surface of the earth. The tunnel vision of the helmet made me feel like a bobble head doll. As we bounced and rolled with the changing terrain, we swept back and forth between rows of trees until we met the open area above timberline. The smooth, fluffy surface was soon disturbed and carved with the lines of the tracks we left behind.

We rose over rolling hills of snow, catching pockets of air before bumping back down and sending up a splash of snowflakes. The roar of the engines pierced through the solitude of the scene. Looking back over my shoulder, I watched as we painted the mountainside with our presence, knowing by morning nature would take back the mountain and erase the signs of our existence.

Each time I was able to steal a look at Cole, his face showed the awe and excitement of a child facing a new discovery. The grin never seemed to leave his face, and there was no indication he was finding this excursion anything but thrilling. Miraculously, I'd left my worries behind and focused on the fun.

The machine climbed toward the peak of the mountain, following the crevasses and valleys, rolling up on its side as we turned and rotated, redirecting our route in elegant moves. The sun glowed against the surface of snow, its rays forming a blue halo against the sun visor of the helmet and a kaleidoscope as it passed through the spray of snow.

Massive chunks of rock rose from beneath the blanket of snow, splitting up the mountain, lifting as jagged arrowheads pointing up into the sky. As I looked down from near the peak, tall white mushrooms pushed up out of the earth; the trees draped in winter cloaks. Heading back down, we picked up speed like a bullet heading for its target, floating up, dropping down, rolling with the rollercoaster landscape. We shifted back and forth across the mountain, reducing our speed, entering back through the timberline. We weaved through the trees like a slalom course.

When we pulled up back at the complex, Cole had his helmet off in record time.

"That was freaking awesome!" He screamed, incapable of holding back any longer.

I just smiled taking in his exuberating cries of pleasure. More animated than I'd seen him in months, he raised his hands triumphantly.

"Sophie, can you believe that? Wasn't it just amazing?"

"Yes, Cole! It was great!"

"Great? Great doesn't even begin to describe it. It was fan-freaking-tastic!"

Shayla leaned near me and whispered in my ear.

"I told you he was in good hands."

I nodded.

Jim helped Cole off the snowmobile and back into his chair. Cole took his hand.

"Thank you so much. I can't tell you how much I enjoyed that."

"My pleasure. I hope you'll come back."

I wasn't sure how I was going to settle him down long enough to get him back to the condo, but somehow we made it. He didn't stop talking about the experience the whole way back.

"Looks like your folks are still out. What do you want to do now?"

"How about taking that dip in the hot tub?"

I shrugged.

"Sounds fine to me. I'll go change."

We met back in the living room, both wearing the robes provided by the resort.

"Ready?" I asked.

"When you are," he urged.

When we got down by the hot tub, he unwrapped his robe, and I helped him out of his chair. He slid down into the bubbling water.

"Oh my gosh. This feels so good," he said before glancing back at me.

I watched his face as I removed the robe to reveal the bikini I was wearing underneath. I thought his eyes were going to pop out of their sockets. I'd been self-conscious of wearing it. Though we'd been together at the pool many times, it was still a little daring. I wasn't sure how to gage his reaction. I tossed my inhibitions aside and allowed myself to explore a side of me I'd been hesitant to accept; the girly side. He gazed silently as I stepped down into the swirling water; its warmth caressing my skin. When I reached the bottom of the tub, I slid on down beneath the surface of the water, lifted my head and pushed my wet hair back out of my face.

"Oh my gosh, I thought I'd just stepped into a scene from *Fast Times At Ridgemont High*," he oozed. "That's the most beautiful thing I've ever seen."

"At least I got your attention long enough to take your mind off the snowmobiles."

"Oh, you've had my attention for a long, long time."

"You know, Shayla asked me a question and I wasn't sure how to answer it."

"What was that?"

"She asked me what my relationship was to you."

"Did you tell her you were the most important person in my life?"

"I told her you were sort of my boyfriend. I told her it was complicated."

"It might seem that way, but I don't think our relationship can be described with a few simple words. You mean everything to me. You are my life blood. You give me strength and courage. You make it all worthwhile."

His hand went to the back of my head and pulled me to him. Our lips met. It was complicated, but it was incredible.

My hand traced across his chest, to his arm and down to rest on his thigh. Something in his eyes caught my attention.

"What is it?"

"Move your hand."

I smiled.

"I, uh, didn't mean anything by that," I assured him.

"No, I mean, move your hand. Touch another spot."

I slid my hand further down his thigh, closer to his knee.

"I can feel that," he whispered.

I sat stunned.

"What?"

"I can feel that. Just kind of like pressure, not really touch, but I can feel it."

"What about the water? Can you feel that?"

"Kind of a tingle."

"Can you feel the heat?"

"No, just the tingle and the pressure of your hand."

I moved to his feet, lifting them into my lap. I ran my finger over the bottom of his foot.

"Can you feel that?"

"Kind of vague. Not the way I would expect it to feel, but something."

I massaged his feet between my fingers; his toes pressed against my belly, his heels lying in my lap. I worked my way up his legs rubbing the muscles, squeezing, pinching them. He described the sensations as my hands explored over his skin.

I moved up beside him and took his arm, draping it over my shoulders. Snuggling against his chest, I kissed his wet skin.

"Should we go back?" I asked.

"Back where?"

"Home and get you to a doctor?"

"Why?"

"They may need to see you."

"For what?"

"To help. Maybe they can help you get your feeling back."

"It's coming back," he said, his eyes staring off into the distance.

"But maybe they need to do something to help it come back quicker."

"I don't think it works that way. I think it will just have to come back on its own."

"Well, we need to tell your parents."

"I don't know."

"What? Why don't you know? They should know."

"I don't want to spoil their trip."

I rose up to look him in the eye.

"Spoil their trip? It will make their day!"

"Yeah, but they'll want to do just what you said. They'll want to go home. They'll cut the trip short, and they need this trip. They needed to get away."

"Cole, you can't keep something like this from them."

"I won't. I'll tell them when we get back."

"This is too exciting to keep to ourselves."

"I still can't move them."

"Maybe that will come with time."

"What if it doesn't?"

"Then you are no worse off than you were an hour ago when you were one of the happiest guys on the planet."

He turned to look at me, a smile growing on his face.

"That was awesome, wasn't it?"

"Yes, it was," I said remembering back to the look on his face when he pulled the helmet off.

He took my hand.

"Please, help me keep this a secret for now. I'll tell them as soon as we get home. I just don't want this trip to end yet, for them, but also for me."

He paused.

"I had a good time today and there're some other things I can do. Jim told me that they have adaptive ski boarding and helicopter rides. And we can spend time together like this."

"So, you like having me around, huh?"

He smiled.

"It's complicated."

I leaned over and kissed him.

"Yeah, it is."

Chapter Twenty-Five

We had a wonderful Christmas there in the mountains. Cole wasn't content to sit around; he was constantly pushing for adventure, whether exploring the shops downtown or searching ways to get up on the mountain. I think I enjoyed the time we just sat around together the most. The setting was perfect. I'd always wanted to spend Christmas in the mountains. The white glow of the lights along the streets reflected off the snow covered walks and the large flakes which floated down each evening. The naturally flocked trees hung down heavily, and the tops of the buildings looked like iced gingerbread houses. There wasn't a more picturesque place on earth to spend Christmas.

In the down time, we clung to each other, and I was content to nuzzle against Cole's chest with his arm draped over my shoulders, his warmth creating a peaceful feeling within me. I could feel his breath against the top of my head, and his heartbeat thumped against the back of my shoulder. Those were the moments I treasured and in my most somber thoughts, I hoped they would be there forever.

By the time we headed home, I could see the excitement and adventure had taken a toll on him. He seemed to be more tired than usual. He slept a large portion of the way back. It worried me that he pushed himself so hard, but I could tell he seemed more content than he had been in months.

Jenna and Craig were beyond excited when they found out about the sensations Cole had been feeling. And as expected, they contacted the doctor's office right away. The doctor visit went much as Cole expected it would, largely allowing that time would tell. His physical therapy was to continue with some slight modifications. It appeared to be his best option for improving his condition.

The sensations continued to increase. It started with a sense of pressure and developed into real feelings of touch. Some movement in his toes and then his legs gave us every reason to hope for the best.

Meanwhile, he continued his treatment for his tumor. His tests looked good, and there were no signs of cancer in his blood tests. Still, his stamina seemed to weaken with the treatments bearing down on him.

"Are you feeling okay?" I couldn't help quizzing him, though he continued to brush it off.

"Yeah, I'm fine. Just a little tired. I had a rough night."

"Did you have trouble sleeping?"

"Yeah, I get strange smells in my nose. It's almost as if I can smell the radiation."

"You can smell the radiation?"

"Well, they say you can't. It's supposed to be ozone or something."

He seemed uncomfortable.

"I know it sounds crazy. Maybe it is. It's probably just my imagination. With those pills, they have me on I get kind of messed up. I have these strange dreams. I get a little disoriented."

"Has this been going on long?"

"A little while. It seems like it gets a little worse the longer I'm on the pills."

He paused.

"I wake up scared sometimes. I'm not sure where I am. My thoughts seem all jumbled and I forget stuff."

"Why didn't you say something earlier? I thought you were over that when you left the hospital."

He shrugged.

"I didn't want to bother you with it."

I looked at him trying to decide if I was astonished or angry.

"How could you think you'd be bothering me? I thought we knew each other better than that. I want to be there for you, no matter what you need."

A guilty look lifted across his face.

"I know. I shouldn't be selfish. I know this affects you too."

"I'd hardly call it selfish, but I do want you to know that I'm there for you."

He nodded.

"I know."

We were silent for a moment.

"Is there anything else?"

He smiled shyly.

"I sleep better if I take short naps than if I try to sleep a long time."

I looked into his eyes. They were tired. Reaching over to him, I placed my hand over his head gently pulling him to me. He moved slowly, his head following my direction until it pressed against my chest. My fingers stroked up the side of his face.

"Go to sleep. I'll stay with you."

Cole slept peacefully for two hours. I watched television while he dozed. I stroked the smooth surface of his scalp. My fingers traced over the raised surface of his scars. I couldn't help thinking about what he was experiencing; fatigue, disorientation, nausea, hair loss, all reactions to the efforts to cure him. He was still Cole; positive, persevering, Cole. He had his bouts, as anyone would, but it hadn't broken him.

When he stirred, it was with a slight start. I stroked his chest.

"Shh. It's okay."

He looked up at me and smiled.

"I wish you were here every time I closed my eyes," he whispered.

His words sent goose bumps over me. It was an incredible feeling to hear him say something like that to me.

"I wish I could be," I whispered back, my lips grazing over his forehead.

It was true. There was nothing I'd like better than to be there for him each and every time he needed me. The thought caused me to consider once again how much this young man had come to mean to me and his role in shaping who I was and what I believed. I wasn't the Sophie who had first met him on that day just after biology class. She had shaped and morphed into someone else.

When Sophie Carter arrived on the scene, she was determined to live life through a test tube. She didn't believe there was any reason to struggle to hold onto life. She didn't see any real purpose other than those which existed in nature's cycle of life. She was studious and boring, and she was floating through life with no other goal than to learn.

Now she had a purpose, but she was hopelessly and wonderfully lost, lost in love. In love. What a concept! How many lines had I crossed in the last few years? I know Cole would never accept what had happened to me as an example of evolution; I'd tried that route once before, but I certainly had evolved as a person. Maybe things aren't always black and white, right or left, up or down. Maybe there is a place for a happy medium. Maybe science, religion, and a contented lifestyle can exist together. And maybe, just maybe there are things which simply can't be explained by tests, analysis, or study. Maybe they were never meant to be explained; maybe they were meant to be accepted with faith and wonder.

Wonder -- To be filled with admiration, awe, or amazement. To marvel.

It was almost an epiphany. That's the beauty of life isn't it? Sure there is a certain amount of wonder at learning how things work and why, but the real beauty is just simply taking it as it is. Take for example the opportunity to stand on a mountain peak. As one looks out on the majestic valley below and watches the lifting of an early morning fog rise and dissipate, she can either be absorbed in the incredible event it is or she can be dulled by dissecting and examining the scientific principles involved. Each response has its place in the world, but allowing one to overshadow the other simply takes away from the enormity of it all.

Sophie's journey had taken a turn somewhere a few miles down the road, and that turn was leading her off in a direction she never expected to experience. The catalyst for that change, the actual fork in the road was lying there against my chest. Cole Allen had stood right there in the middle of the road, holding his ground until he forced me to make a choice; the choice between the two directions I wanted to travel.

I glanced down at his face. My fingers brushed tenderly against his skin. He was a wonder. He translated into the definitions of the word with ease.

His skin felt strangely cool and clammy against my fingertips. My hand brushed down his face, his neck and to his chest. I felt my heart skip, my breath freezing in my lungs as I felt for movement from his chest. There was no lift or fall to his chest, just a faint thump, thump, thump against my fingertips.

I slid from underneath him, and he fell limp to the floor. Taking his shoulders in my hands, I shook him.

"Cole. Cole! Cole, wake up!"

Jenna appeared at the bedroom door.

"Sophie?"

I glanced up at her.

"He's not waking up and he's not breathing!"

The horror in my eyes must have shaken her into action as she raced for the phone.

I could hear her frantic voice speaking into the phone, even while I tried to rouse him.

"Cole," I called out as I gently slapped at his cheek. My mind was rolling in panic. I took a deep breath and pushed emotion aside, trying to think through what I needed to do.

"He's not breathing," I thought. "I need him to breathe."

I closed my eyes and took a deep breath.

"CPR. He needs CPR, Sophie." My brain started kicking in, thinking methodically.

I worked to stretch his body out flat. I placed my hand under his neck, lifting his head, opening his airway. I went back to the training I'd taken, my mind directing me through the steps.

I checked his pulse; it was weak, but present. My fingers clamped over his nostrils. Chin up, mouth open, I gave him four quick breaths, watching his chest lift and fall with each one. My fingers went to his neck; the pulse was still the same. He still wasn't breathing on his own. Five more breaths.

Jenna was at my side.

"Pulse still weak. Not breathing." I called out before placing my mouth over his once again.

"Cole! Cole, Baby, wake up," Jenna said shaking his shoulders.

His pulse remained the same and I continued the breathing. I was still providing CPR when the paramedics arrived and took over for me. I stepped out of the way; my hand over my mouth, my lungs frozen as I watched them work on him. Jenna pulled me to her side; her arm wrapped around me.

"What's wrong? Why isn't he breathing?" I asked to no one in particular.

"What happened?" Jenna asked.

"He was sleeping. I just noticed he wasn't breathing. I felt his skin. It was cool. And I...I don't know."

I turned to look at her.

"What could be wrong? He had seemed fine before he went to sleep. Tired, but fine."

I could see Jenna's lips silently moving and I knew she was praying.

"Male patient. Respiratory arrest. Possible pulmonary embolism." I heard the paramedic say into his radio.

"Patient is bagged," was another snippet my mind grabbed just before they wheeled him out on a stretcher. One of the paramedics continued to squeeze the bag pressed over his nose and mouth.

"Can I go with him?" Jenna asked the paramedic.

"Yes, ma'am," he assured.

"Sophie..." She started trying to explain.

"It's okay. I'll call my mom. We'll be right behind you."

Jenna kissed me on the cheek and whispered in my ear.

"Don't forget to pray," she urged.

My eyes caught hers.

"I have been."

I dialed my phone as they were closing the ambulance doors. When I heard Geneva's voice, I broke down.

"Mom? Can you come and get me at Cole's house?" I asked between the sobs.

The paramedic had been right. Cole experienced a pulmonary embolism which had sent him into respiratory arrest. They placed him on a ventilator and started drugs to break up the clot.

"How much more is he going to have to go through?" I asked Jenna.

"Baby, we don't know. We just have to be patient and supportive."

"How long will he be out?"

"I'm not sure."

"Will there be any damage?"

"They don't know yet. They think they caught it in time."

My mom sat next to me; Jenna was in the seat across from me. The smell of stale coffee wandered through the air. The waiting room was eerily silent; something I'd grown used to over the past several months. Our quite thoughts were interrupted when the doctor entered in green scrubs.

"He's doing pretty well. We'll watch him until we're sure he's out of danger."

He looked over at me.

"Are you the young lady who performed artificial breathing?"

I nodded.

"You know, you probably saved his life. Three minutes without oxygen can lead to permanent damage. Seven minutes and he could have died. He's fortunate you were there."

Jenna smiled at me. I could only imagine what was going through her mind. Thinking back through all of the conversations we'd had, it seemed she was always trying to prove to me how important I was to Cole. Still, I could only see how much he'd done for me.

After the doctor had left, she winked and whispered, "I told you. Thank you, sweetheart."

It hit me, but not as hard as it did later when I was alone with Cole in his hospital room. He was asleep, and Jenna had gone home for a while. The room was quiet, and I simply sat taking in his image. The question came to me, "What if I hadn't checked on him? What if I hadn't been there?"

He would have been gone. Life would have continued that process I used to believe in and Cole would have simply ceased to exist except as a memory. I had saved a life. Me, Sophie Carter. I had stepped in and helped life to continue, and it felt good to know I had done that. Where was that girl; the one who didn't understand the need or desire to go to the ends of the earth to save a life?

It had a profound impact upon me. Cole's entire journey had created diametrically opposing versions of who I was and who I had become. As to where this would lead me, I had no idea. All I really knew was that it felt incredible to know I had a part in saving another person's life. It wasn't an arrogant "look what I did" feeling, but rather a humbling, examination of how one life truly affects another.

It seems everywhere I looked there were little reminders that each of us had a role and a contribution, and maybe...just maybe...a plan. Although I didn't feel like a lifesaver, I couldn't argue with the doctor. All I really did was react and use those lessons I learned back when I was in school in California.

I glanced back at Cole's peaceful form. Whatever my role, I was grateful I could be used to help save his life.

Chapter Twenty-Six

His mother had to have been as excited as she was the day he had taken his first steps as a toddler. Although, as a toddler, he probably looked less awkward than he did as a teenager, it was a wonderful experience to see Cole standing upon his previously lifeless legs. He took no more than a couple of steps before he was forced to grip the parallel bars for support, but it was progress. He didn't give up. Once he had gathered his courage and his strength, he took another stab at it. It took nearly fifteen minutes to traverse the length of the bars, and he was soaked with perspiration when he dropped down into the chair at the end.

While he worked his way down the bars, I stole glances at Jenna. There were moments when she looked like she was ready to bounce up and down with excitement. There were other moments when her heart seemed to be racked with compassion toward the courage and determination her son was showing. In those moments, her face tensed with concentration as if she were willing Cole all of her strength. It was an emotional thing to behold, and though I wasn't his mother, I understood the feelings. I felt myself doing the same things, holding my breath, clenching my muscles, and willing every ounce of energy I had in Cole's direction.

Panting he sucked oxygen into his lungs, breathing as if he'd just ran the first leg of a two-mile relay. Once he regained his breath; he looked over at me and smiled. Then he was up on his feet to go at it again.

It took weeks for him to move without the support of the bars, but he didn't give up. And in between all of that work, he was still taking his treatments of chemo. When we were at his house, he slept almost constantly. I worried he was pushing too hard, but he didn't let up. How he found the strength, I don't know.

I watched him as he slept, sometimes deep and still, other times restless and fitful. He still claimed to be plagued by strange dreams and it nearly broke my heart to see him in those fitful moments knowing he was likely being haunted by the hallucinations and nightmares of which he had spoken. Still I was fearful of waking him, knowing how desperately he needed his rest. He'd lost fifteen to twenty pounds, and there were times his face looked nearly hollow, his eyes rimmed with darkness.

As his chest rose and fell with each breath, I ached to have him back; completely back. I longed for more of those carefree moments we so often shared together. At times, I felt the urge to place my hand upon his chest; to feel him breath; to feel his warmth; to let him know I was near. It was nearly as wearing as waiting around in the hospital, wondering and watching.

Then the next day he would push himself through once again, school, therapy, treatment. This went on day after day; week after week. The almost seemingly endless battle continued pushing forward, pulling at his strength and tugging at my heart.

One day while he was sleeping I stepped into the kitchen where Jenna was working on dinner. She glanced up as I entered.

"Sleeping again?"

I nodded.

Her lips turned in a strained smile.

"He pushes so hard."

She spoke as she stirred at a bowl of mashed potatoes.

"Sometimes I worry he pushes too hard," I said, my voice nearly cracking under my concern.

"I know, Honey."

For a moment, the room was silent with only the sounds of her preparations cutting through the heaviness weighing upon me.

"How do you think he's doing?" I finally asked.

"I think he's tired, but I know him and he won't let up until he feels he has given it his best."

Again the silence as I struggled with whether or not to voice the feelings inside.

"You don't think he'll make himself too weak to fight it?"

There it was in words, my biggest fear. That time I couldn't hide the emotions milling around within me. Jenna heard them, and she saw them too. She set the bowl she was working on down on the counter and came to me, pulling me to her. I tried, straining back the lump in my throat, feeling the tears pooling behind my eyelids, but her simple act was just enough to weaken my resolve.

"It's okay," she said softly.

I felt the guilt building up in me like bile and then next thing I knew I felt like a blubbering idiot.

"I'm trying, Jenna. I'm trying so hard. I'm trying to stay positive, but I struggle. I see him so weak, and it worries me."

Jenna shushed me.

"Being concerned, caring, that's not the same as giving up, Baby."

"But he needs me to be strong."

I felt her gentle push and her hand against my chin as she lifted my eyes up to hers. She brushed the hair away from my eyes with her finger, tucking it behind my ear.

"You are strong, Sweetheart. You've been strong for him. I know you've been a comfort to him. I can't imagine how much harder this would have been on him without you here. He looks so forward to seeing you each day. It gives him strength."

"But look at me," I blubbered. "I'm an emotional wreck and he's the one who has to endure all of this. How's that being strong for him?"

"You're emotional because you care."

"But you care and you're not bawling on someone's shoulder."

"I have Craig and you don't know what I do in the quiet of my room."

She took my hand in hers.

"Come here," she said as she led me over to the dining room table.

I sat down next to her, and she held my hand in hers.

"I have my moments, just like you. And sometimes I need to release them, just like you. None of that makes me weak or unfaithful. It makes me human."

"But, do I doubt when I'm this worried about him? Shouldn't I be able to convince myself that everything is going to be okay?"

Jenna smiled, but there was sadness behind it.

"Honey, we don't know how things will turn out for Cole or anyone else. We just have to have faith things will work out for the best for all of us. I believe Cole will be healed and be okay, but I can't promise that; it just isn't in my control. Still, I must have faith in those hopes and prayers."

"But how can you have faith if your prayers aren't answered?"

"Prayers aren't like rubbing on a magic lamp. God isn't a genie who does our bidding. He has his plan and sometimes we don't know how that plan is going to work or even why things go the way they do. From our side of it, things like Cole is going through seem cruel, and we don't understand why people have to endure those things."

I certainly understood that much.

"We have things which work in our world, death, sickness, evil. Those things exist as a part of our world. Sometimes God works through those things making the best of them. Cole's illness will work in some way to further God's plan. It may be through his healing; it may be through some other way."

"I don't understand. If God made this world, why isn't it perfect? Why do those things exist?"

"That's a pretty big question. I can't give you a solid answer. I can only offer my opinion and understanding."

"Okay, I can start with that."

"You understand free will, right? We have the ability and freedom of will and choice. If we didn't, we would just be robots, following orders. Well, with free will there has to be different choices and outcomes. Right and wrong, left or right, good or bad, those are all choices we make and with each direction in which we go there is an outcome. With this free will comes a degree of randomness. A perfect world wouldn't be random; it would be completely ordered; there would be no choice; no potential for different outcomes. Though we can see design and function in our world, we don't have a perfect world. And we can't expect to if we expect a world of choice. If we want a world free of disease, free of evil, hurtful and dangerous outcomes, then we are asking for order and control."

My head was reeling. I felt like I was talking to Cole, and that thought made me want to go back into his room to check on him. Ever since his embolism I was a little reluctant to leave him alone.

"I'm sorry; I didn't intend to turn that discussion into a dissertation on theology," Jenna said apologetically.

I laughed.

"It wasn't that bad and I'm interested in what you have to say. I just don't know what I believe anymore. There's a lot to understand."

She nodded.

"Take your time.   The understanding will come to you."

Then she winked and added, "A little prayer might help."

"I guess it never hurts, does it?

Chapter Twenty-Seven

As spring waited around the corner, it teased us with little moments which echoed its return. A couple of days of wicked winter weather would be broken by warm, wonderful sunlight and powder blue skies. I didn't know whether to be thankful or angry at the deceitful wiles of nature around me. I'd grown weary of the cold, biting wind, but the disappointment which followed when the warmth disappeared once again was nearly as vexing.

On those days when winter took a break we slipped outside to bask in the sun's glow or took small walks around the block. Cole moved with a stiffened gait, but he seemed to show improvement all the time. Most of the time I let him set the pace of our walks. It was just such a thrill to be holding his hand as we actually walked together.

"It's amazing that a little thing like walking around the block can wear me out like this. This time last year I was running wind sprints," he said contemplatively.

"You've been through quite an ordeal, Cole. I know it seems slow sometimes, but you're making progress."

He nodded.

"My appetite is improving, too. I actually felt hungry when I smelled the food mom was fixing for lunch."

I smiled.

"Well, if things ever go back to normal, I'll be watching you suck down burgers at the Dawg before you know it. I can't believe you could eat so much."

"Hey, in my defense, I was building a lot of muscle back then."

I rolled my eyes.

"Yeah, whatever. You ate like a pig. I've never seen anyone eat like that and not pack on the pounds. Your metabolism must have been double normal."

"You make it sound like I disgusted you."

"No, you amazed me. I was thinking you might be able to win one of those hotdog eating contests hands down."

He stopped and looked at me.

"You know what I want? I want a cherry vanilla Coke."

"I can go down to the Dawg and get you one."

"Why don't we go down there together?"

"Are you sure you're up for it? Aren't you too tired?"

"Nah, I'm good."

A few minutes later we were sitting on the deck at the Grumpy Dawg sucking down a couple of sodas. It wasn't long before we'd gathered a crowd around us. Cole seemed to attract attention when he went out. Long past the popularity struggles of those early years of high school, he

was the center of attention, and even after all he'd
been through he was the life of the party.

"So, Cole, you going out for track this year?"
Taylor teased him.

"No, I don't think so, Jordan. I think I'm
going out for the fishing team this spring."

"Allen, we don't have a fishing team."

"Well, then I shouldn't have a problem making
first string." Cole teased back.

"Seriously, I think I'm just going to take it
easy and enjoy life."

Jordan smiled slyly and nodded in my
direction.

"You're probably going to enjoy more than
just life."

Cole looked over at me.

"Yeah, probably," he said with a contented
smile.

"Lucky guy," Jordan offered making me blush.

"Geez, guys. Way to talk like I'm not here."

Cole leaned over and placed his arm over my
shoulder, pulling me close to his side. Then he
looked back at Tate and stuck out his hand.

"The luckiest guy in the world."

Tate grabbed Cole's hand in his.

"I'm glad you are, man."

It was great being out with Cole again. I
wouldn't let him stay out long. I was too worried
about him getting tired or catching something with
his weakened immune system. Still, it was nice.

As expected, the nice weather didn't last, but
we knew there were better days on the horizon.
Soon spring would be in full swing and by then
Cole would be getting stronger and moving better.
As the end of winter grew closer, so did prom and

after that, graduation. Life continued to move on leaving the past in a blur.

Chapter Twenty-Eight

A year earlier, both Cole and I were agonizing over going to prom. Suddenly, I found myself more excited about it than I ever would have imagined. After the year we'd had, I couldn't think of anything more wonderful than walking up that promenade with my arm anchored securely in his. Even Geneva was amazed at the anxiousness I displayed at finding just the right dress. We'd searched store after store, and though there were so many beautiful dresses, I just couldn't seem to find the right one.

Time was growing shorter and shorter, and if I didn't make a decision soon, I'd be walking up the promenade in a pair of blue jeans. Of course, Cole found plenty of humor in my dilemma. He never hesitated to make fun of me or needle me for making it more complicated than it needed to be. I'd searched the internet, visited shops, and looked at catalogs until I was blue in the face. I just couldn't find the right one.

"You know I'd be happy if we just showed up in blue jeans," he teased.

"You'd like that, wouldn't you?"

"Well, we both thought it was a good idea last year."

"We were both rebelling against society last year. This year is special. We need to celebrate."

"What are we celebrating? Indecisiveness?"

I tilted my head and tensed my brow.

"No, we are celebrating the fact that you are still here, in my life. I could have lost you, Cole. We need to make the most of every little experience."

The amused look on his face told me to prepare for another dig at my transformation.

"We are celebrating life? That unimportant, chemical process that isn't worth fighting for?"

"Okay, okay. Do you have to rub it in at every little opportunity? I was wrong. You were right. I'm going to say a lot of things over the years that will prove the point, but I don't need you reminding me every time I do."

His expression was apologetic, and he almost looked sorry for digging at me.

"Okay. I'll try to cut it down to every other time."

I rolled my eyes.

"You're incorrigible."

"You wouldn't love me if I were any other way."

I smiled.

"Mmm. Well, I might love you, but I like you the way you are."

"So, back to the dress. What's so hard?"

"I don't know. I want something that is elegant, but fun. You know? I don't want something stiff or too formal, but I don't want it to be 'in your face' radical."

"Oh, you want to rebel against society without looking like you're rebelling against society."

I smiled.

"Yeah, I guess so."

"Well, if you ask me, the place to look is Audrey Hepburn."

"Huh?"

"She was a symbol of elegance, the most desirable woman, but it came naturally."

I gave him a contemplative look.

"You know, you might be right."

He gave me a knowing look.

"Of course I'm right."

Oh, geez. Here we go again. He really was annoying sometimes, but he made life interesting.

"Okay, yeah, that was a given."

"Glad to see you're coming around."

"Do I have a choice? So, where do you suggest we start?"

"Let's look at some of her old pictures and see if we can find what you had in mind?"

I have to admit it; he was right. We skimmed the internet for pictures, and we found the perfect dress.

"That's it!"

"Pink?"

My mouth twisted.

"Yes, pink. What's wrong? You don't think I can wear pink?"

"No, no. It's lovely. I just never pictured you wearing pink."

My hands went to my hips.

"It's soft lavender pink and I can wear pink as well as any girl."

He put his hands up in defense.

"Seriously, no offense intended. I think you'd look ravishing in that dress. You have just the shape for it and the... uh..."

"Chest?"

"Something like that."

It was a 1950's style strapless tulle evening dress. It had a creamy white bodice, and it looked great on the mannequin. I just hoped it looked as good on me. Geneva measured me, and we ordered it online. I was so excited when it showed up and as soon as I tried it on, I knew it was perfect.

"Oh my gosh, Sophie. That dress is gorgeous on you. It hugs your shape perfectly," Geneva oozed.

"What about the color?" I asked with just the slightest amount of apprehension in my voice.

"Excellent. It looks great against your skin. I don't think you could have found a more perfect dress."

"Do you think Cole will like it?"

She just stared at me like I was suddenly the most ridiculous person on earth.

"Are you kidding? That boy would love you if you went to the prom wearing a potato sack."

"Okay, I know Cole loves me and accepts me, but will he like the dress?'

"Sophie, he will love the dress. He is going to feel like the luckiest guy in the world."

So, Cole was right, and Geneva was right. The dress was perfect and for one of the few times in my life I felt like I was actually pretty. I mean, I don't have that much of a self-esteem issue that I think I'm ugly, but I'd generally consider myself more average than pretty. That dress made me feel pretty. Against my lightly tanned skin and with my hair drawn up in back, I have to admit, I was pretty hot.

I thought the way our night went the year before was incredible. I learned I could never underestimate Cole's ability to create romance. If high school was any example of what he was capable of, the rest of life was going to be incredible. Yeah, I said that. I was actually thinking about being with Cole for the rest of my life. Maybe it was stupid or immature, but I just couldn't see life without him and I'd almost had to find out what that would have been like. That's why that prom was so special.

When he came to pick me up, I was expecting to see his pickup sitting out front. Instead, he had borrowed Coach Curtis' 1953 Oldsmobile Super Eighty-eight convertible. It was baby-blue with wide whitewall tires. It was a sweet ride, and it got a lot of attention.

His tux, which I didn't help pick out, was a 50's version as well. Black with thin lapels and the small bowtie, he was looking like a member of the Rat Pack. Between our apparel and the car, it almost seemed as if we'd stepped back in time. It was the most incredible way to celebrate our last prom together. Geneva had picked out a boutonnière in pink and cream for Cole, which I pinned on him with relative ease and no blood drawn. On my wrist, I wore a matching corsage.

We cruised up with the top down, and Cole stepped out to open my door. We made our way to the community building amidst cheers, applause, and catcalls. As far as proms go, it was nice. We danced together most of the night, with Cole being cut in on only a couple of times. I loved the slow songs the best when I could just press my head against his chest and feel at peace with the world. It was my favorite place to be, against his warmth, wrapped in his arms.

After his surprise ending to last year's prom, I had no idea what might be in store for me this year. As soon as we left the building, Cole took me by my house.

"You may want to change into something a little more comfortable," he said as he put the convertible in park and turned to look at me.

I'm sure the look I gave him was more than a little inquisitive.

"No dancing in our formals?"

He gave me that coy smile that always shows he's up to something.

"Not tonight, Angel."

"What should I wear?"

"Whatever makes you comfortable. Sweats and a t-shirt are fine. I'll go change, and be back to get you in ten minutes."

With Cole's imagination, there was no way to know what was on his mind, but I trusted him, and I knew whatever it was it would be wonderful and memorable. I was ready when the convertible came rolling down the street. Man, that was a sweet car.

We took the highway out of town for a few miles before turning down a blacktop road. As before, this area appeared to be an abandon homestead, but it had a nice gravel drive. He pulled the car up on a little rise which caused the headlights to point up into the night sky. Then he reached over the back of the seat and started hauling things up into the front seat – his laptop, a small projector, a picnic basket, a small ice chest, and a blanket.

He got out of the car and pulled a projector screen and an extension cord out of the trunk. With the extension cord plugged into a box on the side of a telephone pole, he attached a long cord to the projector before placing it in the center of the hood. Then he set up the screen in front of the car.

He placed the laptop, which had been hooked up to the projector, in the seat on the other side of me. While the computer booted up, he dug into the picnic basket. I knew the smell as soon as he lifted the lid of the basket. He handed me a tub of hot, fresh buttered popcorn. From the small ice chest, he pulled out two large bottles of pop. Then he started the movie and spread a blanket over me as I cuddled up against him.

You know there's something to be said for those old cars. They had big comfortable seats just right for snuggling up together. As Breakfast at Tiffany's started, I looked around at that wide open dark sky, not a light for miles except the twinkling of the stars and the moon shining bright. What an incredible way to watch a movie; it was like being at our personal drive-in.

"You know, you really know how to impress a girl," I whispered as I kissed his cheek.

"There's only one I'm interested in impressing."

"No worries, Dear Heart, you do that every day," I offered with adoration. "Where do you come up with these ideas?"

He shrugged.

"I don't know. I guess I just try to think of things that will make you happy."

"You make me happy by just being here and by being who you are."

After Breakfast at Tiffany's, we watched A Walk to Remember, one of my favorite movies, but honestly I fell asleep before the end. I woke up with my head against Cole's shoulder just as the sun was about to lift its head over the horizon. It was so serene waking up in Cole's arms and just for a second, I allowed myself to imagine what it might be like to do that every day.

"We better get you home. Your mom's going to kill me for keeping you out all night."

I rolled my eyes.

"Cole, how many times do we have to cover this one? My mom would rather I am with you than at a party. She knows if I'm with you I'm safe."

He chuckled.

"Okay, then we better get me home before my mom kills you for keeping me out so late."

"I don't think that's going to happen either," I said grabbing his arm as he started to get out of the car to load things up. "Can we just sit here and watch the sun come up first?"

He smiled and nodded.

As we sat there with our bodies pressed against each other, the sun slid up from the horizon casting its glow against the atmosphere and causing the sky to burst with its yellow-orange color. A few minutes later, I reluctantly lifted myself away from Cole so he could get everything put back in order.

"You didn't spill that popcorn all over the coach's car did you?" he asked as he got back in the car.

I looked at the seat where I'd been leaning against him.

"Oops, there's a piece in the seat."

"Better not mess it up, he won't let us borrow it again."

"And when would we need to borrow it again? That was our last prom."

"Oh, I don't know. I might just want to take my girl out for a Sunday drive. Or maybe we'll use it for the wedding?"

"Wedding?"

"Well, we might someday."

"That's kind of getting ahead of things isn't it?"

"It might be too early to talk about it, but it isn't too early for me to know who I want to marry."

"You think so?"

"I can't imagine anyone else, Sophie."

I smiled at the thought. Me and Cole? Married? It could happen.

We didn't talk much on the way back. If I were to guess, he was thinking about the same things that were going through my mind. School would be ending soon. What would happen to us when high school was over? I was sure we'd both go off to college; maybe even in different directions. I couldn't imagine Cole being away from me or even dating other girls. He was too much a part of me. But the truth was most people drift away after graduation. It left me with a somber feeling as he dropped me off, and I kissed him goodbye.

I watched him ride away in that baby-blue Olds, with the big whitewall tires. Yeah, it was a sweet ride.

Chapter Twenty-Nine

There we were; eighteen of Prairie Blossom's finest standing on the threshold of our future. Dressed in our red satin gowns and flat-topped caps, tassels dangling in front of our faces, we were like every other graduating class. There would be those among us who would spend their lives struggling to survive. Others would soar to the heights, stretching their wings and their minds. Steps which had once been guided by parents, teachers, and clergy would soon be ours to take.

Our world was about to change. Soon, we would be faced with decisions; simple decisions like "do we wash whites and darks separately" and the more difficult decisions of "what occupation will provide a living." Each of those decisions would somehow allow us to realize how protected and supported we were. Keeping a roof over our heads, feeding ourselves and our cars, deciding which paths to take – concepts many of us had never had to worry about were about to fall on our shoulders.

Though I'd been raised to think independently, I still didn't know if I was ready to venture from the safety of high school into the rest of the world. My thoughts on the future had developed and changed over the years, still I was not sure what I wanted to do with the rest of my life. In some ways, I was more unsure at that moment than I was four years earlier. The equation had changed, there were new things to consider; most importantly among them was my relationship with Cole.

I stood waiting for my moment to speak. As the valedictorian, it was my place to summarize our class, offer our final farewell, and put into words the feelings we shared. I'd gone over the speech so many times I knew it by heart. My nervousness was based less on what I had to say and more on what I was thinking. The anxiousness which gripped me had tossed and turned my stomach into knots.

At my introduction, I stood and proceeded to cross the stage on the three inch heels both Tisha and my mother insisted I wear. The fear of falling in front of a crowed gymnasium crossed my mind several times in the few seconds it took to take my place at the podium. Of course, I had to take a glance at Cole before I began. His smile seemed to wrap around me like a warm fluffy blanket in the winter.

I tried to keep my mind centered solely on the words I had to offer. It was probably the first time I had actually listened to what I had written. I'll not share the whole speech, but there are a few lines which grabbed hold of me, even though they were my words.

"Our journeys will take us down many different paths. They will send us all in different directions; directions which will shape and change us from who we are into the mature individuals we choose to become; a spiritual evolution from a child to an adult. Truly, throughout this process, there is only one constant. Love brought us to where we are, and love will lead us on into a bright and glorious future. In life things change, people change, situations change, the world changes, but love remains. Over the course of time, I have learned true love, love born in the soul, remains when all other things have been left behind."

I wrote that. Those are my words. Who was that girl who once believed love to be a jumble of emotions, emotions which were merely a chemical reaction? Where did she go? I felt so sad for her and yet so happy she had come to understand the depth and meaning of living. She would never have known any different if it weren't for a boy with a quirky sense of humor. He had changed it all, and yet, in all reality, he was merely the instrument from which the music came. The music itself was there all along.

And so, my thoughts returned. What would happen after high school? Would Cole and I go our separate ways? I hoped with all my heart that would not be the case, but I also knew we would be okay. If our paths were to take different directions, we would still have that love we had known from nearly the very beginning. We might change. Our situations and our needs might change, but the love would remain the same.

As I walked out of the gym that day, my eyes were filled with tears. They were tears of goodbye for things which would no longer be. They were tears of hello for things which were soon to come. They were melancholy and triumphant; anxious and apprehensive. They were salty paths from the past and moist drops for the future. They were hopes and dreams and memories colliding. They were the chemical reaction which takes place when heartache meets with exuberance.

When I turned around and saw my parents, I knew in some ways they felt the same. When I turned the other way and fell into Cole's embrace, I knew I was in the one place I would never want to leave.

The rest of the day was a whirlwind of activity. We shook hands, ate cake, drank punch, opened gifts, hugged and cried, and at the very end of it all; we danced. We danced slow, savoring every touch, every breath, and every beat of our hearts. We danced fast, celebrating life and its growth. We laughed, and we wept. We remembered, and we promised. And then, we parted.

I remember that day, when I started as an outsider. I remember how the rabbits scurried to the other side of the room and looked at me as if I'd just stepped into their protected space. I remember the boy who made me laugh and forget my discomfort. I remember feeling so lost and alone when I arrived. This place that was so different from all I'd ever know, now seem so much like home I was terrified to leave. How does that happen?

I still have moments when I miss the beach or the seafood. There are times when I wish there were more things to do, and civilization wasn't so far away. But this is comfortable. It is friendly and small and protected. The real world, the one we see on television where people are bitter, hurried, and unattached, seems a billion miles away. In this world, we take things as they come. Here drinking a soda with a friend is like taking a big sigh. Cuddling up with a bowl of popcorn and a DVD are sacred moments. No one honks if old Mrs. Webber is moving too slow. Politics is something to argue about over a cup of coffee and the titles Republican and Democrat come second to the title American.

It may seem like a lazy little town, but people around here know hard work. They do it every day. When they support something, they do it completely and unselfishly. Their kids mean the world to them, and they are there for them every step of the way. They come together in times of need and offer their hearts, their prayers, and their resources.

This little town is a symbol of the heart of America. It is the muscle that keeps the blood flowing. It is the spirit that keeps the traditions and values alive. This is the place that gives birth to the independence and strength flowing through the veins and out to the appendages. The big cities on the coast may be the fingers, hands, feet, and toes, but without the heart we all know the body would die.

With these things in mind, it was going to be hard to leave it all behind. I'm a former city girl, scared to venture back into the world of traffic, concrete, and shadows. How would I ever make it on my own?

"It'll be alright," Cole assured me in one of my more anxious moments.

"You are strong and independent. It's just a change. Life is full of them."

I smiled weakly.

"But what am I going to do? I have no idea what to do with my life."

"Think about it. Pray about it. It'll come to you. There is something you were meant to do, and if you are open to it, it won't pass you by."

He made things sound so easy. Cole was just like the little town from which he came. He took things as they came; one step at a time. He was fearless; confident. He didn't let things get him down, not even cancer.

It is strange how apprehension can make it seem like things are hanging over you, slowing down time. In that way, the summer before college seemed to creep by slowly. It was like trying to go to sleep, but looking at the clock every hour to see how much time you have left. When you finally fall asleep, it seems morning showed up a lot quicker than you expected. Two weeks before college, the anxiety seemed to rush over me, and I felt I had squandered the time I had to make up my mind.

I'd followed Cole's advice. I'd thought and prayed, but I wasn't sure how open I'd been. My mind had been such a jumble that it didn't seem I could have received any message if it had hit me like a brick. But then one day when I was thinking back over the past year, I realized there was one moment when I felt I'd been absolutely happy with something I'd done. It was an epiphany. I knew what I wanted to do, as crazy as it seemed. And when I shared it with Cole, he didn't think it was crazy at all.

Suddenly, I was looking forward to going off to college. I had something to work towards, and though it would be tough, the future didn't seem so daunting.

The week before I left for college, Geneva was in a shopping frenzy. We bought bedding and furniture, appliances and clothes. It seemed like every day she was making another list. My bedroom was starting to look like a warehouse, and I was starting to worry that I'd never fit everything she was buying into a dorm room. When it came time to leave our little sleepy town, we loaded up my Mazda and still had to put some of it in the back of Cole's pickup with his stuff.

Cole and his parents helped with my move to the dorm and then my family helped him move in. We were going to separate schools. I hated the thought of not seeing him throughout the day. I'd grown so used to being with him. We would be in different worlds and who was to say he wouldn't meet someone in that world he might find more interesting than me?

If Cole could have listened to my thoughts, all he would have said is, "Here you go again."

Life is just full of those little moments; those moments when we can let our minds wander off on those tangents that can twist us up. I hope I learn to deal with them better as time goes on. It simply doesn't pay to worry about what is yet to happen. There is so much more to focus on today.

Chapter Thirty

The mild Oklahoma fall afternoon was accented by a gentle warm breeze which lifted strands of my curly brown hair. I waited patiently under the shade of the large cottonwoods at the front of the zoo entrance. Cole was running late from his last class at Oklahoma Christian University. Since we'd moved down to the Oklahoma city area, we had spent almost all of our free time together even though his dorm was in Edmond and mine was in Norman.

It was a Friday, and we were both excited to do something other than meeting for dinner and then hitting the books. A trip around the zoo holding Cole's hand was just what I needed to relieve the stresses of a week of classes, lectures, and nearly unending hours spent with my nose in a book. Though, I'd always considered myself studious, the world in which I found myself was like high school times ten. I'd never I had to buckle down to maintain my grades. My only relief and sanity was in the time I spent with Cole.

"Hey, Beautiful."

His voice made me smile even before I saw him. When I felt his hands on my shoulders as he moved up behind me, a wave of calm flushed over me. His touch brought a flood of warm energy flowing into me. His fingers began to knead at my tensed muscles, and I rolled my head back.

"Oh my gosh, that feels so good."

He whispered into my ear.

"Wanna skip the elephants?"

"Umm. Don't tempt me, but you better stop, or you'll have to carry me through the park."

He kissed my neck.

"Come on. The hippos are waiting."

Cole paid the entrance fee and handed me a ticket stub.

"Hang on to this or they won't let you back in," he said with a teasing smile.

"Thanks for looking out for me, Sweetheart."

"Don't mention it, Babe."

As we strolled along, I watched mothers pushing strollers with toddlers. I couldn't help but smile at the wide, excited eyes. Cole must have noticed.

"That's a pretty interesting look you have on your face. Kind of motherly."

I smirked.

"Are you going to take a stab at me again?"

I just knew the subject of my 'worldview' was about to be explored once again, not that there was much of it left.

"No, I just think it looks good on you. I think you'll make an excellent mom someday."

Me? A mom? It wasn't something I would have given a lot of thought to a couple of years earlier. Now it didn't seem so farfetched. I always assumed I would eventually consider having kids, but with my clinical way of looking at things, I hadn't considered myself as 'motherly.' For most of my life, being a mother seemed more like an act of perpetuating the species.

I looked up into Coles wonderful brown eyes.

"You really think so?"

He nodded.

"Yeah, I do."

I reached up and pulled him to me, giving him a peck on the lips.

"Thanks."

He blushed with the realization he had said something that touched me so deeply.

"So, how's school?" He quizzed with a change of subject.

"Brutal."

"Sophie Carter, classic geek, struggling with school? Doesn't seem possible."

"Biochemistry is kicking my tail."

"Oh, come on. You can handle this."

"I don't know, Cole. I've never had this much trouble with a course."

He squeezed my hand.

"You've got this. I'll help. I can quiz you on terms."

I rolled my eyes.

"Sure, Cole."

"Nucleotide?

I gave him an annoyed look.

"Nucleotide?" He prodded.

"Monomer of a nucleic acid."

"Amino?"

"Functional group that acts as a weak base."

"Proton?"

"Attracts electrons."

He offered that mischievous look I loved so much.

"Lepton?"

I couldn't hide the smile.

"Green suit, red beard, Irish accent," I answered with a giggle.

"See, you got this," he said with a knowing smile.

I took his hand and squeezed.

"Yeah, I got this."

"Seriously, you can do this, Sophie. You'll make a great doctor."

"I've got to get through pre-med first, Cole."

"You will."

We were quiet for a little while as we walked hand in hand. My thoughts wondered.

"Can you believe I'm Pre-Med at OU?"

He nodded.

"Yeah, I can."

"I can't," I admitted. "Four years ago, I never would have believed I'd have any desire to go into medicine. I couldn't have even fathomed the idea; I would have seen no purpose to being a physician."

"That's just what life does to us, Sophie. It takes us down this journey and reveals to us the person within. You were meant to do this, Sophie."

I smiled.

"The plan?"

He nodded.

"Yeah, the plan."

I hugged him as he pulled me in against his chest and lowered his lips to mine. They were warm, wet, and wonderful. His touch could still send chills through me, and I had little doubt it always would. I felt my face flush. When he pulled back to look into my eyes, I felt his warm breath against my skin.

"Come on, Pastor Cole. The elephants are waiting," I encouraged, my words shaking with my breathlessness as they came out.

"Hey, hold up a second," he said tugging on my arm and pulling me toward a bench. "I need to talk to you about something."

"What? I wanna see the elephants," I teased.

I looked up at his face; it was almost stiff and incredibly serious, possibly nervous. It was rare for Cole to take on such a lifeless expression. I felt a sick feeling moving in my stomach, and I knew immediately it was being stirred by fear. I felt my chest tighten. In the back of my mind, I had this thought, and if that's what he was going to tell me, I didn't want to hear it. I tried to calm myself as I sat down and took his hand in mine.

He tried to smile, but I could tell he was anxious about what he had to say. When the words came to his voice, there was a roughness to the sound.

"I… uh." He ran his hand through his hair.

Silently I prayed, "God, please don't let it be back."

It was amazing how easily prayer came to me in time of need these days.

He took a deep breath and let it out.

"Man, I just knew I could do this with no problem."

I squeezed his hand.

"I had this all thought out and I knew exactly how I was going to deliver this. But now my emotions are catching up with me, and it isn't coming out the way I wanted it. I don't know why my nerves are giving me such a fit right now."

"No, please, no," I silently pleaded.

Another deep breath.

"I guess it's because this is one of the most important things I've ever had to say."

I closed my eyes trying to prepare myself.

"You know I love you with all my heart and always will, right?"

My eyes locked on his as I nodded.

"Well, we've been through a lot together, and I guess I'm asking you to go through a lot more with me. I just can't imagine going through all that without you."

"Here it comes," I thought. I could feel the empty pit which had once been my stomach.

He lifted his hand to my cheek, placing his thumb just under my eyes. I could feel the pools I was trying to hold back lifting as he stroked his thumb lightly back and forth. My heart was pounding in my chest, and my skin was riddled with goose bumps. As the fear inside rose, I could feel my lungs starting to constrict and my hands going clammy. I knew I was close to hyperventilating and if I didn't get a grip I'd pass out.

Then I felt the anger rising. It wasn't fair. We'd already been through this. He'd paid his share. I heard the argument in my head.

"God, you can't do this. You can't let this happen. It's our time to be happy."

Cole continued to work at getting out what he needed to say.

"Sophie, what I'm trying to say is that I want you there with me no matter what I face; no matter what we face."

My hand trembled as I lifted it up to his cheek. I tried to gather my courage. I told myself, "We can do this. We can get through it again."

"Dang, I'm not getting this out like I want, and that's really not my style," he said fidgeting with the button on his jacket.

He moved from the bench and knelt between my legs, looking up at me. Then he reached into his jacket pocket and pulled out a black velvet box.

"Sophie, I want you to marry me."

"Oh my God!" I exclaimed, allowing all my pent up frustration to escape. I jerked my hands back and clasped them to my chest. My heart was beating wildly and I was nearly out of breath.

"God, I'm so sorry. I'm so sorry," I repeated.

Poor Cole. The startled look on his face at my reaction would have been amusing under other circumstances, but at the moment it was heartbreaking.

I didn't know whether to laugh or cry. I'd worked myself up so much, I should have been ecstatic, but all I felt was relief.

"Uh, Sophie…"

I closed my eyes and took a breath to calm my feelings. Then I looked up at him and smiled.

"How could you possibly expect me to say anything but yes, Cole Allen?"

I could see his face relax as he reached up to kiss me.

He opened the box and slid the diamond solitaire on my finger.

"I love you, Sophie."

"I love you, too, Cole."

I won't claim to know what our future holds. I can't foresee the challenges or obstacles. I don't know what other hardships I will face, but I do know who will be beside me along the way. Somehow, whether I stumbled upon the path or I was drug down it unknowingly; I ended up in the right place. My journey led me from the west coast to a lonely little town in the Panhandle of Oklahoma; to a place I would never have chosen on my own. And then it led me straight into the arms of the one soul on earth that was meant for me. He is my perfect match; he is my completion.

Though the old Sophie would have dismissed our initial encounter as pure coincidence; the Sophie I have become sees it much differently. She knows things work together for a reason, because the universe shows us the signs of design and purpose; something not merely mechanical, but rather a place and home for vessels filled with spiritual beings.

Love is an emotion, but it is also real and true. It isn't just a process or a chemical reaction. It rises above all things. It binds souls and spirits. I've learned so many things on this journey with Cole. One of those things is from my favorite passage in First Corinthians, chapter thirteen, verses two thru seven.

"If I have prophetic powers, and understand all mysteries and all knowledge, and if I have all faith, so as to remove mountains, but have not love, I am nothing. If I give away all I have, and if I deliver up my body to be burned, but have not love, I gain nothing. Love is patient and kind; love does not envy or boast; it is not arrogant or rude. It does not insist on its own way; it is not irritable or resentful; it does not rejoice at wrongdoing, but rejoices with the truth. Love bears all things, believes all things, hopes all things, endures all things."

I've come to the conclusion that science and religion don't have to be at odds with each other. As a species, we have gathered so much knowledge from scientific discovery, but there's still so much which can't be explained. For all it's worth, science often relies on theories and suppositions as a point of origination. We may never have all knowledge. There may always be things that escape our understanding. When we compare man's knowledge to the knowledge contained within the universe, it is but a sliver. We would be extremely naive to believe we could fathom it all within the confines of our physical brains.

Life can always throw things at us which we don't anticipate. I may have other moments when I face the fear of cancer making its angry return. That question may always hang in the background, or it may be Cole who at one point has to face the fear of loss. Life will challenge us with an unending number of concerns and fear will cast its shadows in other ways, but whatever we face, we will face it together. When faced with darkness, love will light the way. The flame which burns within our hearts cannot be extinguished. We will endure all things; Cole and I... a team with a plan... for this crazy... silly... wonderful... mixed up...some kind of life.

About the Author

C.E. Lemieux, Jr. is the author of bittersweet love stories. His novels are emotionally charged and heartwarming. He has four previously published novels—Whispers in the Wind, Loving Deacon, There's Something About Henry, and The Ladder Climber.

He is the father of four. He and his family, make their home in Oklahoma where several of his stories are set. In addition to writing, C.E. enjoys fishing, camping, and baseball.

His books are available on Amazon, Barnes and Noble, and other online retailers. All books are available for Kindle. Whispers in the Wind and Loving Deacon are available for Nook.

Visit C.E. Lemieux, Jr. at www.lemieuxbooks.com or www.bittersweetnovelist.com. On twitter visit @celemieux. Like him on Facebook at Whispers in the Wind by C.E. Lemieux Jr.

As with all authors, C.E. Lemieux, Jr. appreciates hearing from readers. Book reviews are the best way to show an author how you feel about their work. With that in mind, please take a moment to offer your feelings and opinions on this novel. Thank you for taking the time to offer a review and spending time with C.E. Lemieux, Jr. and his characters.

Made in the USA
Charleston, SC
11 March 2016